A GIFT TO CHERISH

"I daresay the time has come for me to select a gift for you, sweetheart."

They were approaching a small shop with a window full of sparkling jewels. Pausing before it, Lord Rathbone slipped an arm about Chelsea's slim waist and drew her closer to his side. "Just there," he said, pointing a gloved finger. "What do you think? Do you like it?"

"I-I'm not sure which piece you mean," Chelsea said quietly.

"Just there. The heart-shaped locket with the tiny diamond in the center. I realize it isn't a'tall showy, but upon our marriage, you will, of course, inherit a good many lovely pieces from Mother. In the meantime, I should like to give you something that you might wear every day." His voice grew hoarse. "To remind you how very much I love you," he concluded, his final words just above a whisper.

"Oh-h," Chelsea breathed, longing with all her soul to echo the sentiment. "It's . . . beautiful. I shall be very proud to wear it . . . always," she added sincerely.

Lord Rathbone's chest expanded proudly. "Then, it's yours."

* * *

Praise for *Bewitching Lord Winterton* by Marilyn Clay:

"[A] sweet and tender tale. The intrigues give spice, and the supporting characters are enchanting."

—*Rendezvous*

WATCH FOR THESE ZEBRA REGENCIES

LADY STEPHANIE   (0-8217-5341-X, $4.50)
by Jeanne Savery
Lady Stephanie Morris has only one true love: the family estate she has managed ever since her mother died. But then Lord Anthony Rider arrives on her estate, claiming he has plans for both the land and the woman. Stephanie soon realizes she's fallen in love with a man whose sensual caresses will plunge her into a world of peril and intrigue . . . a man as dangerous as he is irresistible.

LORD DIABLO'S DEMISE   (0-8217-5338-X, $4.50)
by Meg-Lynn Roberts
The sinfully handsome Lord Harry Glendower was a gambler and the black sheep of his family. About to be forced into a marriage of convenience, the devilish fellow engineered his own demise, never having dreamed that faking his death would lead him to the heavenly refuge of spirited heiress Gwyn Morgan, the daughter of a physician.

A PERILOUS ATTRACTION   (0-8217-5339-8, $4.50)
by Dawn Aldridge Poore
Alissa Morgan is stunned when a frantic passenger thrusts her baby into Alissa's arms and flees, having heard rumors that a notorious highwayman posed a threat to their coach. Handsome stranger Hugh Sebastian secretly possesses the treasured necklace the highwayman seeks and volunteers to pose as Alissa's husband to save her reputation. With a lost baby and missing necklace in their care, the couple embarks on a journey into peril—and passion.

Available wherever paperbacks are sold, or order direct from the Publisher. Send cover price plus 50¢ per copy for mailing and handling to Penguin USA, P.O. Box 999, c/o Dept. 17109, Bergenfield, NJ 07621. Residents of New York and Tennessee must include sales tax. DO NOT SEND CASH.

Brighton Beauty

Marilyn Clay

ZEBRA BOOKS
KENSINGTON PUBLISHING CORP.

ZEBRA BOOKS are published by

Kensington Publishing Corp.
850 Third Avenue
New York, NY 10022

Zebra and the Z logo Reg. U.S. Pat. & TM Off.

First Printing: June, 1996
10 9 8 7 6 5 4 3 2 1

Printed in the United States of America

One

"I should like to speak with Miss Grant," demanded Miss Alayna Marchmont, a cool gaze directed at Mr. Merribone, the proprietor of Merribone's Millinery Establishment in London.

"Ah, yes," Mr. Merribone replied proudly, a quick glance taking in the exquisitely gowned young lady before him. "Miss Grant is our most popular designer. I shall fetch her for you straightaway, madam."

He turned and headed for the workroom of the small, but fashionable, millinery shop, located near Bond Street. On the way, he paused before another Quality customer browsing in the store that morning. A few seconds elapsed as he waited patiently for the woman to acknowledge him. Receiving at last the encouragement he sought, an almost imperceptible nod of her elegantly-coiffed head, Mr. Merribone smiled broadly. "Good day, Lady Carstairs! And how are you this fine morning? If I may direct your attention to the lovely Semptress, my lady." He pointed to a pretty Italian straw confection bedecked with bright red cherries and a splash of *coquelicot* ribbon. "And, just there is another of our original designs, a frilled Coburg. Both bonnets were created by our Miss Grant."

"Hmmm," Lady Carstairs murmured, at once snatching up the Semptress, while another finely turned out lady, whose ears had also perked up at the mention of Miss

Grant's name, made what could only be described as a lunge for the high-crowned Coburg.

Though pleased, Mr. Merribone cast an anxious glance toward the attractive young lady who had initially sent him on his errand, and noting the impatient press of her lips, he hastened his step. Reaching the curtained partition at the rear of the shop, which separated the display area from the workroom, he pulled aside the blue damask drapery, his eyes seeking those of his most popular designer, Miss Chelsea Grant.

An exquisite beauty with intelligent brown eyes and porcelain skin, Miss Grant was a rose among weeds in the cramped little work space. Five other women, of various ages and sizes, were crowded around the work table nearly lost beneath its burden of bare straw bonnets, spools of delicately spun lace and ribbon, miniature birds, waxed fruit and pastel-tinted flowers.

"Miss Grant," the proprietor said, a sharp gaze telling the other women, who had all looked up from their work when he spoke, to carry on. "Another customer is asking to see you this morning, Miss Grant. If you will come this way, please."

Completely ignoring her employer's bidding, Chelsea Grant merely bent her golden head lower over the lilac-satin rosebud she was industriously stitching onto the stiff straw brim of an Oldenburg bonnet.

"Miss Grant!" Mr. Merribone said again, an irritable edge creeping into his tone this time.

Still, Miss Grant did not move, did not even raise inquisitive brown eyes to meet his. However, upon hearing the insistent swish of the damask drapery being yanked shut behind him, she risked a tentative peek upward.

"As you can see, Mr. Merribone," she said evenly, "I am quite busy just now."

"*Busy!* You will come this way at once, Miss Grant! At once, I say!"

Chelsea felt her breath grow short. A moment ago, she had not only heard, but clearly recognized, the demanding feminine voice that sent Mr. Merribone scurrying to fetch her. *How on earth had Alayna Marchmont uncovered her whereabouts this time?*

Six months ago, when Chelsea had disappeared from the Marchmont town house in Bath, she had purposely taken the precaution of informing the coaching office where she had booked passage to London, that she would *not* be staying in England, but was on her way to the Continent where an Important Position as governess awaited her. It was a lie, of course, and Chelsea had loathed telling it, but she had to be got rid of Alayna Marchmont's continual interference in her affairs. She simply *had* to!

"Miss Grant, may I remind you that you are—"

Chelsea's stomach churned. "Mr. Merribone, I feel I must refuse your request just now and complete my work on the Oldenburg. As you know, Lady Hepplewhite will be calling for it within the hour."

The proprietor's eyes fairly bulged from his head. "Annie Richards will finish the Oldenburg. *You* will follow me!"

Terror gripped Chelsea's middle as she cast an apologetic glance at poor little Annie Richards, then with a weary sigh, she rose obediently to her feet and stepped through the curtain that Mr. Merribone was holding open for her.

Chelsea's knees grew weaker with each step she took. Less than a year ago in Brighton, it had taken but a few well-chosen words from Alayna Marchmont to relieve her of her post as paid companion to the elderly Lady Hennessey. It had been Chelsea's first employment since both she and Alayna had left Miss Farringdon's Academy For Young Ladies in Brighton. True, Alayna had been instrumental in helping secure the post for Chelsea, but that did not give her the right to continue to order Chelsea about afterwards, did it?

Catching sight of her former schoolmate standing just inside the doorway of the shop, Chelsea's heart hammered in her ears. As usual, Alayna looked lovely. Today, she wore a pale blue woolen pelisse over a fitted gown of matching blue serge. Chelsea took especial note of the blue silk Huntley that topped the fringe of curls gracing Alayna's brow, curls that were the exact same shade of gold as Chelsea's.

Unconsciously, she smoothed the folds of her dark merino skirt, aware of the rough feel of the fabric beneath her fingers. Since she departed Bath last winter, which is where Alayna insisted Chelsea accompany her on holiday that fateful day she had called at Lady Hennessey's, she'd not been able to afford a single new frock for herself. Just managing food and lodging was an arduous enough task. Still, she was happy with her new life in London, and proud of her growing reputation as a talented bonnet designer. She forced her chin up a notch. She would not let Alayna Marchmont ruin this position for her. She would not!

"Miss Grant and myself at your service, madam," Mr. Merribone said in a fawning tone.

Chelsea held her breath as Alayna directed a cool gaze her way.

"How do you do, Miss Grant. I am Miss Alayna Marchmont." The look in her steel-blue eyes challenged Chelsea.

Chelsea blinked. *Alayna pretending they were not acquainted? How very astonishing!* "H-how do you do, Miss Marchmont," she managed.

"Very well, thank you, Miss Grant. Now that I have located you, that is."

The icy smile on Alayna's lips filled Chelsea's stomach with dread. *What would Alayna say now?*

The pretty blonde flicked a gaze at the shopkeeper. "It seems all of my friends in Town are wearing Miss Grant's designs," she said sweetly. "And, I daresay I am quite eager to acquire a number of them for myself." She paused, her ice blue eyes cutting again to Chelsea. "I understand Miss Grant is from Brighton."

Chelsea's heart fluttered wildly in her breast.

"As it happens," the young lady continued, "I, myself, attended school in Brighton."

"Ah, what a fascinating coincidence, indeed, Miss Marchmont! Surely you are aware that our Miss Grant is the granddaughter of the famous philanthropist from Brighton, Sir George Andover. You must know of the gentleman. Quite generous he was, quite generous, indeed!"

Chelsea's breath lodged convulsively in her throat. It was the very opening Alayna was contriving for. She had used the same tack with Lady Hennessey. If Alayna said *one* disparaging word about Grandpapa Andover today, Chelsea feared she would lose all control. No, she was *certain* she would!

The smile on Alayna's lips turned calculating. "Indeed, I have heard many glowing accounts of the eminent Sir George. Still, one can only wonder if Miss Grant has told you . . . *everything* about her famous grandpapa?"

"Oh, there was hardly a need for Miss Grant to elaborate," Mr. Merribone gushed. "Everyone who *is* anyone is acquainted with that gentleman's altruism. Quite widespread his reputation was, quite widespread, indeed."

"Hmmm," Alayna murmured, a sly gaze still fixed on Chelsea. "You must feel fortunate, Mr. Merribone, to have such a famous personage in your employ."

"Oh, indeed, I do, Miss Marchmont! Indeed I do!"

Chelsea fought for control as Alayna continued to speak calmly.

"I should like to invite Miss Grant to take tea with me this afternoon, Mr. Merribone." She favored the round-faced shopkeeper with another charming smile. "I am all a-tremor to view for myself Miss Grant's latest sketches. I am staying with my aunts in Town; number 12, Portman Square. A goodly number of my aunt's friends will also be present this afternoon. I daresay, they are as eager as I to own bonnets designed by Miss Grant."

Mr. Merribone's smile was so wide it nearly split his face in two. "Your wish is my command, Miss Marchmont! Indeed, it is!"

Suddenly, Chelsea's voice cut in. "I am sorry to disappoint you, Miss Marchmont, but I am far too busy to leave my post today."

"Miss Grant!" Mr. Merribone gasped. "Begging your pardon, Miss Marchmont. I assure you, Miss Grant did not mean what she said. She shall be honored to take tea with you this afternoon. You have only to name the hour, Miss Marchmont. Only to name the hour."

Alayna turned a triumphant smile on Chelsea. "Four of the clock will suit nicely, Mr. Merribone."

At half past three, Chelsea rose stiffly from her place at the workbench and reluctantly reached for her own flat chip bonnet, which she had recently refurbished with a new green ribbon. After tying a perfect bow beneath her chin, she woodenly gathered up her reticule and sketchbook and quitted the millinery shop, headed for fashionable Portman Square on foot.

If her stomach were not churning so frightfully, she might enjoy the free feeling of being out-of-doors in the middle of the afternoon. As it was, the sharp sting of an April breeze whipping color to her cheeks and causing the long folds of her skirt to flap noisily against her legs as she walked, only irritated her further. She hugged a light woolen shawl closer about her shoulders. It, too, was an unwanted reminder of Alayna, being one of a number of cast-off items Alayna had given to Chelsea this past winter in Bath. *Oh! Was she never to be rid of Alayna Marchmont's interference in her life?*

Upon arriving at the Marchmont house, Chelsea was

shown up to an elegantly appointed drawing room and told
that Miss Marchmont would join her presently. Far too angry to sit down and wait patiently, Chelsea nervously paced
the room. That she was the only person here did not surprise
her in the least. Alayna had obviously used the tea party as
a ruse to whisk her from beneath Mr. Merribone's nose. *If
only she knew the reason for Alayna's subterfuge this time!*

If it were Alayna's intent to ruin her reputation in London
with tales of her late grandfather Andover's indiscretions,
why had she not simply repeated the untruths to Mr. Merribone and been done with it? Blurting out the lies had
worked in an instant with Lady Hennessey. Chelsea had
been dismissed on the spot.

Pacing from the hearth to the row of mullioned windows
and back again, she at last heard the drawing room door
slide open behind her. Whirling about, she watched as
Alayna glided toward her, a sweet smile on her admittedly
pretty face. Of a purpose, Chelsea did not return the smile.

"What do you want this time, Alayna?" she demanded.

"Why, Chelsea, dear, what a positively insolent greeting.
Do sit down, I shall ring at once for our tea."

"I am not staying for tea, Alayna. I insist you tell me
straightaway what it is you want from me."

Alayna's sugary smile did not waver as she turned from
the bell rope she had already pulled. "I shall reveal my plan
to you over tea, Chelsea. Do be a dear and sit down." A
hand indicated a pale lemon-yellow settee situated before
the low-burning fire in the hearth.

Pressing her lips tightly together, Chelsea edged onto the
settee while Alayna took a seat in a striped wing chair opposite.

"Now, then," Alayna began. "I must say, I was shocked
to learn that you were employed at a millinery shop, Chelsea. Making bonnets"—she pulled a face—"how dreadfully
dull. Still, I recall, you did have somewhat of an artistic
flair at school. No doubt, Miss Farringdon would think you

quite a success now. You always were her pet pupil, but we
know the *real* reason for that, do we not?"

Chelsea's nostrils flared. "What is it you want, Alayna?"

Alayna made a dismissing motion with one hand. "We've
plenty of time to discuss that, Chelsea, dear. I'd much rather
you tell me why you simply disappeared from us in Bath?
Aunt Lettie was quite beside herself with worry. We all
were. You can be such an ungrateful girl at times. I, for
one, thought it quite generous of my aunts to offer you
employment after the unceremonious manner in which Lady
Hennessey dismissed you.

"Dismissed me?" Chelsea's eyes flashed. "And who do
I have to thank for that?"

"Why, I only wished you to accompany me on holiday,
Chelsea. I cannot think why you are still angry with me
over such a trifling matter. It was well past a year ago. Why,
I still think of you as my dearest friend in all the world."

Chelsea chose not to respond to that. It was true she and
Alayna had once been dear friends. Both orphans, they had
naturally gravitated to one another at Miss Farringdon's
Academy, but their differing circumstances now created a
chasm so wide no childhood friendship could hope to
bridge.

When Chelsea was a child of ten, both her parents had
been killed in a common carriage accident outside
Brighton—common because spills and upsets on the road
to London were an almost daily occurrence considering the
frivolous manner in which gentlemen pitted their gigs and
curricles against one another. After her father's enormous
debts had been paid, what little remained of her Grandpapa
Andover's vast fortune was set aside for Chelsea's educa-
tion. With no family to care for her, the unfortunate child
had been placed with the spinster Farringdon sisters at their
academy in Brighton, a school which her Grandfather Andover had generously supported during his lifetime.

The elder Miss Farringdon had seemed especially glad to have Chelsea with her. And, therein lay Chelsea's problem.

Though she never believed a word of it, it was widely rumored at the school that her grandfather, Sir George, who had died when Chelsea was seven, had not only funded the school, but had also engaged in certain illicit studies of his own with the elder Miss Farringdon. Because Chelsea had adored her lovable grandpapa, she grew white-faced with anger whenever any of her schoolmates taunted her about her grandfather's supposed *tendre* with the prim and proper Miss Farringdon. Some even questioned the legitimacy of Chelsea's lineage. *That* was more than she could bear. Grandpapa Andover was Chelsea's only link to respectability and she would not let anyone mar his good name.

"Did you know that I am to be married?" Alayna asked suddenly, jarring Chelsea from her reverie.

"Hmmm." Chelsea sniffed.

Alayna smiled. "That is the reason I invited you to tea today, Chelsea dear; to inform you of my plans."

"I see." Not at all certain whether to believe Alayna was telling the whole truth or not, Chelsea shifted nervously on the settee. "I expect congratulations are in order."

"Why, thank you!" Alayna responded brightly, then turned to attend to the tea service which the butler was carrying in. After depositing the silver tray on a lovely rosewood table at Alayna's elbow and nestling the pot in the server, he silently vanished, leaving the two young ladies once again alone.

Alayna poured two teacups full of the steaming brew, and after handing one to Chelsea, settled back to sip from her own cup. "Are you not curious to know *who* I am to marry?" she asked.

Though she honestly did not care a whit, Chelsea said, "I am simply dying to know, Alayna."

Alayna giggled. "Oh, Chelsea, you always were an abominable liar! I am to marry a cousin of mine, Rutherford

Campbell. He is the sixth baron. I have not seen him since I was a child, and to say truth, I do not care for him in the least. Though, he is extremely well-put. Or . . . will be. Our marriage releases his inheritance." She smiled roundly. "In a month, I shall be a baroness and you shall have to address me as Lady Rathbone."

"In a month, I hope not to be addressing you at all."

"Oh, Chelsea." Alayna laughed again. "You can be so very droll at times." She leaned forward to set her teacup down. "Rutherford has vast holdings in Honduras, a mahogany plantation, I believe"—she wrinkled her nose in distaste—"so, of course, I have no intention of joining him there. I should go quite mad in such an uncivilized place. I have not yet told Rutherford of my plans. I see no need to inform him until after the ceremony." She smiled conspiratorially. "I expect it will be too late by then, won't it? My Aunt Lettie and Aunt Millicent, Rutherford's mother, arranged the match. Rutherford and I are both agreeable to it; though we have only discussed the matter by letter.

"As I said, we have neither of us laid eyes on the other since we were children—I was a mere child of ten or eleven when last I saw Ford. Though, following our betrothal last month I sent him a lovely miniature of myself. It was the best likeness of me yet!" she enthused. "If I had known of your whereabouts, Chelsea, I could have shown the picture to you before I sent it. At any rate . . . this is where you come in."

Her teacup halfway to her lips, Chelsea's hand froze in mid-air. "Me?"

"Why, of course, dear. It's the rest of the reason I invited you to take tea with me today."

Chelsea's heart pounded afresh.

"Do not look so alarmed, Chelsea dear. I am sure you will be agreeable to what I propose. At the very least, it will remove you from that horrid bonnet shop where you now spend your days."

"I have no intention of leaving my post, Alayna, and I will thank you to stop meddling in my—"

"It will only be for a month, Chelsea. That is—" she smiled wickedly "—unless you refuse."

Chelsea's heart plummeted to her feet. "And if I refuse?"

"Why, I shall have to pay another call on Mr. Merribone, of course."

Chelsea sprang to her feet so fast she nearly toppled her teacup. Her hand shaking furiously, she deposited the clattering cup and saucer onto the tray.

Watching her, Alayna wore a sly smile. "You appear overset, Chelsea. Do sit down, I have not yet told you the whole of it."

Chelsea glared at Alayna. "No! I shall not sit down! And I refuse to let you spoil my living for me here as you did with Lady Hennessey in Brighton!"

"Why, Chelsea, I meant to spoil nothing for you there, and I do not mean to here. Unless, of course . . ." her voice trailed off again.

Chelsea's bosom rose and fell with heated anxiety. "What do you want from me, Alayna?"

Alayna turned another sweet smile on her guest. "It is such a simple request really. I merely want you to travel to Chester. Do, sit down, and let me explain."

Chelsea's heart thundered in her ears. As usual, Alayna's way of putting things left her with no choice but to do as Alayna asked. Glaring at her hostess, she edged back onto the settee.

"Now, then," Alayna began sweetly, "as it happens, Rutherford and I are to be married by *proxy*—in that musty old chapel at Castle Rathbone. You know how I detest the country. So dreadfully rustic. At any rate, because Rutherford will not be present, the marriage ceremony is merely a formality. Aunt Millicent will be there, of course, but no one else of consequence, except myself, and the clergyman. A stranger—perhaps even a servant—will be standing in for Ford. But . . . in order to be married in this fashion, by proxy, one of us must reside for an entire month beforehand in the parish where the wedding ceremony is to take place. And, since Ford is in Honduras, that leaves only *me* to satisfy the silly residency requirement. Surely you can see my problem, Chelsea."

"You wish me to keep you company for the month you are to be in the country," Chelsea muttered flatly.

Alayna nodded, though a bit coyly.

"Well, I simply cannot, Alayna. I cannot just up and leave my post on a whim. I am not like you. I must work to earn my keep, and I cannot—"

"But, I am prepared to pay you, Chelsea. Double what Mr. Merribone does," she added.

Chelsea's lips tightened. She would not do it. Not for any amount of money.

"I shall pay you a hundred pounds!" Alayna interjected shrilly. "I promise I shall!"

Chelsea thrust her chin up. No. She still would not do it.

Alayna leaned forward, her blue eyes angry. "If you refuse me, Chelsea, I shall have no recourse but to *insist*. And then, you shall have no post to come back to."

Chelsea's nostrils flared. Alayna did not make idle threats. She would do exactly as she said. Oh, why did Alayna persist in interfering in her life? At length, Chelsea inhaled an uneven breath. "Well, I—I suppose, I could ask Mr. Merribone to grant me a month's leave of absence in order to accompany you to Chester."

"Accompany me? Oh, I shall not be going, Chelsea. I have other plans for the month. You shall be going to Chester *instead* of me."

Chelsea's brown eyes widened. "Instead of you?"

Alayna nodded. "You shall pretend to *be* me while you are in Chester. We are the same size and have virtually the same colouring. Not that it would matter a whit. No doubt, you will not see a single soul who knows either of us, but in the event that you do—"

"But, Alayna, I cannot—you said yourself I am an abominable liar. I could never carry off such a pretense! Not to mention that it would be an outrageous lie!"

"Oh, you mustn't think of it in that manner, Chelsea. Think of it as . . . acting. As I recall, you are a . . . fair actress. Not nearly so accomplished as I, of course, but you did win the title of 'Brighton Beauty' while we were in school. I never forgave you for that, you know, I thought my Lady Macbeth far superior to your Juliet, but all the same—"

"It was my *one* triumph at school," Chelsea cut in, elevating her chin to a height equalling Alayna's. "And it has nothing to say to anything. I could never convince your Aunt Millicent that I am you! And it most certainly would be lying," she maintained.

"Oh, Chelsea," Alayna leaned forward, "of course, you could do it. Aunt Millicent hasn't seen me since I was a child, and besides, she is practically blind, spends all her days sequestered in her bedchamber. I have everything arranged. You shall take my carriage, wear my clothes. Why, I have already packed a trunk. And my own abigail, Dulcie, shall accompany you. Dulcie is delighted with the prospect of hoodwinking Aunt Millie. She has a half-sister at Castle Rathbone who says my aunt isn't the least popular with the servants. She is far too nasty and cantankerous; doesn't get along with a soul these days. So, you see, it is a perfect plan."

"I see nothing of the sort, Alayna," Chelsea replied frostily. "And furthermore, I do not see why you cannot go yourself."

"Because I—" Alayna paused, considering, as she chewed on her lower lip. "I think it wiser that I do not divulge my whereabouts to you, Chelsea. Suffice to say that

I shall also not remain in London. If my plan should go awry, you may honestly say you have no idea where I am."

Chelsea stewed. She knew very well it was asking far too much to expect Alayna to tell the whole truth, besides, she was too upset over her own situation to even care what mischief Alayna was up to. Her own world had come tumbling down around her feet, and for what? A ridiculous scheme, that's what. If she refused, Alayna would see to it that she lost not only her position with Mr. Merribone, but her reputation in Town would be ruined as well, and then what would she do? At least, this way, if Mr. Merribone agreed to her request, her good name in London would remain intact and she would still have a means of support once she returned to Town. Still . . . she hated letting Alayna think she was giving in so easily.

She thrust her chin up another notch. "I cannot imagine what could be more important to you, Alayna, than marrying your cousin, a wealthy, titled gentleman. Surely you relish the idea of setting up your own household—" Chelsea felt a prick of wistfulness as she realized how very unlikely such a prospect was for her.

"Oh, fustian! You have never met my cousin Rutherford. No young lady in her right mind would be a-tremor to marry him. He is a bore of the first order. Cross and demanding, and not the least bit entertaining. For the most part, I left off reading his letters ages ago. They were full of nothing but the dull goings-on in that horrid place where he lives. How he can abide living there, I cannot think. Though, if you must know"—Alayna's eyes took on a wicked gleam—"I do consider myself quite fortunate to be marrying him. I shall be well set up, after all. And, I shall have all of the freedom—though none of the responsibilities—accorded to a married lady. I shall be free to do as I please."

Chelsea blushed. She knew exactly what Alayna meant, and it was an arrangement that would never suit her. A man and his wife belonged together. "How very cold-hearted you have become, Alayna."

"Moi? Rutherford has the cold heart. He is only marrying me to benefit himself. At eight-and-twenty, he can suddenly wait no longer for his inheritance. I expect he means to increase his holdings in Honduras, or some such nonsense."

Chelsea said nothing further on the subject of Alayna's marriage. And, neither did Alayna, except to reassure Chelsea again and again that she would, indeed, arrive at Castle Rathbone in time for the proxy wedding ceremony. Two stand-ins would never serve.

At length, after Alayna had outlined Chelsea's travel plans to Chester, Chelsea rose to take her leave. The prospect of telling an untruth to Mr. Merribone in order to be granted a month's leave of absence loomed like a dark cloud before her, but, as usual, she had no choice in the matter. Still, as she scurried back to the millinery shop that evening, she reminded herself with some relief, that at least, this time, if Mr. Merribone agreed to her request, she would have a position and a living to come back to.

Two

As expected, Mr. Merribone was not pleased.

"I view your request as quite out of the ordinary, Miss Grant," he replied coolly. "And, by all that is right, I should not allow it."

"I understand your position completely, Mr. Merribone. But, you see, my . . . my aunt is ill. I am told she rarely leaves her bedchamber these days, and I . . . I am her only living relative. I assure you it will be only for a month, after which I shall be returning again to London and to my post, if . . . if you will have me," she added contritely.

Mr. Merribone continued to protest. "Such a lengthy absence, Miss Grant, will serve only to diminish your popularity with the *ton*. They are a fickle lot, professing undying allegiance one day, then abandoning the very proprietor they declared a favorite the next."

Chelsea fidgeted. "Perhaps if I sent along new designs every week, Mr. Merribone. Annie and the others could make them up just as if I were here. I expect to have plenty of time in the coming days to attend to my sketching," she added with a smile, hoping to sway him with charm. It had worked for Alayna. "My absence would hardly be noticed. I assure you, Mr. Merribone, I shall be returning to my post, just as soon as . . . I find someone to properly care for my aunt."

Mr. Merribone's lips pressed tightly together, but at length, he acquiesced to her plea. After thanking him profusely and assuring him once again that she did, indeed, mean to return to London, Chelsea left the shop. Deceiving her employer in so shameless a fashion went against all she stood for, but in this case, she saw nothing else for it.

After a quick bite to eat that night, Chelsea packed up her few belongings and climbed into bed. She'd leave a note tomorrow for the landlord explaining her sudden exit. No doubt, she'd be obliged to find new lodgings upon her return to Town, but that was the least of her worries now. The Marchmont coach would be arriving for her at first light in the morning, and for the month following, everything—including her name—would change.

The journey to Chester took three days. All in all, it proved to be a less than dreary ride; the Marchmont equipage with the fancy gold crest on the side door was plush and comfortable. Though Chelsea was still not particularly happy to be here, she had to admit, she half enjoyed the trip. Alayna's abigail, Dulcie, was agreeable. About seventeen, she was light-hearted and amusing, and even managed to make her nineteen-year-old companion smile upon occasion.

Chelsea's smile faded, however, when late on that final afternoon, the dusty black coach wheeled onto a narrow, overgrown road that caused the elegant high-sprung carriage to jostle and sway dangerously. So shaken was Chelsea that she barely noticed a weathered sign hanging limply from a wall that spelled out Castle Rathbone in dim letters. When next, the great coach rumbled onto a rickety wooden bridge, which Chelsea rightly assumed must have once spanned the castle moat, she found herself fearing for her very life and wishing she'd queried Alayna further about her illustrious ancestral home.

In a matter of minutes, the carriage drew up in front of a crumbling stone relic that was covered top to bottom with a tangled growth of gnarled old vines and brown-tipped ivy. Several wings of the castle jutted from either side of the foremost tower, but all the narrow windows were shut up tight with ill-fitting shutters and, in some cases, pieces of discolored clapboard. Sucking in her breath with dismay, she wondered how even she was to bear spending a month here?

Suddenly, the carriage door flew open from the outside, causing her further alarm. Stepping tentatively to the ground, she became aware of the rapid pounding of her own heart in her breast. A quick glance about revealed the pitifully kept yard inside the bailey. At the moment, it was rapidly filling up with what appeared to be peasants, most of them unkempt and dressed in tattered garments. Adding to the confusion was a pack of mongrel dogs, whose excited barking and tail-wagging told Chelsea she must be the first stranger to visit here in quite some time.

She shrank when an especially filthy footman stepped forward to usher her into the castle foyer. Dulcie lagged behind as other servants began to unload the many trunks and boxes Alayna had sent along with Chelsea.

Indoors, she blinked into the semi-darkness, beginning to understand further why Alayna had been so loath to come here. Thus far, Castle Rathbone could only be described as grim and oppressive. The cool, dank foyer was almost bare of furniture, only a few high-backed chairs were positioned here and there before the cold stone walls. Suddenly, a solemn-faced gentleman dressed completely in black appeared out of nowhere.

"Miss Marchmont, I presume?" the man said, gazing the length of a pinched nose at Chelsea.

She gulped. "Y-yes."

"This way, miss."

Lifting the folds of her skirt a bit, Chelsea followed the man down a dark, narrow corridor, its meandering length seeming to take her deeper and deeper into the bowels of the high-ceilinged tomb. The clicking sound of Chelsea's half-boots on the bare stone floor echoed like bells in the eerie stillness. Feeling a sudden chill overtake her, she ran a gloved hand up one arm in an effort to ward it off.

Glancing warily at her surroundings, Chelsea absently noted a row of dusty portraits hanging on the wall to her left, their expressionless faces and hollow eyes seeming to follow her progress through the castle. At intervals on the opposite wall, single candles in sconces flickered as Chelsea and the man in black passed beneath, their movements stirring the stale air trapped within the castle walls.

Other eyes watched her—brighter, human eyes, glittering from shadowy corners and through cleverly concealed hidey-holes in the dimly lit corridor. But, absorbed in her own thoughts, Chelsea was also unaware of them.

After she and the butler, who, she assumed this man to be, had ascended an ancient staircase, sans railing, they moved silently down yet another long corridor, crossed a room lined all around with musty-smelling books, and even passed through a secret passageway hidden in a cobbled wall. At length, the man paused before a set of immense wooden doors, whose huge ornate hinges looked sadly in need of polish.

Chelsea waited breathlessly as the butler rapped insistently on the door. For a farthing, she would turn around and flee, though there was some doubt in her mind that she'd be able to accurately retrace her footsteps to freedom. Instead, she willed her pounding heart to be still and drew in a long breath in an effort to bolster her courage. She had come this far; she must at least present herself to Alayna's Aunt Millicent, and then hope for the best.

As the butler rapped again, louder this time, Chelsea nervously smoothed a wrinkle from the skirt of her gown, which wasn't her gown at all, but one of Alayna's—a lovely beige travelling suit, with York tan gloves, and a matching casquet bonnet. Though she felt quite elegant wearing the attractive ensemble, she knew the lovely gown could do nothing to diminish the fear and trepidation wrinkling her brow.

Suddenly hearing what could only be described as a 'bellow' coming from the other side of the closed doors, Chelsea jumped with fright. By way of response, however, the butler merely pushed open the creaky door and stepped inside.

"Miss Marchmont has arrived, my lady," he said, solemnly.

The unexpected reply to this pronouncement made Chelsea recoil with fresh fear.

"Well, show her in, you fool!"

A lesser mortal would have taken umbrage at the tone, let alone the words, but this manservant merely turned again toward Chelsea and said evenly, "Her ladyship will receive you now, Miss Marchmont."

Her brown eyes wide, Chelsea prayed for additional courage as she advanced one small step into the room. Here, the darkness seemed to envelop her. Blinking into it, her eyes were drawn to the one bright spot she saw, a low-burning fire on the hearth. Above the massive mantelpiece, hung a tattered tapestry, the top partially covering two narrow windows that stretched nearly as high as the vaulted ceiling.

"Well, what are you gawking at, gel?"

Whirling about, Chelsea caught sight of an ancient canopied bed dripping with hangings which at one time may have been lovely, but were now soiled and squalid. Propped up in a sea of pillows was a very old lady. Strewn about her on the coverlet and on the floor were piles and piles of yellowed newspapers and books . . . *books!* Chelsea blanched as heightened terror washed over her. *Alayna had said her aunt was practically blind!*

"Come here so I can get a close look at you, gel!"

Too afraid to move, Chelsea barely managed, "H-how do you do, Aunt Millicent?"

"Aunt Millicent! As I recall, you used to call me Aunt Millie." Squinting at Chelsea, Lady Rathbone reached to steady her spectacles. "You appear to be quaking, gel. Sit by the fire if you feel a chill. I'll have Jared bring us a pot of tea. *Jared!*"

Chelsea jumped again, but upon hearing a muffled noise coming from outside the closed bedchamber door, her round brown eyes cut that direction.

The door opened and the same stone-faced gentleman stepped inside. "You bellowed, madam?"

Chelsea thought she heard a chortle coming from the old lady on the bed, but she couldn't be sure. It might have been a cough.

"Tea, Jared! Bring it up. And don't spare the butter on the toast." She directed another squinty-eyed gaze at Chelsea, who, as commanded, was edging toward the crackling fire. "I assume you brought a maid with 'ye, gel?"

Chelsea nodded tightly. "Yes, ma'am."

"Put the girl in the west wing with the other maids, Jared, and see that she's properly fed. Have my niece's trunks taken to the green suite in the east tower. But, bring our tea before you attend to the other duties. Miss Marchmont seems to have caught a chill."

When Jared had backed away and had, as quietly as possible—considering the squeaky hinges—closed the bedchamber door, Chelsea turned a terrified gaze on the thundercloud still reclining on the bed. It went without saying that Aunt Millicent was not the least as she'd expected.

"Well, I still haven't got a proper look at you," Lady Rathbone grumbled, flinging back the coverlet and snatching up a cane which had been leaning against the commode beside her bed. Then, with less effort than Chelsea would have expected from someone purported to be bedridden, the old woman rather agilely limped across the room, headed for a faded brocade sofa positioned near the fire.

Taking no thought for her actions, Chelsea hurried to

fluff the cushions at the old woman's back and help settle a warm woolen shawl about her frail shoulders.

Appearing somewhat astonished by her niece's thoughtful gesture, Lady Rathbone twisted to look up at her. "I daresay, you've changed considerably, Alayna. I seem to recall you being an especially selfish child. Not given to thinking of anyone but yourself." Her lips pressed tightly together as she reached to steady her spectacles.

Chelsea hastened to seek out a chair situated a bit apart from Lady Rathbone and slipped nervously into it. Then, during the brief moment of silence that followed, her anxiety grew as she felt the old woman's eyes boring holes through her.

At length, Lady Rathbone said, "You've become a passing fair young lady, Alayna. Rutherford will be pleased to see it."

Chelsea blinked. "Rutherford? But, I . . . I shan't be *seeing* him, shall I, madam; I mean, Aunt Millicent?"

Lady Rathbone squinted narrowly. "Well, of course you shall see him, peagoose. Husbands and wives generally do meet up, on occasion."

Chelsea felt her insides begin to tremble once again. The interview was not going at all well. Valiantly, she tried to recall Alayna's sentiments regarding her forthcoming marriage, and summon the proper tone to voice them. Elevating her chin a notch, she managed to announce evenly, "Well, if you must know, Aunt Millicent, I have no intention of spending any length of time with Rutherford."

To Chelsea's surprise, Lady Rathbone threw her gray head back and laughed aloud. "Can't say as I blame 'ye gel! I doubt my son's temperament has improved with age. A more demanding young man, I never saw." She fussed with her shawl. "Just like his late father in that regard, though I believe Ford is a jot more principled. As a prospective husband, I mean. You could do worse, gel."

"Hmmm." Chelsea wracked her brain for something additional to say on the subject, but could think of nothing plausible, so elected to remain silent for the moment. After a pause, she said, "I wonder when you last heard from my cousin?"

"Not since he wrote saying he'd agreed to the match. Of course, I haven't seen my son since he became a man. Suffice to say, I shouldn't recognize Rutherford today if I met him in the corridor." A gnarled finger touched her spectacles again. "Have only had these less than a twelvemonth. Not that they'd help matters any."

"Hmmm," Chelsea repeated herself, then cast an anxious glance about . . . and saw *another* stack of books piled near Lady Rathbone's feet! "It . . . appears you do a good deal of reading, ma'am, uh, Aunt Millie."

A sharp gaze on Chelsea, Lady Rathbone nodded assent. "Been trying to catch myself up. Still find reading difficult, however, in spite of being spectacled."

"I should be happy to read to you, ma'am," Chelsea blurted out, then caught herself. *Alayna would never have offered to read to her aunt.*

"Read to me, eh? Well, that would be quite lovely."

Chelsea stewed. She simply must keep her wits about her! Shifting uncomfortably in her chair, her eyes flitted nervously over the room. Again, she felt Lady Rathbone studying her the entire time.

"I detect a marked difference about you, gel," the woman remarked.

Chelsea held her breath. Was Lady Rathbone about to question why Alayna's sky blue eyes had suddenly turned midnight brown?

"Can't quite name it though," the old lady muttered thoughtfully, "however, I expect it will come to me soon enough."

Chelsea tried to still her rapidly pounding heart. She was making a shambles of pretending to be Alayna. There must be *something* she could say, or do, that would reassure Lady

Rathbone that she was, indeed, her niece. Suddenly, she sprang from her chair and flounced across the room. "Whatever do you suppose is keeping Jared?" she exclaimed with a huff. "I declare I am simply parched. I have been three days shut up in a stuffy carriage and I am sick to death of just sitting about!"

"Anxious to get to the stables, are you?"

Chelsea froze. "The stables?"

"Riding. Lettie tells me you dash to the stables the minute you arrive in Bath. Why, I recall even as a child, your riding skills put Rutherford's to shame."

Chelsea winced. She hated horses. Had been frightened to pieces of them ever since her parents' unfortunate accident which involved a huge stallion and a run-away team. "Uh," she hedged, "well, if you must know, Aunt Millie, I rarely ride these days. It isn't necessary in Town, you know."

A gray brow shot up.

"Though, I admit," Chelsea added airily, "I should like to go into Chester." She began to prance mindlessly about the room, pausing to examine the ancient tapestry, then flitting to a table upon which rested an old leather-bound volume whose title she couldn't quite make out.

Twisting about on the sofa to watch her niece, Lady Rathbone said, "Would hardly expect the Rows to interest you, young lady."

"You are quite right, Aunt Millie. I expect the shops in Chester look much the same as they did the last time I visited." Truth to tell, Chelsea had never seen the famous Rows, and would like nothing better than to browse through the multitude of shops there, however, she was quite certain Alayna would find such an excursion dull beyond words. Chelsea exhaled an exaggerated sigh. "I should simply like to purchase a few things," she said. "A sketchbook, perhaps. I must find something useful to do with my time these coming weeks."

"Useful!" Lady Rathbone exclaimed, pursing her lips.

"You are considerably altered, indeed, Alayna. For the better, I might add," she muttered beneath her breath.

Chelsea grimaced. She was botching things frightfully! She could only wonder why Lady Rathbone hadn't already confronted her and demanded to know the truth. For the moment however she was spared further conversation when the chamber door creaked open and Jared reappeared with the tea things. Chelsea gratefully returned to her chair and didn't mind a bit when Lady Rathbone asked her to serve. It was something to do.

"Well, I see your years at Miss Farringdon's Academy were not wasted," the older woman remarked after Chelsea had handed her a perfectly poured cup of tea and a small chipped plate piled with buttered toast and two greasy tarts of some sort. "Your aunts have no doubt put your talents to good use these last years, I expect. A young lady with exemplary social skills is sure to be an asset in Town."

Sipping her tea, Chelsea murmured a nervous agreement to that sentiment, then managed to evasively answer additional questions regarding Alayna's aunts, Lettie and Hermione, both of whom Alayna had remembered to tell Chelsea were spending the spring and summer months in Brighton.

"And Eudora? Is she still in London?"

Chelsea paused. She did not recall Alayna mentioning Aunt Eudora. Yet, Eudora must have been in London, else who had Alayna been staying with in Portman Square?

"I asked about Eudora, gel!" Lady Rathbone fairly shouted, then waited as Chelsea carefully set aside her teacup. "Good God, gel, you just came from London, is Eudora well, or isn't she?"

"Umm . . . she is well enough, I expect, Aunt Millicent, but . . . suddenly, *I* am feeling quite out of curl." It was not a lie. "I should like to retire to my chamber now, if you please."

Behind her spectacles, Lady Rathbone's gray eyes narrowed. "Oh, go on with you then." She waved Chelsea away with her cane. "We've a month of Sundays to talk of the relatives, I expect. Never mind that I haven't had a visitor this age," she grumbled. "I should think the least you could do is catch me up on the family." She set aside her own teacup, then struggled to rise to her feet.

Chelsea couldn't bear to watch the feeble old lady struggle so. Springing to her feet, she reached to help. "Allow me to assist you, Aunt Millicent," she said gently.

Lady Rathbone's eyes cut round, but she said nothing further. After Chelsea had helped her into bed and tucked the coverpane about her, she excused herself and left the room.

She found Dulcie awaiting her in the corridor. "Thought you might need help finding your way to your suite, miss," she said, her voice lowered in case Jared, or someone else, may be lurking about and overhear her.

Chelsea exhaled a relieved sigh. "Thank you ever so, Dulcie. I admit I quite forgot to scatter breadcrumbs on my way here."

Alone in her bedchamber that evening, Chelsea mentally reviewed the disastrous interview she'd endured with Lady Rathbone. Though she knew she had made a muddle of it, she couldn't help feeling sorry for the old lady. With only her books and a stone-faced butler for company, it was more than obvious that the old woman was lonely. But what could Chelsea do about it? Alayna would never lift a finger to help.

Though she spent the next few days learning her way around the centuries-old castle, Chelsea continued to stew over Lady Rathbone's situation, making a point of visiting the formidable old woman at least once each day, generally at tea time. On the second day, she made good on her word to read to the woman and was pleased when they laughed together over an amusing article in an outdated copy of *The Times*. As the days passed, Lady Rathbone ceased asking questions that Chelsea felt hard put to answer, and instead seemed merely glad for the company.

Chelsea took her meals in her own quarters, a large suite of rooms located in an interesting round tower in the east wing. Clearly evident to her was the fact that the rooms had not been in service for a while—the heavy wine draperies were a haven for dust mites, as was the faded carpet that covered the smooth stone floor of her bedchamber.

It took a bit of doing, but Chelsea finally pressed four of the housemaids into removing the draperies and rug and carting them outside for a much-needed cleaning. The bulk of Lady Rathbone's servants, Chelsea had discovered, were an uninspired lot, given to slothful habits and in the absence of their employer, blatantly shirking their duties.

Even Dulcie—who after the second night, took to sleeping on a cot in the dressing room next to Chelsea's bedchamber, telling Chelsea that she wasn't accustomed to sharing a bed, even if the bedfellow was her own half-sister—commented on the lackadaisical attitude of the castle servants.

"Ain't a one of them does a half-days work!" she exclaimed hotly. "Miss Marchmont would sack 'em in a minute, she would."

Chelsea knew that was true. Alayna wouldn't stand for the laziness or half-completed tasks. Thinking further on it, Chelsea reckoned there were at least twenty-five or thirty people who lived in relative ease inside the castle, and counting the outside stablehands and the groundskeepers that number would likely swell to fifty. Still Chelsea couldn't bear to see a single one of them lose their positions. So, after some thought, she decided to handle the matter not as Alayna might, but in her own singular fashion.

Jared, she had observed, had few duties other than to loiter about the corridor outside Lady Rathbone's chamber, in order to be on hand when the woman bellowed. It had not taken Chelsea long to ascertain the reason for her unorthodox habit of shouting when she wished Jared to appear. Not a single one of the bell pulls in the castle worked.

On the afternoon that Chelsea intended to put her plan into action, she approached Jared, as usual, to request an audience with Lady Rathbone.

"Do come in, dear," the woman said, after Jared had announced her. It had been some days since Lady Rathbone had bellowed at Chelsea. "My, is it tea time already?"

"No, ma'am, I have come about another matter," Chelsea replied, a warm smile on her lips.

"And what might that be, dear?" Already, Lady Rathbone had sat up in bed and was reaching for her cane, apparently intent upon joining Chelsea at their customary place before the fire. "Do you require something?" she asked pleasantly, as Chelsea reached to assist her to a standing position.

"No, ma'am; not for myself." Chelsea walked slowly alongside Lady Rathbone, then adjusted a cushion at her back as she eased onto the sofa. Chelsea slipped onto a nearby chair.

"Well, then, what is it?" Lady Rathbone asked expectantly.

In a confident tone, Chelsea began. "I have come to ask if you would consider opening the dining hall, Aunt Millicent, so that you and I might take our meals together? And," Chelsea rushed on before the woman could object, "I should like us to take our tea in the drawing room from now on. I located a perfectly good Bath chair belowstairs, and I am certain that with Jared's help, and perhaps one of the footmen, we could wheel you about the corridors, and perhaps even venture outdoors. A breath of fresh air on occasion would bring color to your cheeks, Aunt Millie."

A slow smile moved across Lady Rathbone's face. "Why, I think that a capital idea, Alayna. You are a positively dear girl for thinking of me. We shall begin this very evening. *Jared!*"

* * *

Leaving the old lady's hide-away moments later, Chelsea smiled to herself. A bit of life about the castle and she felt certain the servants would once again be inspired to take pride in their work.

Supper in the dining hall that evening proved a somewhat haphazard affair, what with the servants not being accustomed to properly serving or clearing. However, breakfast and luncheon the following day went a bit smoother; and though tea in the drawing room that afternoon came a little too soon for the draperies and carpets to have been aired, Chelsea helped dispel some of the gloom by drawing aside both the curtains and shutters and allowing some much-needed air and light in.

Over the next days, Dulcie assisted Chelsea in transforming the gloomy castle into something that more closely resembled a home. Chelsea saw to cleaning the bed hangings and linens in Lady Rathbone's chamber, and brought in armloads of colorful wildflowers and arranged them in vases throughout the castle. She also supervised the dusting of portraits, and polishing of all the brass hinges on the great oaken doors. Though Jared's stoic countenance never varied, Chelsea began to sense his approval of her brightening up the place.

She also became aware of a certain respectful camaraderie that existed between that gentleman and Lady Rathbone. On one afternoon, as she was sitting with Lady Rathbone in her chamber, a particularly high wind came up. Not an uncommon occurrence in this part of England, wind seemed to whistle about the crumbling castle walls with disturbing regularity. However, on this particular afternoon, it loosened an outside shutter from its moorings and caused it to fly straightaway to the ground, where it landed smack on the head of a sleeping pig and killed it. In minutes, the entire castle was in an uproar, the few eyewitnesses to the happening being consulted by vast numbers of inside servants, eager for a detailed recounting of the bizarre occurrence.

Jared delivered the news to Lady Rathbone. "Most disturbing, I should say, my lady," he concluded, his expression impassive, both hands clasped calmly behind his back.

Chelsea had found the tale quite amusing and Lady Rathbone had laughed aloud. However, when Jared did not join in the levity, Lady Rathbone chided, "Come, come, Jared, I see your eyebrow twitching. I take that to mean you are as astonished as the rest of us, perhaps even shocked."

Chelsea watched the drama unfolding before her with growing fascination.

"Whatever you say, my lady," Jared replied smoothly, without so much as a blink of an eye.

Her lips twitching, Lady Rathbone turned to Chelsea. "I expect it has not escaped your notice, my dear, that our Jared does a perfectly splendid imitation of a statue. He thinks I suspect nothing, but I have been on to him for quite some time now. These, of course—" she reached to touch her spectacles "—have given me a decided advantage. I daresay, I once saw Jared's eyebrow lift a good eighth inch. I took it to mean he was near to hysteria."

Chelsea couldn't smother a laugh as her gaze cut to Jared. There she caught an almost imperceptible movement about the corner of his mouth. Something told her it would be an outright smile on anyone else.

When the first Sunday rolled around, Chelsea was obliged to attend early services in the parish church, in order that Alayna's banns could be read. The past week, she had become so caught up in brightening up the castle and yes, *enjoying* her new-found footing with Lady Rathbone, that she had nearly forgot the real reason she had come to the castle. Yet, it all came tumbling down around her the minute she and Dulcie set foot inside the church.

Amid shy stares and a few tentative greetings, being addressed as Miss Marchmont, of course, Chelsea felt renewed mortification over the lie she was living. The second the last Amen was sung, she gathered up her reticule and prayer book and hastily exited the church, poor Dulcie scurrying along behind her in an effort to keep up. So overset was Chelsea when she returned to the castle that she spent the remainder of the day sequestered in her bedchamber with a megrim.

She felt a bit better the next morning, having come to the realization that with the most difficult week of the month behind her, all that remained now was for Alayna to return and the actual wedding ceremony to be got through. As far as explaining the faradiddle to Lady Rathbono, Chelsea felt that was Alayna's concern, therefore she would not waste time worrying needlessly on that head.

Dressing for breakfast that morning, she further decided that she'd venture into Chester that day and purchase the new sketchbook and pens she needed so she might make good on her word to Mr. Merribone. In a few days' time, she should have quite a number of fresh designs to post to London, with explicit instructions for Annie and the others, to make up.

However, upon reaching the ground floor of the castle on her way to breakfast, Chelsea again found the castle in an uproar. Why, the commotion this morning was enough to make the pig incident of last week pale by comparison!

Three

Her brown eyes a question, Chelsea proceeded toward the little nook off the old hall where she and Lady Rathbone had been in the habit of taking their morning chocolate and buttered scones. That today the nook was empty surprised her greatly. Entering the corridor again, Chelsea came upon a literal parade of maids and footmen scurrying thither and yon.

"Mary, what is it?" Chelsea asked one of them. "Has something happened to Lady Rathbone?"

"No, miss." Mary bobbed a quick curtsy. "It's him, miss. 'E's arrived."

"He?"

"Must go, miss. 'E wants 'is coffee now." Mary bustled away.

Two steps more, and Chelsea came face to face with Dulcie. Her blue eyes were round as she drew Chelsea aside.

"What is it, Dulcie? What's happened?"

"It's 'im, Miss Grant. Lord Rathbone. Miss Alayna's intended."

"Oh!" Chelsea clamped a hand over her mouth.

"There's more, miss." Dulcie glanced about, apparently not wanting to be overheard. " 'E's been asking for you, Miss Grant, or rather for Miss Marchmont. 'E's quite the ill-tempered bloke, I'll say."

Chelsea was so overset she thought she might expire on the spot. "Where is Lady Rathbone? Is she—?"

"Her ladyship's with him. Both of them's in the dining hall. It's a proper breakfast they're havin'."

Just then, she and Dulcie's tete a tete was interrupted by a masculine shout that rivaled Lady Rathbone's in volume and tone. *"Jared!"*

Dulcie jumped. "You'd best go now, miss."

"But, Dulcie, I—"

"Good luck to you, miss."

"Jared!" came the angry shout again. "My eggs are cold and the pork is underdone."

Apparently Lord Rathbone and his mother were having the last of the pig for breakfast, Chelsea thought, as she hurried toward the dining hall, on the way, making a valiant attempt to quiet her pounding heart before she entered the cavernous chamber.

Advancing bravely into it, the greeting Lady Rathbone directed her way seemed altogether usual. "Ah, there you are, Alayna dear," the woman said, a smile creasing her weathered cheeks, her Bath chair pushed up to one end of the long oaken table. At the other end . . .

Chelsea's frightened gaze flitted toward the dark-haired gentleman seated there. Though he made a cursory effort to rise, his dark brows were pulled together in a decided frown. "So . . ." He studied Chelsea through the narrowed slits of his eyes. "This is my betrothed, cousin Alayna."

Chelsea winced as she slid into the chair a footman was politely holding out for her. "My lord," she murmured, then hastily lowered her gaze to her lap.

"Look at me!" the man shouted.

Chelsea instantly obeyed.

Silence hung between the two for a spell, then an angry brow shot up. "Eat your breakfast, Miss Marchmont."

Chelsea felt a footman hovering near her elbow, but knew she was far too overwrought at the moment to consume even a bite of the hard-cooked eggs and thick cutlet the man was lifting onto her plate.

"Rutherford's arrival in the wee hours of the morning has taken us all by surprise," Lady Rathbone said evenly, apparently addressing Chelsea.

"Hmmm." A nervous smile wavered across Chelsea's face.

"Mustn't look so alarmed, Miss Marchmont," the man snapped. "I shan't be staying. As soon as you and I are wed, and"—his black eyes cut to Lady Rathbone—"certain documents have been handed over to me, I shall be on my way again."

Chelsea searched for something appropriate to say. "You . . . have come to collect your inheritance, then," she ventured.

"Correct, my dear."

At his term of endearment, Chelsea blanched. For some reason, she did not wish to be regarded as this man's dear. He was rude and crass, and Alayna had not been wrong in her assessment of him.

Suddenly, the man startled her by slamming his fist onto the table once more. Twisting in his chair to address the footman who had just filled his cup with coffee, he snarled, "I said *hot,* you fool, this is tepid!" Turning back around, he directed a sharp look at Chelsea. "What are you staring at, missy?"

She flinched.

"Eat!" he ground out.

Nervously, she picked up her cup and forced a sip of warm tea down as he gobbled the mountain of fresh food on his plate, his eyes fastened on her the entire while.

"No appetite, eh, Miss Marchmont?" he chided, talking coarsely around a mouthful of bread and jam.

Chelsea thrust her chin up. "I am rarely hungry in the morning, sir."

"Do cut line, Rutherford," Lady Rathbone put in. "She is obviously taken aback by your presence this morning.

Neither of us expected to see you here today. You have given us all quite a jolt."

"A jolt was hardly my intent, Mother," the brash man replied, then snapped his fingers, indicating to the footman that hastened to his side that he desired still more ham and eggs on his plate. "I have merely journeyed to England to collect what is rightfully mine, and"—a sidelong gaze cut to Chelsea—"the means by which to collect it." With that, he dove into his food, noisily wolfing down the meal as if he had eaten nothing in a fortnight.

From the corner of her eye, Chelsea watched him. This man was anything but a gentleman. His dark hair was over-long and greasy, his shirt-front soiled, and his frockcoat and vest not the finest cut. Suddenly, the man's sharp eyes darted her way again.

"You'd best leave off staring at me, missy, and eat your meal. We leave for London within the hour."

Chelsea blinked. "Excuse me?"

He swiped a sleeve across his mouth, then seemed to remember himself and snatched up the cloth napkin lying beside his plate to finish the job. "London. We are to be married as soon as possible."

"But, the banns were read only yesterday," Chelsea protested weakly.

"Which signifies nothing!" the man bellowed, slamming his fist onto the table to emphasize his point—a large, rough fist, Chelsea noted. "We shall obtain a special license in London and be married at once. I understand that is common practice among the gentry."

Chelsea's finely arched brows pulled together. For a gentleman, that seemed a singularly odd thing to say. There was much about this man that did not ring true. She glanced toward Lady Rathbone. Apparently, she saw nothing amiss.

"You have only just arrived, Rutherford," the frail old lady said. "Now that you are here, I had hoped you and

Alayna might have a proper wedding in the castle chapel.
Your father and I exchanged our vows there and—"

"I have no desire to follow in my father's footsteps!" the
man spat out. He glared at Chelsea. "We leave within the
hour!"

Hurrying toward her bedchamber a few moments later,
Chelsea was certain something was vastly awry. The man
calling himself Rutherford Campbell was no gentleman. He
was crude and uncivil and he had abominable manners. Perhaps Lady Rathbone had lived too long in the country to
see it, but Chelsea had not. She was certain this man was
no more Lady Rathbone's son than she was her niece. Yet,
as things now stood, she had no choice but to obey the
man's every command.

In her suite, she and Dulcie made hasty preparations to
leave immediately for London. Perhaps at an inn along the
way, Chelsea could alert someone to the danger they were
in, or better yet, conceive a plan to escape. For now, the
most she could do was remove this vile creature from Lady
Rathbone's presence. She would not, *could* not, let any harm
come to that dear old lady!

In less than half an hour, she and Dulcie breathlessly
descended the stone stairwell and took up a position in the
foyer as they waited for the ill-bred man to join them.

His belligerent voice preceded him before long strides
brought him into view. Alongside him, Jared was pushing
Lady Rathbone's Bath chair. "It was my understanding the
documents were here at the castle!" the man stated angrily.

The squeak of Lady Rathbone's chair drowned out her
reply, but Chelsea and Dulcie exchanged alarmed glances
anyway. Approaching them, the man registered surprise at
finding Dulcie standing beside Chelsea, both of them obviously prepared to leave.

"You are not to bring a maid!" he announced.

Chelsea had opened her mouth to protest when he interrupted.

"No maid! You'll not need one where you are going." His tone was harsh.

Chelsea's lips thinned. She had had about enough of this contemptible beast. "Either Dulcie comes or I do not!" she replied hotly.

The man scowled. "You will do as I say . . . and I say, no maid!"

Chelsea's bosom rose and fell, but she managed to hold her tongue. Perhaps it was for the best. She did not wish harm to come to Dulcie either. And if she were to attempt an escape later, it might be more easily accomplished if she were alone.

Just then, the wide castle doors creaked open and a pock-faced man stuck in his head. "Horses are saddled, 'yer lordship."

Chelsea thought she detected a gleam of treachery in the man's eyes when he said 'yer lordship'. She thrust her chin up. "I don't ride."

" 'Ye'll do as I say, wench!" the dark-haired man sputtered.

"Rutherford," Lady Rathbone put in coolly, "you know very well that your cousin, Alayna, does not ride."

Chelsea turned frightened eyes on Lady Rathbone, but the warmth and acceptance she usually found there was missing. The look of cold, hard hatred she saw now made her shiver.

Bouncing along in the Marchmont coach, Chelsea was thankful for small favors. She had no idea why Lady Rathbone had said what she had, or who she suspected Chelsea was now, but, at least, she had protected the old woman from harm.

After several hours on the road, the men riding alongside

the carriage on horseback directed the lumbering coach into the busy yard of a roadside inn. Chelsea was about to step to the ground when a rough hand shoved her back inside.

" 'Yer not going anywhere, missy."

Her brown eyes widened with fresh alarm as she edged back onto the bench. The man calling himself Rutherford Campbell crawled into the carriage and pulled the door shut behind him. "Who are you, wench?" He glowered at her.

Chelsea stiffened.

"I know you ain't Miss Marchmont. So, who are you?"

"Who are *you?* " Chelsea returned hotly. "It is perfectly clear that you are not my cousin, Rutherford."

"Oh, that's clear, is it?"

"Indeed, it is. And *I* demand to know what you have done with him."

"You demand?" He snorted. "You ain't in no position to do no demanding, missy. Now, tell me who you are a'fore I—"

"I am Alayna Marchmont"—Chelsea returned his icy gaze—"and I have no intention of marrying you."

" 'Yer mighty uppity for an impostor, missy." Eyeing her, the man grinned wickedly, his uneven, yellowed teeth making Chelsea cringe. "Tell me the truth and I might be persuaded to share the spoils with you."

So, that was his scheme, Chelsea thought. He meant to marry Alayna so that he might abscond with Lord Rathbone's inheritance himself. "I *am* telling the truth," she maintained coolly. "I am Alayna Marchmont, and I shall marry no one save my cousin, Rutherford Campbell."

Grunting, the man reached into his frockcoat pocket and removed a small, flat object wrapped in brown paper. Chelsea watched as he unfurled the wrapping to reveal a gold-encrusted miniature, which he waved beneath Chelsea's nose. "This, my pretty trickster, is the real Miss Marchmont. And," he added triumphantly, "the likeness don't resemble you one whit!"

Chelsea gasped. It was the miniature Alayna had sent to Rutherford following their betrothal. Indeed it was a perfect likeness of her. Suddenly, she felt faint with fear. Had the man . . . *killed* Lord Rathbone in order to obtain it? Oh, she dared not think it! "H-how did you come by the portrait?" Chelsea barely breathed.

"How I got it don't signify. That I have it is the important thing. Now, I put it to you again, missy, who are you and what have *you* done with the real Miss Marchmont? I don't want no fashionable ladies turning up in London laying claim to what's mine!"

Chelsea stared at the charlatan defiantly. "I refuse to tell you a thing."

"So," his eyes narrowed with fury, "don't tell me nothing, then." He jammed the portrait back into his pocket. "But, be forewarned, missy, I have no intention of abandoning my plan. And, don't think to cheat me out of the bounty neither. I come a long way for this and I don't mean to leave emptyhanded."

Flinging a last contemptible look at her, he crawled out of the coach and slammed the door shut behind him.

Chelsea's heart sank. If she were not to be let out of the carriage for even a second, how could she possibly engineer an escape?

As the long hours of afternoon dragged by, she grew increasingly uneasy. What if these wretched men had indeed killed Lord Rathbone? What would she tell Alayna, and Lady Rathbone? And what did the killers intend to do with her?

Near nightfall, they stopped again to change horses, and after proclaiming a dire need to use the necessary, Chelsea was, at last, permitted to leave the coach. Both the false Rathbone and his man waited outside the privy door and quickly ushered her back to the coach. She was thrust inside and given a wedge of stale bread to eat. She wished now she had been able to eat more of her breakfast. As it was, she was so frightened she could barely swallow the morsel of dry bread in her mouth.

As the great coach skimmed over the countryside, an ominous veil of darkness seemed to settle about her. Apparently they would not be stopping at an inn for the night. She only hoped that once they reached London, she would be set free . . . that is, once she had . . . agreed to the wretched man's plan to marry.

Suddenly, she was startled by a deafening explosion ripping through the crisp night air. Sitting bolt upright on the bench, Chelsea peered wide-eyed from the coach window, but in the darkness, could make out nothing. When another blast rang out, the huge carriage lurched forward at an even faster pace.

Twisting about on the bench, Chelsea tried to see through the small pane of glass at her back. What she saw from this vantage point made her gasp with alarm. Five, maybe six, men on horseback were chasing the large coach. *Highwaymen! They were being chased by highwaymen!* The flash of moonlight gleaming on the barrels of their upraised pistols sent her heart plummeting to her feet.

When Chelsea heard yet a third shot ring out and then the thud of a body being toppled from the coachman's platform to the ground, she screamed with terror and threw herself onto the floor of the coach, grasping for something, *anything* to hold onto.

"No!" she cried, as the huge, driverless coach began to career dangerously across open countryside. Suddenly, she knew exactly how her mother and father had felt those last horrifying moments of their lives. "Help!" she screamed. "Somebody, please help!"

Tossing to and fro on the floor between the benches, Chelsea's bonnet toppled askew and she felt her long golden hair come tumbling down around her shoulders. Upon hearing the shouts of upraised voices, she stiffened with fear. Was she now to be robbed, or *killed,* by the highwaymen?

A second jolt of the carriage told Chelsea someone had leapt to the platform and in seconds, the run-away coach was brought to a somewhat shaky standstill.

Chelsea's eyes were wide as she raised herself to her knees, wondering what would happen next. She gasped when suddenly the carriage door flew open from the out-side. Silhouetted in the bright shaft of moonlight that spilled into the coach, she found herself gazing into the dark eyes of yet another tall, dark-haired man, only this time, the man's face was full of concern as he looked in upon her.

"Thank God, you are unhurt, Alayna!" At once, the stranger reached to pull her close to him, his strong arms folding her trembling body to his hard chest.

"Oh, sir! You have saved my life!" Chelsea cried, pressing herself against him, her sobs of relief muffled against the man's massive shoulder.

"Do you not recognize me, little one?" the man breathed, his deep voice just above a whisper, his warm cheek nestled in the soft cloud of her hair. "It is I, Rutherford."

Far too overset to have heard the gentleman's words, Chelsea, at last, drew away. Her breath was still coming in fits and starts when she felt his gloved finger gently brush away a tear that lingered still on her lashes. Raising grateful eyes to his, she murmured, "F-forgive me, sir . . . I—"

"Alayna, darling, it is I. Rutherford."

"Oh!" Horror-struck, Chelsea sprang from him.

The gentleman's lips pressed tightly together. "Well," his tone became brusque, "I am pleased to see you, as well, Cousin." He turned to call over his shoulder. "Miss Marchmont is safe. I need a driver here. We are off for Castle Rathbone."

With that, the powerful man climbed into the coach and settled his large frame on the seat next to Chelsea. She snatched up her bonnet from the floor and hurriedly secured the ribbons beneath her chin. Though she felt vastly in-debted to this man for saving her life, discovering that he was the *real* Lord Rathbone suddenly made the idea of being set upon by highwaymen a less frightening prospect than she'd first thought it would be.

Four

Feeling exhaustion about to overtake him, Rutherford Campbell fell back against the squabs. Three days of chasing Sully's tail had left him bone-weary and irritable. He hadn't wanted to come to England, hadn't even planned to be here for his own wedding, but after learning of his former overseer's plot to steal his inheritance, he'd had no choice but to drop everything and make the arduous journey to England at once.

The sea voyage from Honduras had been long and treacherous. High winds and stormy conditions had plagued the passengers and crew the entire way. But, at last they reached shore, and once near Bristol, Lord Rathbone came near to overtaking Sully and his men, only to lose them again when another storm blew up and dashed all hopes of capture.

Feeling certain that Sully was on his way to the castle, Lord Rathbone had sent a message to the authorities in Chester asking that the constable there alert his mother and betrothed to the danger they were in, but either the warning had come too late or word had never reached them.

Exhaling a weary sigh, Lord Rathbone turned a sidelong gaze on his cousin. Thank God, he had arrived when he did. He had no doubt that before Sully was done, he would have ruined her.

"Are you certain you are all right, Alayna?" he asked, his voice full of concern.

By the dim moonlight engulfing the carriage, he watched

the young lady at his side lower her golden head, her still-frightened eyes refusing to meet his. An odd tightness caught in Lord Rathbone's chest. Alayna was more delicate and fragile than he remembered. In fact . . . a sweeping gaze took in her flushed cheeks, the small tilted nose and trembling full lips, she was as near to perfection as any woman could be. Suddenly, the memory of her throwing herself into his arms a moment ago beset him. With it came an unwelcome longing that the steel-hearted Rathbone had not been prepared to feel. Not for Alayna. Not for any woman.

Swallowing tightly, he turned away.

Theirs was to be a marriage of convenience, a contract between two agreeable parties that would benefit them both. After the ceremony, Alayna would join him in Honduras, of course, she was to be his wife, but even that arrangement was calculated merely to fulfil the second part of the agreement, to beget him an heir. Beyond that, he expected nothing from her, that is, not in the way of sentiment. As a planter's wife, she would have certain duties, but Rathbone was rather looking forward to the fact that neither of them would be bothered with the complication of falling in love with one another.

Rathbone was perfectly content with the life he had carved out for himself across the sea. Ten years ago, he had left England and, completely on his own, had created a mahogany empire that was second to none. The release of his inheritance now would enable him to increase his already vast holdings, to build better homes for his workers, and schools for their children. Rathbone took pride in what he had accomplished and in the fact that he was a man of vision, whose noble thoughts and honest deeds placed him head and shoulders above many Englishmen of his time. For the most part, he did not miss his homeland. He was a self-sufficient and self-contained man, and beyond the satisfying of his own normal sexual appetites with women who were more than willing to accommodate him, he had wasted no time in pandering to the fairer sex.

He glanced again at his cousin. Having a wife would not change that, he vowed. Not even a wife as beautiful as Alayna.

"Are you . . . quite certain you are unharmed?" he asked again, finding it somewhat difficult to speak around the odd tightness in his throat.

When she refused still to look at him, he knew a prick of disappointment, but with decision, thrust it aside.

Finally, the young lady said, "I am fine," but her gaze remained fixed on her lap.

"And Mother?" Rathbone persisted. "Was she as fortunate as you? Sully did not harm her, I trust?"

Watching his companion closely, he noted her eyes, beneath unbelievably long lashes, cut round to the corners, but still she did not look at him.

What had happened? Five minutes ago she had flung herself into his arms!

"Good God, Alayna!" he exploded. "Can you not even look at me?"

When she at last directed a tremulous gaze upward, the abject fright Rathbone perceived in the depths of her dark eyes caused him to regret his outburst. "Forgive me, Alayna. I should not have shouted. I have not slept in days and I admit I am exhausted from sheer lack of rest." He paused. "I should merely like to know if Mother is well, or not. Surely you can put my mind at ease on that score."

A pause followed, then, "She is . . . well enough, sir, or, at least, she was when last I saw her."

The young lady had deigned to lift her chin, and for the space of a second, their gazes locked. Suddenly, Rathbone was near to overcome by a compelling urge to gather his betrothed into his arms again and hold her close.

He swallowed. "I expect this ordeal has overset you beyond endurance, Alayna," he murmured. Unable to quell the unsettling urge completely, he did stretch an arm across the back of the seat and gently laid a hand on his cousin's shoulder to urge her toward him. But, at once, he felt her stiffen beneath his touch.

His jaws pressed together with disgust. "It was not my intent to molest you, Alayna. I merely sought to offer comfort."

With that, he withdrew his arm, and folding them both across his chest, he slid down on the bench in order to rest his own head against the squabs. "I should like to sleep a bit. I've been days, nay weeks, chasing Sully's tail and I am near fagged to death."

He closed his eyes, but was startled into awareness a second later when Alayna said, "You are . . . acquainted with the man?"

Rathbone opened one eye. "Sully? Of course, I am acquainted with him! He has been my overseer these past eight years, until he grew so lazy and insolent I was obliged to release him. Surely you recall my writing to you about it. At length, as I recall."

Another pause followed. When it became apparent that no response was forthcoming, Lord Rathbone lifted his head to look at his cousin. "Am I to infer from this that you have *not* been reading my letters, Alayna?"

He watched her twist her small hands together in her lap. "O-of course, I have been reading your letters, sir, it's just that . . . h-how was I to know that *he* was Sully?"

"He had no trouble identifying you."

He noted she seemed to experience some difficulty drawing breath. Finally, she said, "But . . . he carries m-my miniature in his waistcoat pocket. The . . . the portrait I sent to you following our . . . b-betrothal."

"Hummph." Rathbone slid down onto the bench. "I never saw it."

"You . . . never saw it?"

Rathbone's eyes closed again. "Sully has been intercepting my letters. Must have been in the last packet. The man is an unprincipled scoundrel with no regard for anything decent. I shall see him hanged for this treachery."

"Hanged?"

Lord Rathbone's head jerked up. "Surely you can have no objection to that, Alayna?"

"But . . . sir"—her eyes were especially large and round—"no harm was done. Lady, I-I mean, Aunt Millicent was unharmed, and, as you can see, I am . . . I am—"

"What are you babbling about, Alayna?" Rathbone snorted his impatience. "Sully is vile and contemptible. Despite the fact that he has not yet killed a man, I would still insist he hang. Apparently you have forgotten that deception is the one thing I cannot forgive!" With that, he pulled the brim of his hat down over his eyes, the action signaling the end of the discussion.

Beside him, Chelsea tried to still the rapid pounding of her heart. Deception! *Hanged!* Oh!, she had never felt so distressed in all her life! If she were to divulge her true identity to Lord Rathbone now, he would think her one of Sully's accomplices and have her hanged, as well! Most especially when neither of them could produce the *real* Miss Marchmont! Oh! This horrid coil was becoming far too complicated to bear, let alone unravel. If only she could think what to do.

After spending what seemed like hours reviewing her options, which weren't many, she decided that whether she liked it or not, she had no choice but to continue playing her part in the faradiddle. When Alayna returned to the castle, she could explain the whole silly business to her aunt and cousin. In the meantime, it was to Chelsea's advantage that Lord Rathbone had *not* seen the portrait of Alayna, and that, thus far, he seemed to accept that she was, indeed, his betrothed. But, what would happen when the incriminating miniature turned up? She dared not think about that.

* * *

Russet fingers of light had begun to stretch across the early morning sky when the dusty black Marchmont coach lumbered onto the rickety-wooden bridge spanning the castle moat. The jostling of the heavy carriage awakened Lord Rathbone from a deep slumber.

"Bridge is frightfully bumpy," he muttered, his voice sleep-heavy. "Must have fallen into disrepair."

Beside him, Chelsea had been wide-awake most of the journey. "Much about the castle needs attention," she returned quietly.

Lord Rathbone was glancing from one side of the coach to the other. "Bailey's overgrown. Why haven't the grounds-keepers kept the brush under control?"

Chelsea saw no need to respond. There was such a lot to be done at the castle. She wondered if perhaps Lord Rathbone would see to the repairs now that he was here.

"Well, I can see my work's cut out for me," he mumbled.

Chelsea cast a glance his way. "Will you be staying long, sir?" she managed to ask evenly.

He snorted. "Hadn't planned to."

At that, Chelsea's spirits rose the veriest mite. If the gentleman did not mean to stay, she might indeed be safe.

When the carriage drew up in front of the castle, Chelsea was grateful when Lord Rathbone insisted she retire to her bedchamber at once, saying he would explain matters to his mother once she was up and about.

"Thank you, sir," Chelsea murmured, striving to keep her head down as she spoke. With daylight fast upon them, Lord Rathbone might still be inclined to question her identity. There remained the matter of her eyes being brown, instead of the clear blue Alayna's were.

Indeed, as he reached for her hand to assist her to the ground, Chelsea was acutely aware of Lord Rathbone studying her. Without looking at the tall gentleman, she moved quickly to the stone steps when, with a single word, his voice halted her.

"Alayna."

Her breath in her throat, Chelsea waited as determined strides brought him forward.

"Alayna," he said in a low tone, "we are betrothed, consequently it is perfectly acceptable for you to address me by my Christian name. 'Sir' has a far too formal ring to it."

"Yes, si—I mean . . . as you wish, Rutherford."

His lips pursed and after turning to fling hasty instructions to the coach driver and a sleepy footman, he stepped into the darkened foyer alongside Chelsea.

Alone with her indoors, he continued, "I must also ask that you look at me when you address me, Alayna. As a planter's wife, a certain authoritive air about you will be expected. I find your habit of ducking your head when you speak quite lowering, to say nothing of being dashed annoying. You are an"—his own authoritive tone suddenly took on a raspy quality—"an attractive young lady." With that, he abruptly ceased speaking altogether.

Chelsea could not think what her looks had to say to anything, but she obliged the gentleman by tilting her chin upward. Suddenly, the deafening silence surrounding them grew excessively loud. That there were no servants about at this early hour was not unusual. What was unusual Chelsea noted, was the fact that she had travelled an entire night in the presence of this gentleman and had not noticed how very attractive *he* was.

Quite tall and powerfully built, his aristocratic features—well-shaped nose, square jaw, and thick, dark hair—closely resembled a number of other Campbell's whose portraits hung in the picture gallery just beyond the foyer. Recalling with some embarrassment the unrestrained manner in which she had flung herself into this gentleman's arms when he bravely rescued her from Sully's clutches, she felt the colour in her cheeks deepen and her eyelids involuntarily dropped again. The memory, she realized, was not altogether unpleasant.

In truth, she was deeply indebted to this man, but because she had been so preoccupied with worry about what would happen once he uncovered her subterfuge, she feared she had not properly thanked him for saving her life, not really. "I am very grateful to you . . . Rutherford," she began, "for rescuing me as you did." She struggled to lift her eyes. "You were . . . very brave. I was so awfully frightened. I have always had a fear of . . . perishing in a carriage accident."

She found Lord Rathbone's gaze still fixed upon her face, the expression in his dark eyes unreadable. "I did not know that about you, Alayna," he murmured.

Listening to him, Chelsea suddenly realized she had been speaking from her own heart. If she were to successfully carry on the pretense with Lord Rathbone, she must remember to play her part in a manner more befitting Alayna. With renewed decision, she lifted her chin and inhaled deeply.

"Well, I expect there are a good many things we do not know about one another, Rutherford. It has been such a very long time since we were together. I was what . . . ten? when last I saw you." She sighed loudly. "But now *I* am feeling quite tired. I did not spend the entire night sleeping as you did, Ford." She put great emphasis on the shortened form of his name as Alayna often used it. "I should like to rest now," she added.

Her sudden flippant tone seemed to shatter Lord Rathbone's thoughtful one. "Of course, you must be exhausted, Alayna. Well then, sleep well, my dear."

Cocking her head in a saucy manner, Chelsea pranced across the room, leaving Lord Rathbone to stare at her backside as she sashayed the length of the corridor away from him.

Upstairs, she hurriedly undressed, climbed into bed and fell at once into a sound slumber. Upon awakening, however, she was once again sharply aware of the hard knot of foreboding that sat like a rock in the pit of her stomach. Last evening, she may have convinced Lord Rathbone that she was indeed his cousin Alayna, but when she left the castle the previous morning in Sully's company, Lady Rathbone had appeared none too sure.

Glancing at the clock on the mantelpiece, she saw that it was already half past noon. Not bothering to call for Dulcie, she dressed quickly, wondering all the while what had transpired this morning while she slept.

Upon setting foot in the dining chamber a few moments later, she was vastly surprised when Lady Rathbone greeted her quite cheerfully.

"Good morning, Alayna, or should I say, 'good afternoon'." She laughed, her gnarled hands wrapped around a warm teacup. "I hope you had a good sleep, my dear." She glanced toward the sideboard where Rutherford was heaping his plate with the delicious looking meal of roast beef and steamed vegetables that was laid out for them.

"Rutherford has been telling me all about the frightful episode you suffered with that reprehensible man, Sully," Lady Rathbone continued. "I declare, I was never so shocked in my life! Although, I was equally as shocked when this young man appeared at table this morning, declaring that he was my son! Do sit down, dear," she admonished Chelsea, "I shall have a servant bring you a plate."

Chelsea obeyed without a word, aware that Rutherford was now headed for his place at the head of the table.

Taking his seat, Lord Rathbone greeted Chelsea in a warm tone, then said, "I had not realized your sight had so suffered, Mother, that you would be hoodwinked by that reprobate, Sully."

Lady Rathbone sighed. "I was thankful when spectacles

let me read again, but I would exchange that gladly for the ability to see a face clearly when it is more than six inches from my own. And I thought you had acquired the roughest way of speaking while you were away."

Chelsea squirmed. "We were all taken in," she said quietly, suddenly realizing that in spite of the fact that she had hardly eaten in two days, she was still too nervous to eat.

"That Alayna was taken in is understandable. You two have not seen one another since you were children. But, I feel quite bird-witted for not recognizing the man as an impostor. Still, Alayna," Lady Rathbone gazed expectantly at Chelsea, her tone making her words a question, "you fell in so quickly with the man's plan."

Chelsea struggled to calm herself. "I wished only to remove that horrid creature from your presence as quickly as possible, Aunt Millie. I was quite frightened, actually. For all of us."

"And well you should have been," Rathbone put in gravely. "When provoked, Sully can be a dangerous man. To say truth, I would never have hired such scum had I not been hard put for another Englishman on the plantation. As it was, Sully proved untrustworthy from the start. I once learned he had diverted funds intended for cutting to his own pocket. I should have dismissed him them."

"I wonder that you did not," Lady Rathbone mused.

Rutherford glanced up from his plate. "I expect I was trying to be a generous and forgiving employer, Mother. I recall he put on quite a show of remorse. But I have since learned my lesson. Once a traitor, always a traitor."

Chelsea winced.

After a pause, Lady Rathbone said, "Rutherford tells me the man absconded with your portrait, Alayna. How thoughtful you were to send Ford such a lovely betrothal present. I wish I could have seen it myself. I'm sure it must have been quite beautiful."

A shaky smile wavered across Chelsea's face. Recalling

that Alayna had bragged about the painting being a perfect likeness of herself, she decided it best not to take that tack. "Well, it . . . was not a . . . particularly good likeness, actually."

"I am sure you are just being modest, my dear." Lady Rathbone directed a gaze at her son. "Alayna has become quite a lovely young lady, has she not, Rutherford?"

Lord Rathbone's eyes cut to Chelsea, then darted quickly away. "Indeed," he murmured tightly.

"Well, she will simply have to sit for another picture," Lady Rathbone said. "And, once it is done, I should like to have a copy for myself this time. Perhaps I should have one made of you, as well, Rutherford," she added with a laugh.

"I expect there is an artist in Chester who could paint Alayna's portrait for us, Mother," Lord Rathbone remarked. Laying aside his fork, he reached for his napkin. "The sitting would keep her occupied while I tend to repairs about the castle. I shouldn't like to leave England again without putting things to rights here, Mother. I am quite shocked at how frightfully shabby the castle appears. The bridge looks as if it could go any minute, and the yard and grounds . . ." He shook his head with dismay. "Even the mews and stables are a fright. By the by, Alayna," he turned a puzzled gaze on Chelsea, "how on earth did you persuade Sully to let you travel in the Marchmont coach? I'd have thought Sully would insist you travel horseback. Much faster that way."

A pregnant pause ensued as Chelsea felt both the gentleman and his mother watching her intently. "I . . . no longer ride," she said quietly.

Rutherford's brows pulled together. "No longer ride! Why I can hardly fathom the like, Alayna!"

"It is astonishing, isn't it," put in Lady Rathbone.

Chelsea offered nothing further on the subject, though she did consider fabricating something about an accident in Town that might have caused Alayna to change face on that score. But she just as quickly dismissed the notion. Maintaining one lie was exhausting enough.

"Well," Rutherford said at length, pushing up from the table. "All's well that ends well, I expect. To say truth, it was the Marchmont crest on the coach door that alerted me to your whereabouts. Both a stablehand and an inkeep remarked upon the handsome equipage and the fact that a lone young lady was ensconced inside."

Chelsea seized the moment. "Actually that was my plan all along! I am pleased that it worked so well, aren't you, Rutherford?"

The gentlemen flung her a look, but said nothing. Just as he was approaching the archway leading to the hall, he was intercepted by Jared who had come to announce that a gentleman was awaiting reception in the withdrawing room.

"Ah, I expect it is the magistrate from Chester," Lord Rathbone exclaimed. "No doubt, he has put Sully behind bars and is calling to inquire further about the incident." He directed another gaze at Chelsea. "When you have finished your meal, Alayna, I expect Mr. Wainwright will want to question you, as well."

Chelsea's heart plummeted to her feet. *What must she endure now? What if the magistrate had brought the stolen portrait of Alayna with him? Would Lord Rathbone insist she be put behind bars as well?* Oh! This day was fast becoming as horrid as the previous one had been!

Five

Moments later, when Chelsea pushed Lady Rathbone's chair into the drawing room, she was vastly relieved to find not the authorities as she'd feared, but the familiar figure of the vicar, Mr. Stevens, whom she had met the day the banns were read in church. He and Lord Rathbone were greeting one another cordially.

"Indeed a pleasure to find you here, your lordship!" the vicar enthused. Hearing the squeak of Lady Rathbone's chair, he turned and proceeded across the cavernous room toward the ladies. "My stars! is it Lady Rathbone herself? I admit, I had heard you were venturing down stairs these days, my lady, but I had to see it with me own eyes to believe it! God be praised!"

Lord Rathbone wore a puzzled look as he advanced. "Have you been unwell, Mother?"

"Merciful heavens, no!" the older woman sputtered. "Just saw no reason to leave my chamber, until"—she turned a warm smile on Chelsea—"my niece arrived from London. Alayna's presence has lifted everyone's spirits."

Chelsea coloured deeply, due in part to the fact that everyone's attention was now fixed on her, more for being obliged to, once again, deceive a man of God.

"I see," Lord Rathbone muttered, still gazing at Chelsea.

"Indeed, it is true," the vicar responded heartily. "Miss Marchmont is a charming young lady. More than one of my parishioners remarked upon her beauty following services on Sunday last. Word is Miss Marchmont has completely transformed the castle."

Again, all eyes focused on Chelsea. She ducked her head. "You are being too kind, I'm sure, Mr. Stevens."

"On the contrary," the round-faced man glanced about the room, "appears quite cheerful in here to me. Why, to find the drawing room open and her ladyship receiving is a miracle in itself!"

Lord Rathbone's brows pulled together. "Are you quite certain you have not been unwell, Mother?"

"Do sit down, Mr. Stevens," Lady Rathbone said, indicating with a hand to Chelsea that she'd like her wheelchair moved closer to the fire. "We've such a lot to discuss now that there's to be a wedding in the chapel."

"Are you certain you feel up to it, Mother?" Lord Rathbone asked, taking a seat on a faded silk sofa beside Chelsea, while the vicar settled his large frame on a somewhat tattered brocade side chair. "I had rather thought it would be more expedient if Alayna and I were married in London, on our way back to Honduras."

Chelsea swallowed a squeak of alarm, but upon recovering, put in hastily, "But, Ford, I should *like* a nice wedding. Your parents were married in the castle chapel, and I see no reason why we shouldn't—"

"Alayna is right, Rutherford. And, I'm sure she will see to the bulk of the arrangements, won't you, dear?"

"Of course, I will," Chelsea replied quickly, smiling with relief at the prospect of being kept blessedly occupied.

"From what I hear," the vicar put in, "Miss Marchmont is quite good at organizing and such. Why, just look at the way she's brightened this room up." He beamed at Chelsea again.

Lord Rathbone's lips pursed. "I would appreciate it if someone would please enlighten me as to precisely what was amiss indoors."

Lady Rathbone laughed. "Well, for one thing, there were the portraits in the picture gallery."

"Yes, well, what about them?"

"Why, I had thought all my husband's ancestors' hair had suddenly turned white, until Alayna had the dust rubbed off and now, every last Rathbone in the bunch has hair the color of coal!"

Everyone but Rutherford laughed gaily.

"And, there was the furniture and the rugs, to say nothing of the bed hangings and draperies. Your betrothed, my dear boy, has been a veritable whirlwind of activity."

Lord Rathbone cast another quizzical gaze at Chelsea. "Hmmm."

"And did I not hear something about a pig?" the vicar asked.

"A pig!" Rathbone sputtered. "Don't tell me Alayna has also been frequenting the barnyard."

At that they all, save Rutherford, burst into hearty laughter.

"Alayna, do tell your cousin about the pig," admonished Lady Rathbone. "It was quite extraordinary."

Feeling more relaxed than she had in days, Chelsea smilingly related the story of the high winds, the torn shutter and the slain pig, whereupon everyone, including Lord Rathbone, shared another round of laughter.

Chelsea was struck by how pleasant the sound of Lord Rathbone's laugh was. It came from deep within him, the delicious sound being at once both warm and mellow. Realizing how good it felt to forget her troubles for a spell, she eagerly joined in the merriment. Mr. Stevens was a jolly fellow, not the least bit stuffy or prim as clergymen were so often wont to be. He loved both hearing amusing tales and often told them, even from the pulpit.

After he'd relayed a few more village *on-dits,* they settled down to discuss the details for the wedding ceremony. After that subject had also been exhausted, he turned again to Chelsea.

"I wonder, Miss Marchmont, if you would be good enough to accompany Mrs. Stevens on her rounds this Thursday? Your charming countenance is sure to lift the spirits of many of our more elderly parishioners."

"Oh! Well, I-I—"

"Why, I think that a lovely idea," put in Lady Rathbone. "Alayna has quite cheered me these last weeks. I can't think when I have enjoyed myself half so much. Did I mention, Ford, that your lovely bride-to-be is in the habit of reading to me every afternoon, and often again in the evening before I go to sleep? Why, it was Alayna herself who found this chair and insisted that I venture out and about."

Lord Rathbone turned an approving look on Chelsea. "Is that so?"

"So, it's settled then," the vicar concluded. He rose to go. "I shall tell Mrs. Stevens to call for you at half past two, Miss Marchmont. If that is agreeable with you, of course."

Chelsea nodded, then was startled to hear Lord Rathbone chime in.

"I should like to go along, as well . . . that is, if I am free. Father had several elderly acquaintances in the parish that I should like to see again. It's likely this could be my last opportunity to visit them." He smiled at Chelsea. "I should also like to show off my future bride."

"Splendid!" the vicar exclaimed.

Chelsea blanched, but nonetheless, managed a pleasant enough smile.

Lord Rathbone saw the vicar out and moments later, returned again to the drawing room. "I should like a word with you, Alayna," he said warmly.

Chelsea glanced up at the tall gentleman. He looked quite dashing today in a claret-coloured waistcoat and white shirt, his buff breeches tucked into shining black top boots. A finely turned-out gentleman at the castle was an unusual sight. Up against the slap-dash manner in which most of the footmen and manservants appeared, Lord Rathbone's clean-shaven face and neatly brushed hair was a decided contrast.

"If you will excuse us, Mother?" he said, politely.

"Indeed. I am quite ready to repair to my chamber now for a nap. *Jared!*"

The sheer unexpectedness of his mother's bellow brought a look of surprise to Lord Rathbone's face.

A smile played at Chelsea's lips. "All of the bell-pulls are inoperable," she explained to Ford who was gazing at his mother as if she'd just taken leave of her senses. "I shall fetch Jared for you, Aunt Millie."

Chelsea scampered from the room and returned a moment later with Jared close on her heels. When the butler had pushed Lady Rathbone's chair from the room, Chelsea took her seat and turned an expectant gaze on Rutherford.

He stood with one arm resting on the back of an ancient old corner chair. "I should simply like to say, Alayna, that I am extremely pleased by all I learned about you today. I admit I am a good deal surprised by your . . . selfless attitude, that is, given your . . . privileged upbringing, but apparently you possess a certain talent for household management that I was unaware of. It gives me hope."

"Hope?" Chelsea murmured.

Lord Rathbone nodded. "Indeed. As a planter's wife you will have similar duties in Honduras. And aside from looking after our immediate household, I had hoped you would spearhead certain charitable concerns in the village. We've a long way to go before we are as civilized as England, of course, but I am determined that we shall succeed."

"Oh." Chelsea let her gaze fall to her lap. To say truth, what the gentleman proposed sounded quite intriguing to her, and she'd like nothing better than to throw herself wholeheartedly into such a project, but . . . he was not speaking to her, he was speaking to his betrothed, Alayna.

"Have you nothing to say, Alayna?"

Chelsea lifted a tentative gaze.

"What is it, my dear? You seem to exhibit some reluctance in speaking your mind to me. If you have something to say, I implore you to say it at once."

Chelsea chewed on her lower lip. Though she was loath to do so, she simply must tell Lord Rathbone that Alayna had no intention of returning to Honduras to live with him after they were married. Alayna would not have waited this long to voice her feelings in the matter. She had to tell him.

"Alayna!" Lord Rathbone's dark eyes flashed. "I demand that you tell me at once what is the trouble!"

Chelsea swallowed hard. And rose to her feet. To confront a gentleman as formidable as Lord Rathbone from a sitting position was something she did not think even Alayna could do. "I . . . I have no intention of returning to Honduras with you, sir."

The veins in Lord Rathbone's neck popped out. "That is preposterous, Alayna! Of course, you will return to my home with me. What is the point of our marrying if we are not to live together as man and wife?"

Affecting the mocking posture she had so often seen Alayna wear, Chelsea thrust her chin up. "I was given to understand that the point of our marriage was the release of your inheritance, cousin."

Lord Rathbone glared at her. "You are being insufferable, Alayna. I will not countenance it. I *refuse* to countenance it, do you hear me?"

"Of course, I hear you, Ford. I expect even the servants can hear you."

His dark eyes smoldered with rage as he moved to stand in front of her. For the space of a second, Chelsea feared he might strike her. After all, he had just admitted that in

Honduras people were not nearly so civilized as they were in England.

Instead, he merely planted himself a few inches from her, his narrowed gaze challenging her defiant one. "We remove to Honduras within a fortnight, Alayna. You will prepare yourself accordingly." With that, he stalked toward the door.

But, nearing it, he paused. "By the by," he turned toward her again, the tone of his voice having altered the veriest mite, "if you did not mean to reside with me as properly wedded couples do, how exactly did you propose to live?"

Chelsea took a few steps toward him, giving herself a moment in order to fabricate a reply. "I shall content myself as I have in the past, attending fancy dress balls, frequenting the opera, and . . . and such." Having not spent her days in like manner, she wasn't entirely sure how fashionable ladies did go on. "There is always the Season, you know, and in winter, there are . . . houseparties and hunting weekends."

"I was not referring to your social outings, Alayna. What I meant was . . ." A dark brow lifted.

Chelsea's eyes widened and she felt the already high colour in her cheeks deepen. She knew exactly what he meant now, and she also knew that Alayna would not hesitate to speak her mind on *that* subject, as well. She had not hesitated when Chelsea put the same question to her the afternoon they sat discussing Alayna's forthcoming marriage in the Marchmont drawing room.

Lord Rathbone folded his arms across his chest. "I am waiting, Alayna."

"Well, uh . . . i-if you must know. I . . . intend to live 'freely'. As other married women . . . and *most* gentlemen do," she added, proud that she had thought of it. It was precisely the sort of thing Alayna would say. "Furthermore, though I cannot see where it is any concern of yours, I mean to . . . to fall in and out of love with whomever I please." Aware of her own heart pounding wildly in her breast, she wondered if perhaps she hadn't taken it a bit too far with that last part. But no matter how mortified *she* felt in speaking so plainly to a gentleman, as long as she was pretending to be Alayna, it was likely she could never go too far.

She watched Lord Rathbone's nostrils flare with suppressed rage, then he said, "Are you quite finished, Alayna?"

Chelsea nodded. "Have I not . . . said enough?"

He snorted. "You have said quite enough."

Chelsea steeled herself for whatever might be coming in the way of chastisement. It was plain to see that Lord Rathbone was not the sort of man to let even the contemplation of such improper conduct pass without strong recriminations. In truth, she knew her words had mocked him, had mocked all that he stood for. He had made it abundantly clear that he expected Alayna to make a home with him in Honduras. But, Chelsea knew very well that Alayna would never agree to the sort of life he proposed for her. *Never!*

Lord Rathbone had been watching her closely. At length, he said, "I will not accept your decision in the matter, Alayna."

In a perfect imitation of the young lady she was pretending to be, Chelsea cocked her head to one side. "You have no choice but to accept my decision, sir." For strength, she gripped the edge of a nearby chair, then to remove herself from his piercing gaze, she flounced to a mullioned window and peered out. With her back to him, she said, "Our engagement has already been announced in the London papers and the first reading of the banns was Sunday last. You are far too honourable a man to cry off now, Rutherford Campbell."

The silence hanging between them grew so heavy that Chelsea, at last, turned around. Lord Rathbone was staring hard at her, his eyes dark with anger.

Chelsea watched his jaws grind together and thought again that Lord Rathbone was a very handsome man.

Finally, he said, "There is something you are not telling me, Alayna."

Stunned by his astuteness, Chelsea felt her knees go weak beneath her skirt, but nonetheless she managed to gather enough courage to breeze past him. "I am telling you everything, sir. I have told you I have no intention of removing to Honduras and how I propose to live. What more could there be?" she tossed off airily. But, stepping into the corridor, she cringed when she caught sight of a sly smile softening the stern lines of his mouth.

"I haven't a clue, Alayna. But, I will tell you this much, I shall not rest until I have uncovered the whole truth. Whatever that may be."

Something was vastly awry, Lord Rathbone told himself as he headed for the library. Alayna was resisting him, but not for the reasons she'd given. A moment ago, he'd nearly laughed aloud when she said she meant to live "freely," to fall in and out of love with whomever she pleased. Not that she was not attractive enough to do precisely that, but, any fool could see that to live in such a fashion was not in Alayna's character. Why, she sounded like a silly schoolgirl with a head full of romantical ideas. Alayna could never live such a life!

In the library, he drew out several large account books from the top drawer of a centuries old desk where he had often watched his father sit and work. Opening the first dusty volume, he had to turn only a few yellowed pages to see that the ledgers had not been dealt with in years.

Reaching for a teetering pile of receipts, he began the daunting task of bringing the account books up to date. But, for some reason, he experienced difficulty concentrating. Lifting his head, he tapped the end of his pencil to his chin.

Alayna looked especially pretty today in a becoming peach-coloured morning gown, her golden hair tied back from her face with a blue ribbon. He inhaled a sharp breath. His cousin had, indeed, become a beautiful young lady. And considering her sheltered upbringing—he lips pressed tightly together—one could only wonder how her head got filled with the fanciful notions she'd outlined to him earlier. The idea was preposterous! Did not bear thinking upon. He set again to work.

Only to pause once more. Truth to tell, if he had received the portrait Alayna had sent to him upon the announcement of their betrothal, he'd have been tempted to sail for England straightaway in order to be here for their wedding. And, for the honeymoon. Feeling an unfamiliar tightening sensation in his loins, he frowned.

Ridiculous! He could not be falling in love with his cousin. Love only complicated matters and he'd not allow it. He'd have no part of Alayna's caperwitted scheme about living apart from one another either!

With decision, he turned again to his work.

After supper that evening, the three of them, Chelsea, Lady Rathbone and Rutherford settled themselves in a cozy sitting room to partake of a second cup of tea.

Lord Rathbone had spent nearly the whole of dinner relaying his findings in the account books to his mother.

Handing a fresh cup of tea to her now, he said, "It is imperative that we hire a trustworthy bailiff, Mother. I am amazed that things have not fallen to complete rack and ruin with only the housekeeper, Mrs. Phipps at the helm. That is not to imply that she is incompetent, but she is a woman, and women know very little of business matters."

Without thinking, Chelsea took umbrage at that. "Some women know a great deal about business!" she snapped.

Both Lord and Lady Rathbone fixed startled gazes on

her. Surprised by her own outburst, Chelsea squirmed. "Er, what I mean to say is that . . . not all women are un-schooled in such matters."

Lord Rathbone's lips began to twitch. "I see. And, I take it you count yourself among the enlightened few?"

Chelsea sniffed . . . and realized she had no idea how to respond. Alayna knew absolutely nothing about estate affairs, and truth to tell, Chelsea knew little enough herself. But, she'd had some experience with household records during her time with Lady Hennessey, and Mr. Merribone had put her in charge of purchasing thread and ribbon for the workroom of the shop. That all counted for something, did it not?

Lady Rathbone spoke up. "I believe Alayna has already exhibited a certain talent for taking things in hand, Rutherford. Why, she set matters to rights here in no time. I never saw such scurrying about and all of it to good purpose."

"So I've been told," Rathbone muttered.

Lady Rathbone wasn't done. "With the exception of Jared, the household servants had become quite slovenly and ill-tempered," she added. "Why, you can see for yourself, the change that's come over them."

Lord Rathbone's lips pursed. "The servants' attitudes are neither here nor there, Mother, what I am speaking about now is organizing the rent collections and reassigning tasks to the outdoor staff. It is clearly a job for a man."

Chelsea bristled, but said nothing further.

She noted when Lord Rathbone turned a calculating look on her. "Of course, if you'd care to assist me until I hire a bailiff, I would brook no objection, Alayna." He smiled coolly. "As my wife, you will be obliged to perform similar duties on the plantation."

Chelsea's lips tightened. Her own folly had ensnared her this time. Besides, to refuse him at this juncture would be the same as refusing to help Lady Rathbone. And, if she were to survive once everyone had abandoned her again, she'd need all the help she could get. Anyone with half an eye could see that the tenants and castle staff had been taking advantage of the sweet old lady for years. To bring the entire lot under control was work enough for several people, and in view of what she had already accomplished, Chelsea was more than qualified to help.

She tilted her chin upward. "I will be happy to assist, Rutherford, however, that does not mean I have changed my mind about removing to Honduras. I shall never agree to live in such an uncivilized place as that. *Never.*"

She watched one of Lord Rathbone's dark brows lift, but all he said was, "I will be making an early start of it tomorrow, Alayna. You may join me at your leisure." Setting his empty teacup aside, he stood. "But be forewarned," he stepped past her, "everyone on the plantation rises early. Once we are there, the same will be expected of you."

Six

Awake at first light the following morning, Chelsea was torn between surprising Lord Rathbone with her eagerness to work or leisurely strolling in after a late breakfast. She could always make the excuse that she had simply forgot the assignation. It was certainly something Alayna would do. That the gentleman still refused to believe that she, or rather, that Alayna, did not mean to accompany him to Honduras was making her wonder if perhaps her portrayal of Alayna Marchmont lacked something vital. *What must she do to convince him?*

Turning the puzzle over in her mind as she dressed, she toyed with the idea of pulling a tantrum and refusing altogether to join him in the library. She had often seen Alayna act in such a fashion. But, going back on a promise was not in Chelsea's character and besides, she had agreed to help on Lady Rathbone's behalf. In the end, Chelsea's sense of honor won out.

In fact, she went the extra mile.

"What's this?" Lord Rathbone's head jerked up as the door to the library burst open and without preamble, Chelsea and two footmen barged in.

"You may place it just there," Chelsea said briskly, shepherding the two footmen, who carried a bulky load between them, into the book-lined room. "That's correct; beneath the window where the light is good."

"Alayna, what the devil—" Lord Rathbone sprang to his feet, his dark brows pulled together.

"No, position it face outward," Chelsea instructed. After the footmen had done her bidding, she waved them both away, then turned toward his lordship. "It's a rent table," she announced smartly. "I chanced upon it the day I found Aunt Millicent's Bath chair. It will make the new bailiff's job that much easier, don't you agree?"

"Well, I—I—" Lord Rathbone stepped from behind the imposing mahogany desk that dwarfed the center of the room, to move toward the smaller piece of furniture that sat beneath the window.

"As you can see, the days of the week and quarter days are still quite readable," Chelsea pointed out, a finger indicating the many labeled drawers marching across the front of the desk, "and the tenant's names can go right here—"

"I know what a rent table is, Alayna," Lord Rathbone snapped. "The marvel is that *you* knew what it was."

Chelsea nearly blurted out that she had often helped Lady Hennessey's housekeeper sort out collection notices at the end of the month, but catching herself, she merely said, "I told you I am not a complete dunce when it comes to household affairs."

The tall gentleman spun around. "I never said you were a dunce, Alayna."

Chelsea's lips pursed. "Well, then. What would you like me to do today?"

Regaining himself, Lord Rathbone set her to the task of entering tiny numbers into columns in the account books. Seeing that she was thusly occupied, he busied himself labeling the cubby-holes in the rent table with the names of the tenants who still maintained farms on the estate.

Twice, when Chelsea was unsure where to enter a figure, she had to ask Lord Rathbone for assistance. Each time, help was freely given. The third time, however, when he took the pencil from her hand in order to set down the number in his own bold, sure script, Chelsea became oddly aware of the gentleman's very . . . masculine presence. In all her life, she had not had occasion to work so closely beside a man. As he leant over her, it was all she could do not to inhale deeply of the scents that engulfed him—a mixture of musk and the slight tinge of tobacco. Upon feeling his strong arm brush against her shoulder, she could not deny that a tingle of pleasure rippled through her. With alarm, she jerked away, but succeeded only in colliding with his massive chest as he leaned forward at her back.

"Oh! I'm so sorry, I did not mean to cause—"

Apparently as unperturbed by the encounter as she was unsettled, Lord Rathbone merely muttered, "No harm done." Laying the pencil aside, he straightened. "You've worked quite diligently this morning, Alayna, perhaps you'd like to rest a bit?"

He strode toward the rent table. "I had meant to drive into Chester today to post a notice for the new bailiff, and to order supplies for repairing the bridge. Perhaps you'd like to come along?"

Chelsea risked a glance his way.

But he merely turned to the window. "Wind appears to be getting up, I should like to get to Chester and back before it begins to rain." He turned toward Cheslea. "What do you say?"

At the moment, Chelsea wasn't sure she could say anything. What was happening to her? It was true, Lord Rathbone was a very attractive man, but . . . she had no interest in him, or he in her. He was betrothed to another. "N-no," she finally managed. "I-I promised I'd read to Aunt Millicent this afternoon."

"Very well, then." Lord Rathbone nodded, bending to gather up some papers on the desk before him. "I shall just be off. If you will be good enough to tell Mother where I've gone, and that I shall be back around tea time."

Chelsea watched the tall gentleman exit the room. What

had come over her? Things were happening so fast she could barely keep up. Thinking again of his long, tapered fingers wielding the pencil as he leaned over her to write, she swallowed tightly. His hands appeared strong and graceful. They were the hands of a gentleman, to be sure, and yet . . . they were more. A disquieting breathlessness swept over her. *What did it mean?*

Chelsea was still perplexed by the strange phenomena when that evening after dinner, the three of them again adjourned to the cozy sitting room. It had, indeed, begun to rain that afternoon, at first coming as a gentle mist. Now, it was cutting up quite nasty, the insistent rumble of thunder constantly punctuated by the startling crack of lightning. The dismal weather outdoors made the intimacy of the red and gold fire crackling here in the grate that much more inviting.

Lord Rathbone had not made it back to the castle before the downpour began, for Chelsea had noted at table that his dark hair was still damp from the drenching he took.

"I'd have taken a carriage," he remarked to his mother as they all sat down now, "but every last gig in the carriagehouse is in need of some sort of repair."

"I seldom go out these days," Lady Rathbone said, by way of explanation.

"Nonetheless, it's important to keep something in good repair."

"You could have taken my coach," Chelsea offered, referring to the elegant Marchmont equipage that was also housed in the out building.

In reply, his lordship sneezed, then sneezed again.

"Oh, dear," Lady Rathbone fretted. "I daresay you've caught a chill, Rutherford. Go and stand by the fire."

"It's nothing, Mother." Lord Rathbone withdrew his handkerchief and began to dab at his nose. Folding the square of linen up again, he added laughingly, "I admit I am not accustomed to having a woman fuss over me."

"There are no women in Honduras?" Chelsea murmured incredulously.

Drawing his wing chair nearer the fire, Rathbone laughed again. "Of course, there are women in Honduras, pea goose. There are men and women and children, the same as there are here."

A pause ensued, then Lady Rathbone said, "I expect Alayna does not know a great deal about your home, Ford. Perhaps you could enlighten us both. I know I should like to hear more about it. Having spent all my life in England, I know very little of foreign climes."

Lord Rathbone looked thoughtful, then with a nod, he smiled, the action serving to soften the sculptured look of his jaw.

"As I said, we've plenty of rain in the tropics," he began, bending an indulgent, smile on his mother, "But, when it isn't raining, we've an abundance of sunshine. My house sits on a hill, surrounded on three sides by tall trees. I am not referring to the common low copse so prevalent here, but sweeping palms, and coconuts with branches that seem to touch the sky. And, of course, a profusion of mahogany."

"But, you do not cut the trees near your house," Chelsea put in quietly, finding the description of his home quite intriguing. She'd never seen a palm, or a coconut, tree.

"No," he shook his head, "indeed not. The trees for cutting lie deep in the forest. In full bloom, the forest is quite beautiful. We've two cutting seasons a year, one just after Christmas, the other in July or early August. I expect cutting will begin this year soon after I return home. Summer is also known as our wet season." He grinned again at his mother. "Consequently, I am often caught in an unexpected shower."

"Well, I hope you change into dry clothes quickly!" Lady Rathbone admonished.

Lord Rathbone laughed. "Not when I am miles away from the house."

"But, what do you do?" Chelsea asked,

He glanced at her. "Carry on, of course. One is often wet in the tropics, and not only from the rain."

"Wet?" Chelsea murmured.

"From the heat. On most days, the least bit of exertion is likely to . . ." he glanced again at Chelsea, perhaps wondering if he might be speaking too plainly for a lady's ears . . . "produce a glow across one's brow," he finished, his lips twitching. "Even dressing can be somewhat of an ordeal, it being necessary to cool down between a shave and drawing on one's clothes. In the tropics, a man cannot leave his chamber in ten minutes as he does here in England. Not if he wishes to be presentable." He laughed good-naturedly.

"Do you not have a manservant, or a valet, to assist you?" Chelsea asked, not realizing she was becoming quite caught up imagining how it might be to live in such an extraordinary place.

"Indeed. There are plenty of servants, the most of them slaves."

"Slaves!" Chelsea sputtered, her eyes suddenly wide with horror.

He nodded. "A planter's slaves, both men and women, are highly valued property. Without them, and our indentured servants, the production and cutting of mahogany would come to a complete standstill."

"But . . . do you not feel guilty about . . . *owning* people?"

Lord Rathbone laughed at his betrothed's seeming outrage. "It is the way it is, Alayna. Most of us provide quite well for our people. I intend to build snug new homes for my workers and their families; and a school house, so the children of my servants will not grow up completely illiterate."

"Perhaps Alayna could supervise the new school," Lady Rathbone put in quietly.

Chelsea squirmed, but said nothing.

"We are not so uncivilized as you may think, Alayna."

Chelsea ventured nothing further and for a long moment, it appeared the conversation had ground to a halt. Then, following a particularly loud clap of thunder, Lady Rathbone spoke up. "I expect it is time I toddled off to bed."

Before she could yell for Jared, Chelsea jumped to her feet. "I shall see you to your room, Aunt Millicent."

Lady Rathbone gazed pointedly from Chelsea to her son. "That won't be necessary, my dear, I shall just—"

At that second Jared appeared in the doorway.

"Ah, there you are, Jared. I was just about to call for you."

"Yes, my lady." The butler's features were as immovable as stone as he stepped forward to push Lady Rathbone's chair from the room.

"Good night, children," she called gaily over her shoulder.

The ping, ping of raindrops hitting the narrow slit of window above the hearth and the receding squeak of Lady Rathbone's chair in the corridor were the only sounds to be heard until Lord Rathbone said quietly, "I believe I have uncovered the real reason for your reticence in returning to Honduras with me, Alayna."

Chelsea's ears sprang immediately to attention.

"You are simply afraid," he said wisely.

"Afraid?"

"Indeed. And, I'll allow that such a response is understandable. I wonder that I did not think of it sooner. To leave your family and friends to travel to such a far-off place must seem a terrifying prospect to you. You are so . . . very young."

Chelsea said nothing. At the moment, she realized that she would sooner travel to the moon than be left alone in this isolated wing of the castle with Lord Rathbone, a man she was beginning to feel so very—she swallowed tightly—drawn to.

She cast a fearful gaze his direction. He looked quite harmless seated peacefully before the fire, the glow from the flames turning his already tanned face a beautiful shade of bronze. His fingers were steepled beneath his chin as he sat gazing into the flames. She had never felt such an odd pull toward a man before. At dinner, she had caught herself a number of times, studying him with acute fascination, her eyes lingering on the disheveled look of his damp hair, the resolute line of his jaw, the strength of his hands as he cut up his beefsteak. It was as if she wished to memorize every detail about his person.

And, a moment ago, as he spoke to them of his home, every time his eyes met hers, she experienced the same trembly feeling in the pit of her stomach as she had this morning when he leaned over her to jot down numbers in the account books. It was most unsettling.

Suddenly, Lord Rathbone leaned forward in his chair, his gaze meeting hers. "Just look at you now, Alayna. You are gazing at me as if virtually terrified." He rose to his feet and strode across the room to the small cellarette that had been placed near a side table.

Withdrawing a bottle of aged sherry, he busied himself opening the bottle and pouring himself a drink. "The logic of it actually came to me this afternoon," he continued. "Other than your little trips to Brighton and Bath and back again to London, you have never been anywhere before. Therefore, the very thought of being uprooted and transported across the ocean must seem horrific to you."

He settled the bottle back into the well, then glanced at Chelsea. "Forgive me, would you care for a glass of sherry? Can be quite good for the nerves, you know."

"Ummm . . ." Chelsea wasn't the least accustomed to strong drink, but her nerves could certainly use settling. "Yes, I . . . I believe I will have a drop, thank you."

After retrieving the bottle again, he poured the drink and crossed the room to hand her a glass. "I was pleased when

Mother asked me to speak of my home this evening," he
said, moving to stand before the fire. "I had already decided
that the more you know of Honduras, the less you will be
inclined to fear it."

After swirling a sip of the amber liquid around in his
mouth, he asked, "What else might I tell you about your
future home, my dear?"

Chelsea delayed a response by sampling the drink he'd
placed in her hands. *She* wanted to know everything about
Lord Rathbone's home, but she knew full well Alayna
wasn't the least bit interested. Yet . . . it was not Alayna
who was ensconced here in the castle with her handsome
cousin. Downing another small sip of the golden liquid, she
allowed herself to enjoy the burning warmth as it seared a
path to her belly. Feeling a good deal more relaxed already,
she managed a look upward.

But Lord Rathbone's gaze was fixed on the crackling
embers. "A night such as this is unheard of in the tropics,"
he said quietly. "To say truth, I rather miss the cold, the
snow in winter and the sparkling gleam of ice crystals in
the tree-tops."

Downing the last of her drink, Chelsea set the small goblet aside and rose, as if compelled, to go and position herself
near Lord Rathbone. "You sound almost poetic, my lord,"
she murmured evenly.

He turned and finding her near him, their gazes locked.
Chelsea likened the burn in his eyes to the sting of the
sherry in her throat. When he held the gaze for quite a
length she finally grew uncomfortable and looked away.

"I admit I have consulted the bard upon occasion," he
said, belatedly resuming the conversation. "There is . . .
often very little to do of an evening. It will be pleasant,"
he added, "to have you read to me, as you do now for
Mother."

Chelsea watched him move from her side to set his own
emptied goblet down on a nearby table.

"I recently acquired a pianoforte," he told her.

"Oh?" Chelsea enjoyed the sight of his graceful, yet completely masculine stride as he returned again to her side. "Is there . . . someone to play the instrument for you? A neighbor, or perhaps the daughter of a servant?"

The gentleman laughed softly. "You have forgotten a great deal about me, Alayna."

Lowering her gaze, Chelsea's eyes squeezed shut. Dear God, how was she to go on? She was forever saying the wrong thing, and now, she had to contend with this . . . this disquieting manner in which Lord Rathbone's very presence affected her. Feeling him inch closer to her, as if on cue, her knees grew wobbly beneath her skirt, and her throat became inordinately dry.

"Alayna," he breathed, so near her she could feel his breath on her cheek.

She didn't dare raise her eyes to meet his now. Yet, when she felt his large, warm hand move to touch her shoulder, she risked a gaze upward. "Yes."

When he turned her to face him, Chelsea was more acutely aware of the warmth from his hand through the soft fabric of her gown than the heat from the fire blazing in the hearth. "You are so very beautiful, Alayna." Both his gaze and his voice were soft and caressing.

Chelsea held her breath.

"You've nothing to fear in Honduras, Alayna. I will always be there to protect you."

Chelsea felt her lower lip begin to tremble. No one, *no one,* had ever said those words to her before. This man had already saved her life once. Suddenly, it was all she could do not to fling herself into his arms again. Gazing up into his warm golden eyes she did not trust herself to speak. When his gaze dropped to her mouth, Chelsea knew he meant to kiss her.

As if reading her thoughts, Lord Rathbone said, "We are

soon to be man and wife, Alayna. You have nothing to fear from me, either."

Chelsea shook herself. *Nothing to fear.* She had *everything* to fear! With a gasp of alarm, she jerked from his grasp. "You forget yourself, sir!" she cried.

"Alayna!" His brows snapped together. "You are behaving like an infant. We are to be married in a fortnight, for God's sake. A certain amount of . . . of contact between a man and a woman is to be expected!"

"I do not expect it!" Chelsea cried, realizing that, for once, she and Alayna were of the same mind in the matter. Her eyes large and round, she darted from the room. Gaining the corridor, she broke into a run and did not stop running until she reached the suite of rooms that had become her home.

Inside her chamber, she flung the door shut and leaned breathlessly against it. She was not safe in this house! Whether pretending to be Alayna, or acting of her own accord, one thing was abundantly clear. She was definitely not safe!

Seven

Though still in a quandary over Alayna's continued resistance to him, Lord Rathbone made an effort to put the puzzle from his mind for the moment and see to the more pressing needs of the castle. After he and Alayna were married and on their way to Honduras, he'd have plenty of time to deal with his new bride's fears.

Early that next morning, he and a small army of workers, set out with the intention of repairing the rickety wooden bridge that served as the only avenue into the castle grounds. Once there, however, Lord Rathbone was chagrined to discover that during the previous night's downpour, the bridge had completely collapsed and all the moorings washed away.

"Drat and bloody hell!" he exclaimed, trudging back up the muddy road toward the castle, his workers following dutifully at his heels. In the yard, he set the men to work reinforcing the side wall of the stable, which looked perilously close to surrendering its thatched roof.

"When you've got that wall upright again," he told them, "we'll see to repairing one of the gigs and perhaps a wagon, or two. We'll need them to bring back additional supplies from Chester in the next day or so."

With that he turned and headed again for the castle. Indoors, he came upon Chelsea on her way toward Lady Rathbone's chamber.

"Bridge is out," he announced without ceremony.

"Oh, my," Chelsea replied. "I expect that means we will not be accompanying Mrs. Stevens on her parish rounds this afternoon."

"Hmmm." Lord Rathbone's dark brows drew together. "I admit I had completely forgot the appointment. Good of you to remember, Alayna. I shall get word to Mr. Stevens somehow."

"Perhaps through the forest?" Chelsea suggested, not at all sure there even was a viable way through the dense thicket of trees at the rear of the grounds.

Suddenly, Lord Rathbone's stern face softened into a smile. "I had completely forgotten that, as well, Alayna. Apparently you remember more than I thought you did about being here." A look of fond remembrance in his eyes, his gaze locked with hers and lingered.

Chelsea grimaced. She had no idea what he was thinking about. "I . . . haven't forgotten everything," she lied.

"Well, I expect we shall have plenty of time to renew old memories, now that we are to be cooped up indoors for a spell." He moved a step away from Chelsea. "Will be no point attempting to rebuild the bridge now until the rain completely lets up and the ground is dry enough to support new timber."

"Hmmm." Chelsea grimaced again. Cooped up in the castle . . . with Lord Rathbone . . . for how long? she wondered. When he bent another smile upon her, a sickish feeling began in the pit of her stomach and spread upward to her throat. How she was to endure such close proximity to him without breaking down altogether she did not know.

To her immense relief, however, she did not have occasion to see much of the handsome baron for the next several days. She was as aware of him as ever though—three times a day at table, often during the day when she'd overhear his deep baritone imparting instructions to one or another of the servants, and always each evening, when the three of them gathered for a last cup of tea, or in Lord Rathbone's case, a snifter of brandy or sherry, in the sitting room abovestairs.

One evening, as Lady Rathbone sat dozing in her chair, the gentleman said, "Perhaps we might get up a game of chess, or backgammon, Alayna. That's another thing I miss in the tropics, having someone to challenge to a game now and again."

"Oh, well, I—" Chelsea racked her brain trying to recall if Alayna was a chess player or not. In the end, she decided it didn't really matter. Nothing that transpired between herself and Lord Rathbone would signify once Alayna returned and the perfidy uncovered. In the meantime, she and the gentleman had to fill the long hours of the evening somehow. At least, this way, there would be the safe barrier of a game table between them.

Lord Rathbone had crossed the room to a corner cupboard and was rifling through it on a quest for the chess pieces or the backgammon suitcase. "Which shall it be?" he asked, his back to Chelsea as he talked.

"Either," she responded feebly.

"Good." Carrying a small box in his hands, he headed for a circular loo table and after tilting the top into position, began to remove the contents from the box. "How about cribbage?" he asked, with a laugh. "It was all I could find."

Chelsea smiled agreeably. "Cribbage is fine. I used to play with my grandfath—" Abruptly she stopped. *She* had played the card game with her Grandpapa Andover many, many times but whether Alayna had played the game or not, she had no idea.

Lord Rathbone was busy dragging a pair of chairs to the table. He glanced up. "You were saying?"

Chelsea swallowed tightly. "I . . . haven't played since I was a child. I hope I haven't forgotten the rules."

Lord Rathbone held a chair out for her. "We shall refresh our memories together, Alayna. As I recall, even as a child, you were a fairly apt pupil when it came to games." He positioned the wooden board between them and divided up the small markers, then reached for the deck of cards and began to shuffle them. "The last letter I received from Aunt Hermione said you had taken up whist, or was it faro? I'm not much on gambling, myself," he continued conversationally. "Now, then, let me see . . ." He began to deal the cards.

Chelsea recalled perfectly how to play cribbage, but decided to let him take the lead in explaining it to her. Afterward, they played silently for several minutes, then out of a clear blue, Lord Rathbone said, "I've been thinking about the *few* letters you wrote to me, Alayna—"

Fear clutched Chelsea's middle. What was he going to ask her now?

"Several of your letters last summer," he went on, "were chock full of the goings-on during your London Season."

Anxiety churned within Chelsea. She knew next to nothing about Alayna's come-out.

As Lord Rathbone continued, his tone grew more serious. "The thing is, Alayna, I do not recall you mentioning the names of any of your suitors, that is, any of the more persistent ones. And with your stunning looks, my dear, there must have been several."

Chelsea ventured nothing on the subject, though his comment on her looks did not escape her notice.

"Well, Alayna? At the risk of sounding inordinately forward, were there any?"

Suddenly Cheslea experienced great difficulty drawing breath. Alayna, she knew, had had several suitors. One in particular. But, as it turned out, the gentleman chose to pursue and finally marry a wealthy heiress from Ramsgate. Nonetheless, Chelsea did not feel obliged to tell Lord Rathbone about it. Especially since Alayna had not. Affecting one of Alayna's familiar put-upon poses, she said, "I hardly see where that is any concern of yours, Rutherford." Without looking at him, she settled her peg into the next hole in the board with an astonishingly steady hand.

When a reply from him seemed overlong in coming, however, she risked a sidelong gaze across the table at him and caught a frightening glimpse of his jaw clenching.

"To quarrel with you this evening is not my intent, Alayna, I am merely trying to ascertain why you . . ." He paused, then sat back in his chair, completely ignoring the fact that it was his turn to play.

Wondering what was the trouble now, Chelsea's heart leapt to her throat as she gazed full at him.

"I am trying to understand why you persist in refusing to comply with my wishes in regard to living in Honduras, Alayna. Your insubordination in the matter is quite troubling. If you must know, I am unaccustomed to disobedience."

Chelsea felt an unwelcome surge of heat color her cheeks. She did not even have to think before replying to the gentleman this time. "I am hardly one of your slaves, Rutherford," she said in a breathless rush. "And what exactly do my former suitors have to say to anything?"

"So," his eyes snapped, "you admit to other suitors?"

Chelsea's lips tightened. "I admit to nothing."

"Dammit, Alayna!" He slammed his cards onto the table. Apparently the volume of his tone, and the sudden action, awoke Lady Rathbone, for across the room, she sat up with a start.

"Beginning to thunder again?" she mumbled from her chair.

Chelsea rose to her feet and moved swiftly to the old lady's side. "No, Aunt Millie, Rutherford was just"—she cast an accusing look at him—"overset," she concluded. "We are playing a game and I expect he drew a bad hand."

Lady Rathbone twisted about in her chair. "Mustn't take on so, Rutherford, it is only a game."

In spite of the gnawing guilt she felt for inciting Lord

Rathbone's intense anger Chelsea silently voiced her agreement to that.

Dammit! What was it going to take to uncover the truth behind her refusal to obey him, Lord Rathbone demanded of himself, as he stalked toward his chamber that night. *And worse, what did it really matter?* Despite her objections to living with him in Honduras, she would acquiesce in the end. She was to be his wife for God's sake and that's all there was to say for it.

Flinging his coat and waistcoat to a chair, he fumbled with the stiff linen he'd so carefully wrapped about his neck before dinner. He thought he had unearthed the reason for her obstinence when he'd decided she was simply afraid to remove to an unknown clime. But, apparently he'd been wrong. Then, when she'd refused to kiss him the other evening, he thought perhaps her reticence was due to her youth and innocence, that perhaps she had never been kissed before. Now, he was beginning to think otherwise. That she had fallen in love with someone and was, therefore, reluctant to leave the gentleman behind in England made more sense. Anger roiled within him as he unbuttoned his trousers. Guilt had been as evident on her face tonight as puzzlement was on his!

Alayna had had a Season, after all, and with her beauty, it was hard to imagine that she had attracted no notice whatever among London's eager young bucks. In fact, it was hard to believe that she had not been snapped up after first being introduced to society at her come-out ball.

He tossed his trousers aside and reached for his dressing gown. Wrapping it about himself, he crossed the room to pour himself a stiff draught of spirits. But downing the drink did not push thoughts of Alayna from his mind. Carrying the bottle with him to the comfortable wing chair positioned before the fire, he continued on in the same vein.

So far as he could see, apart from her extraordinary looks, Alayna had nothing of value to offer a man. The orphaned daughter of an impoverished peer who had had the good fortune to marry a Campbell, she had no funds of her own and no connections to speak of. Which is one of the reasons Rutherford had agreed so readily to the match. Being the only surviving male in the family, he felt a compelling duty to look out for his female counterparts. By marrying Alayna, he was solving two problems at once. She needed a means of support and he needed a wife. Of course, he had not counted on . . . Dammit, he was *not* falling in love with her!

Beyond the insignificant little farradiddle he was attempting to unravel at odd moments of the day, it did not signify in the least that his future bride had once fancied herself in love with another. Did not signify in the least! Still, he would like to know if . . . *dammit!* He slung the half-full bottle of whiskey against the gray stone hearth before him and did not move when the glass shattered, and the amber liquid pooled at his feet. There was a reason behind her stubbornness and he would uncover the truth if it killed him!

The following afternoon, as the three of them partook of an early tea in the drawing room, he looked for a way to broach the subject with her once again. A heavy mist had been falling all day outdoors, consequently he had been forced once again to spend the entire day inside. But, as usual, thoughts of Alayna did not permit full concentration upon the tasks he'd set before him. He feared his patience, which even on a good day was in short supply, was fast running out.

Throughout the small meal, he had been unusually silent, his dark gaze resting fitfully on the blonde beauty, who reposed on a silk sofa opposite him. Just being in her presence these days made thinking difficult. She had the creamiest ivory skin he'd ever seen on a woman, with exactly the right amount of natural flush to her cheeks and lips. That she used no paint to enhance her features was evident. Today, her bright golden hair hung loose down her back, the ends of it a riot of soft yellow curls. Thoughts of pressing those silken tresses to his cheek and tasting the sweet nectar of her lips had driven any appetite he may have had for cold watercress sandwiches and pickled nasturtiums from his mind.

Watching her take a delicate bite from the slice of cake in her hands now made him swallow convulsively. Feeling a sudden tightness in his chest, he rose to his feet and was about to exit the room when the sound of his mother's voice stopped him.

"I have been thinking, Rutherford," Lady Rathbone began, "that I should like to give you children a proper send-off."

Lord Rathbone paused in his tracks. "A send-off, Mother?"

The older woman nodded, her grey eyes twinkling merrily. "I have decided to host a ball. In honor of your wedding. It's been simply ages since we had a soiree here. What do you say, Alayna? Would be quite lovely, don't you agree?"

Lord Rathbone thought he distinctly heard Alayna gasp aloud, but could not say for certain.

"Are you quite sure you are up to such a fete, Mother?" he began. "After all, the wedding is less than ten days away. I should think that will be send-off enough."

"Oh, fiddlesticks! Surely you recall the grand affairs your father and I used to host when you were a boy. And the delightful fairs we held on the castle lawn." Suddenly, she leaned forward in her chair. "Why, we should have a fair, as well! There's been nothing like our fairs since your father passed away. We've plenty of time to put it all together!" Excitement shone on the old lady's face. "Mr. Stevens could help spread the word. And you, my boy, could post notices the next time you go up to Chester."

"Now, Mother, I hardly think—" Rathbone began, his dark head shaking in protest.

But, suddenly Alayna spoke up. And, as usual she was of a differing opinion from him. "I think it a lovely idea, Ford," she began. "Aunt Millicent is right, a fair would be great fun! If nothing else, the planning of it will give us something to do while the bad weather persists."

"And what if the bad weather refuses to let up? All our planning will have gone for naught. Unless the bridge is repaired, no one will be able to attend our grand affair."

"Oh, Rutherford, don't be such a downpin," his mother said fussily. "If Alayna wishes to have a ball, *and* a fair, then we shall have both!"

His lips pressed into a thin line, Lord Rathbone angrily exited the drawing room. That both his mother and Alayna's heads were already bent together excitedly discussing the upcoming events, seemed like one more slap in the face to him. And, Lord Rathbone was not accustomed to being slapped in the face.

Eight

Chelsea and Lady Rathbone spent the next several days working diligently on their plans for the fair, and for the ball, which would be held in the castle's grand hall the night before the wedding. In all her life, Chelsea had never attended a fancy dress ball and watching the elaborate plans for this one unfold, she could not help but wish that she might be on hand to attend. But, of course, that was not likely, for surely Alayna would have returned to the castle by then and Chelsea would be on her way back to London.

The fair, she felt certain, would also be great fun. As a girl at school, Chelsea clearly remembered Alayna excitedly telling her friends at Miss Farringdon's Academy all about the lovely summer fairs held at Castle Rathbone. Aside from various games of chance, there would be jugglers, and knife-throwers, pie-men, a puppet show, plenty of food and drink, and country dancing.

With Lady Rathbone providing suggestions for the wording of it, Chelsea drew up a notice for the fair which she intended to take to an engraver in Chester and have copies printed up which would be posted all around the countryside.

By Sunday of that week, Lord Rathbone had overseen the rebuilding the bridge that spanned the castle moat, though the water beneath was still greatly swollen from the heavy rains that had fallen, filling the cobbled enclosure to the brim.

At breakfast on Sunday morning, Chelsea was inordinately surprised when Lord Rathbone announced that he meant to accompany Chelsea to church services later that day.

"We've a small church in the village near my home in Honduras," he said matter-of-factly. "I often attend services there."

"Ummm," Chelsea murmured, not sure if she liked the idea of him accompanying her or not. Carrying the lie she was living into the very portals of God's house was difficult enough without having the added burden of Lord Rathbone beside her.

"You will mention our fair to Mr. Stevens?" asked Lady Rathbone. "Perhaps he will announce the news from the pulpit."

"I'm sure he will, Mother," Rathbone said flatly.

"Well, you might show a bit more enthusiasm," she scolded. "As a boy, you used to greatly enjoy our fairs. You and Alayna both did. Surely you recall the time Alayna tossed the ball and landed you in a barrel of suds." Lady Rathbone laughed, referring to a game played often at country fairs where the victim perches on a platform and is subjected to a ducking when the rope holding him up is released after a perfect toss of a ball.

Glancing across the table at Chelsea, Lord Rathbone's lips pressed into a thin line. "I can't say as I recall the incident," he muttered.

Feeling a bit mischievous, Cheslea said, "Well, I do. And giving you a much-needed dunking was simply delicious!"

"Humph."

A moment of silence ensued, then Lady Rathbone said, "You must pay close attention to the vicar's sermon today, Rutherford. Your attitude is quite remiss these days."

Chelsea squirmed. Lord Rathbone's attitude may be remiss, but there was no denying that *she* was the one at fault. Her deceptive behaviour and continued resistance to him was clearly the cause of his ill-temper. To say truth, she was beginning to feel increasingly more guilty about deceiving him. Lord Rathbone may have a short temper and be arrogant to a fault, but he was still the most intelligent and honourable man Chelsea had ever met. All on his own, he had accomplished a great deal in his adopted country.

Glancing across the table at him now, she felt her breath grow short. The gentleman would make a . . . a wonderful husband for Alayna. Chelsea could only hope Alayna would realize how lucky she was to be marrying such a man.

After Dulcie had helped Chelsea dress for services that morning, she topped off Alayna's lovely suit of blue serge with a close-fitting casquet bonnet that sported a half veil. The bonnet was not one of Chelsea's own designs, but nonetheless, it was quite charming. Nestling it onto her upswept coiffure, she realized with a fresh surge of guilt that she had yet to make good on her word to Mr. Merribone. In the entire fortnight she had been at the castle she had not yet posted a single new bonnet design to him as she'd promised she would.

Descending the stairs to meet Rutherford in the foyer, she vowed that in the coming days, she'll spend less time in Lady Rathbone's delightful company and devote a few hours of each day to thinking up new bonnet designs for Mr. Merribone. With the bridge now serviceable again, she could go up to Chester herself and purchase the new drawing materials and paper she needed. She lifted her chin with resolve just as she reached the hall and caught sight of Lord Rathbone standing there awaiting her.

Meeting his gaze, she noted his stern countenance soften at once.

"Alayna," he breathed, "you look . . . lovely. Positively, lovely."

Chelsea smiled sweetly. "Why, thank you. You look"—

her sweeping gaze took in his smart blue superfine coat, thigh-hugging buckskin breeches and polished black Hessians—"quite handsome, yourself."

"Thank you, dear. I daresay, we make a grand looking couple."

Chelsea thrilled to his words as she curled a gloved hand around the arm he offered and they stepped onto the sun-dappled drive in front of the castle.

Following services, Chelsea was aware of the tremulous flutter she felt in her middle every time Lord Rathbone smilingly introduced her to the ladies and gentlemen he was acquainted with, as his future bride. She could not deny that a part of her, a *large* part of her, wished that what he was saying were true. But, of course, she was being silly. Once Alayna returned and the perfidy uncovered, she would never see Lord Rathbone again, nor Alayna, for that matter. And *that,* she told herself, was the real reason she was suffering through this torment. To once and for all be rid of Alayna Marchmont's interference in her life. She drew in a long breath. It would indeed feel good to no longer live under the constant threat of exposure, to simply live her life, to earn her keep, to . . . she glanced at Lord Rathbone as they headed for the handsome Marchmont coach . . . to . . . she had nearly said, to never see Lord Rathbone again, but those words caught in her throat.

With effort, she pushed down the roiling bubble of emotion that suddenly swelled her breast, that made her want to . . . to . . . she was unable to complete that thought, as well.

Upon returning to the castle, they, along with Lady Rathbone partook of a light luncheon, then Chelsea felt strangely disappointed when, as usual, Lord Rathbone disappeared into the library for the remainder of the day.

The following morning the sky again dawned blue and sunny. Chelsea actually awoke to the sound of birds chirping and trilling as they perched on the wide stone sill outside the narrow slit of window in her bedchamber. Her bare feet hit the floor with determination. Today, she would make the short journey into Chester to purchase the necessary drawing materials so she could make good on her word to Mr. Merribone.

"I think you should go into Chester today, Alayna," Lady Rathbone announced almost at once after they had all sat down to breakfast.

"Excuse me?" Feeling a sudden flush of alarm color her cheeks, Chelsea stared at the woman wide-eyed. *How did she know—*

"I shall be driving into the village today," Lord Rathbone said absently, "you may come with me, Alayna."

"Splendid!" his mother chimed in. "You may accompany Alayna to the engraver's with the notice about our fair."

For the drive into town, Chelsea, Lord Rathbone and Dulcie climbed into a rather shabby-looking carriage that had recently been repaired. As the poorly-matched team struggled to prance smartly in front of them, Lord Rathbone kept up a running discourse regarding the things he still intended to accomplish at the castle before he departed England.

"I intend to call on a land agent in Chester this morning," he said. "I am counting on him to recommend a competent bailiff to me, whom I shall hire straightaway and then see the man settled in before we leave. With the bridge now coach-worthy, and the outbuildings nearly all repaired, that leaves only cutting away the brush that's overtaken the bailey and lower castle walls. And, then, of course, there is the matter of clipping the lawn and putting up the necessary stalls for the fair. I take it Mother sent along a list of supplies she needs for the ball?"

"Yes," Chelsea replied. "And, I—I have a few errands I should like to tend to myself in town."

"Since you are familiar with Chester, I had thought to let you off at the Rows while I look after my business. By separating to take care of our respective errands, we shall make better use of our time. I should like to be back at the castle before luncheon, which will give me a long afternoon to complete my work. Is that agreeable with you?" He flicked a glance at Chelsea.

She feared all color had drained from her face. *Alone? He was leaving her alone with Duclie to find her own way about Chester?* Her heart hammered frantically as she fought to reply. "I—o-of course, that is quite agreeable with me," she said weakly. "But," she hurried on, "what about the packages? I rather expect I shall have a good deal to carry, more than poor Dulcie could manage."

Lord Rathbone turned to stare at her. "Have you gone completely daft, Alayna? Simply give over your list to the proper merchant, and I shall send a servant back this afternoon to collect the parcels. You don't think I intend hauling a load of fresh lumber atop the coach, do you?"

A nervous giggle escaped Cheslea. "No. H-how silly of me. But, I-I should like to bring my drawing materials back with me," she added in a rush.

"Drawing materials?" He slapped the reins over the backs of the mismatched pair in an effort to urge the cumbersome beasts along at a swifter pace. "Since when are you of an artistic bent?"

Chelsea could not think what had prompted her to blurt out that piece of incriminating evidence. She knew very well that Alayna was not an artist, as apparently, her cousin did. "Uh . . . they are for Dulcie, my abigail. Today is her birthday and I should like to get her something special."

When Dulcie opened her mouth, Chelsea kicked the poor girl's ankle.

"Ah, I see. Come to think on it, I had meant to purchase a gift for my housekeeper. Mrs. O'Riley is a lovely woman, you will like her," he continued. "Despite the fact that she is Irish, she is every bit as competent as any Englishwoman trained in the household arts that I have dealt with. While

I'm here, I expect it would also be a good idea to purchase small gifts for others of the household staff," he added, thinking aloud. "I regret Boxing Day came and went last year and I had nothing for them."

"You generally give your servants gifts." It was more a statement than a question. "What about the slaves? Do you also give them something?"

Glancing down at her, Rathbone half-laughed. "I daresay, you have developed a soft heart, my girl. I admit I never expected such an admirable quality to develop in you."

On Alayna's behalf, Chelsea begged to differ. Alayna may have her faults, but she could be quite generous, at times. "I merely think it fair that if you give your servants gifts, you should treat the slaves equally as well."

Still grinning, he said, "For the most part, the slaves are my servants. You will see how it is once you are there, Alayna." He returned his attention to his driving. "And furthermore you may rest assured, that all of my slaves are treated fairly."

Once they'd arrived inside the walled city of Chester, Chelsea made every effort to stay alert to the sights about her. Making note of the imposing lacy spired cathedral, and numerous half-timbered buildings, she hoped that in the event she had to walk a great distance in order to find her way back to the coach, she could avoid becoming hopelessly lost. As it turned out, when Lord Rathbone turned into the square that marked the entrance to the Rows, she soon saw that she had nothing to fear.

All the shops that she could possibly want to visit were clustered together, nay, stacked one atop another, in a riot of gay profusion.

"I shall leave the coach here," Lord Rathbone said, handing the reins to the livered footman who had ridden the short distance from the castle in the small dickey in the rear. "Will an hour be sufficient for you to complete your errands?" he asked Chelsea.

Wearing a very relieved smile on her lips, Chelsea quickly nodded assent. "Indeed. An hour will do quite nicely."

"Very well, then."

Chelsea stood for a long moment watching Lord Rathbone's tall figure disappear into the busy crowd milling purposefully about the colorful marketplace. When he was gone, she involuntarily inhaled a sigh of relief. For a very brief moment, she toyed with the idea of losing herself as well in the crowd. Permanently.

She just as quickly dismissed the notion. Dulcie was with her and to leave Lady Rathbone hanging in the lurch, and Lord Rathbone to worry over her sudden disappearance would never do.

In less than an hour, she had delivered her shopping lists to the appropriate merchants and selected and purchased the drawing materials she needed, and was on her way back to the coach. Through the surge on the flagway surrounding the cluster of horses and equipages left awaiting their occupants, she caught a quick glimpse of Lord Rathbone striding toward the curb. At the sight of his now all too familiar face, her heart lifted. She bit her lip to quell the rising tide of emotion that of its own accord swelled within her. He was indeed a wonderful man. Surely Alayna would fall in love with him once she saw him again.

On the way back to the castle, Lord Rathbone was again as talkative as he had been earlier.

"I met with a Mr. Wells," he told Chelsea. "He was able to recommend a highly accomplished bailiff to me." Rathbone sounded quite pleased. "I shall meet with the man straightaway. This is certain to solve Mother's management problem. Though I rather expect the gentlemen will serve more as a steward than a mere bailiff," he went on, thinking aloud. "Mr. Wells seemed to think the candidate sufficiently qualified. I do hope things proceeded as smoothly for you in town as they did for me, Alayna."

Chelsea nodded. "I took the announcement for our fair to the engraver. He said he would have the placards printed up by day after tomorrow. You will send someone to collect them, won't you? And I should also like to have them posted."

"I shall be happy to take care of that for you, Alayna." Lord Rathbone smiled magnanimously. "I am certain the fair will prove a great success. You and Mother have worked quite industriously." He turned to press a smile upon Chelsea. "I will admit," he added in a laughing tone, "I am quite looking forward to the festivities. And, to the ball, as well. It's been an age since I attended such an affair."

Chelsea cast a gaze upward, her eyes drinking in the handsome lines of his aristocratic profile. "There are no fancy dress affairs in Honduras?" she asked.

He turned another smile on her. "Not of the type you are accustomed to. Oh, we have our little assemblies, and such. There are a number of English couples living in Honduras. In fact, there are five in our village alone. Lord and Lady Bridleshelm only recently arrived from Africa. Bridleshelm acquired the sugar plantation at the foot of the hill, down from me. And there are a number of other planters whose wives accompanied them. I recall writing to you about that young Mr. Spencer, who originally hailed from Birmingham, I believe. He recently married the daughter of Mr. and Mrs. Fisk. It was our first wedding in the village. English wedding, that is. There are plenty of couples who jump the broom."

"Jump the broom?" Chelsea could not quell a laugh.

Rathbone joined in. "It's a marriage ritual of the Negroes. To seal their wedding vows, the young couple jumps backward over a broom handle. I've no idea why or how the custom originated," he added, with a laugh.

Chelsea relaxed. She had grown to love hearing him talk of his home. It all sounded so foreign, so thrilling, like making a fresh new start with one's life. Gazing up at him with wonder, she held her breath, hoping he would continue, though not daring to encourage him lest he think she was interested.

Apparently he felt her gaze on him for he turned then, and for a long moment, held the gaze. Chelsea did not know what to read into the look, but after a small smile had wavered across her lips, he started up again.

"We Englishmen are quite a gay lot when we gather together. The gentlemen puff on cigars and talk and talk. Occasionally we get up a game of cards, though I am not often amongst the players. The ladies prefer to gather 'round my new piano wanting to sing. And, of course, we dance. The ladies are constantly after us to dance with them." He laughed easily. "I can't think where they get the energy to do so, but I do believe if we'd oblige, the dancing would go on all night." Pausing, he looked at Chelsea again. "You would like that, would you not, Alayna?"

Chelsea turned her face away. *She* would adore it. "I-it all sounds very gay, Ford, but . . . you are forgetting," she said quietly, "I shan't be there."

Upon uttering those words, a sense of doom seemed to press down upon her. She hated to squelch his pleasure, but it would not do to let him think she had changed her mind. She knew it would take more than the promise of music and a bit of dancing to lure Alayna Marchmont away from England.

Once the small coach had rattled across the sturdy new bridge and wheeled past the bailey, Chelsea caught sight of a dusty horse tethered near the mammoth wooden doors that marked the entrance to the castle. At once the feeling of foreboding within her intensified.

"Appears we have a visitor," Lord Rathbone said, his well-modulated tone having grown distant and cool again. "I expect it is the magistrate, Mr. Wainwright. I called at his office just now, only to find that he had journeyed to the castle to see me. Or rather, us."

Chelsea's heart leapt fearfully to her throat as Lord Rathbone halted the team. He tossed the reins aside and hopped to the ground.

"Alayna," he said crisply, reaching to assist Chelsea down, "you will join us in the withdrawing room. Wainwright will want to have a word with you."

Her mouth having gone completely dry, Chelsea had difficulty responding. "D-do you suppose . . . I mean," she knew she was stammering, "will he have m-my miniature with him?"

Rathbone's lips pressed together in a show of disgust. "How vain you are Alayna. Perhaps he will have the picture with him, and perhaps he will not. Your portrait is not that important a piece of evidence, you know. There are any number of more critical things to consider in this case." Long strides carried him into the castle's darkened hall. "I have already said that in due time we shall have another portrait painted of you. Now, send your packages to your chamber and come with me."

Making an effort to swallow the terror that gripped her middle, Chelsea knew that once again, she had no choice but to do as she was told.

Nine

"We were beginning to despair of you," Lady Rathbone, exclaimed as Lord Rathbone, with Chelsea close on his heels, came striding into the room.

"My apologies, Mother," Lord Rathbone said, his hand outstretched as he approached the short, balding man standing near the mantelpiece. "Good day, Wainwright."

"Good day, my lord," the magistrate replied, pumping the hand Lord Rathbone offered.

"I trust I have not detained you overlong."

"Not at all, sir. Lady Rathbone has kept me occupied. She has given me quite a detailed account of her dealings with the prisoner."

"Yes, well, Mother did spend a good bit of time with Sully; but so did Miss Marchmont. Alayna," Rathbone turned toward Chelsea, who was standing quietly to one side, hoping the loud pounding of her heart could not be heard by anyone but herself. "This is my cousin, Miss Alayna Marchmont, the brave young lady whom Sully abducted."

Chelsea took a step forward, fixing what she hoped was a confident smile to her lips. "How do you do, Mr. Wainwright." She fervently hoped that the quavering of her voice was not as noticeable to the others as it was to her.

"Well enough, thank ye, Miss Marchmont. Now that the rain has let up and I can get about easier, that is. And dryer," he added, with a laugh. "Understand your lordship had troubles here, with the bridge collapsing and all."

"Indeed, we have," Lord Rathbone agreed heartily, then his pleasant tone changed abruptly. "Shall we get on with it, Wainwright? I should like to have this nasty business put behind us as soon as possible." With a hand, he indicated a group of straight-backed chairs in one corner of the cavernous room. Leading the way toward them, both Chelsea and Mr. Wainwright followed, leaving Lady Rathbone seated in her chair near the fire.

After everyone was settled, Chelsea, managing for the moment to hold her fierce anguish at bay, forced herself to speak up. "May I say how grateful I was that you and your men were within close range that night, Mr. Wainwright."

"Indeed, Miss Marchmont. You must have been frightened beyond measure that night, what with the shooting and all."

Chelsea nodded tightly, all the while watching the magistrate's face, hoping to read something, *anything* in his expression. But, so far, his ruddy features and burly manner had revealed nothing out of the ordinary.

He proceeded to ask her several questions, general in nature, regarding her dealings with Sully, then he and Lord Rathbone launched into a brisk discussion concerning the man's treacherous plot to make off with Lord Rathbone's legacy. Since they seemed to have forgotten that she was there, Chelsea wondered if perhaps her interview was done. Seizing upon a break in the gentlemen's conversation to excuse herself, she rose boldly to her feet and murmuring something vaguely intelligible, she hastened to Lady Rathbone's side.

"Well, my dear," the woman greeted her with a warm smile, "I hope you and Ford had a nice drive into Chester."

Chelsea drew up a chair and with a relieved sign, sank into it.

"You look as if you quite enjoyed yourself," Lady Rathbone went on, her gray eyes twinkling merrily. "The high color in your cheeks is most becoming."

At the mention of that, Chelsea felt the warm flush on her face deepen. Still working to suppress the unease that fluttered within her, she said, "We had quite a lovely time, Aunt Millicent." Pausing, her nervous gaze flitted across the room to where the gentlemen were still speaking in hushed tones. "I"—she glanced again at Lady Rathbone—"took our notice to the engraver. He said the placards will be ready day after tomorrow," she concluded, trying for a gay tone.

"Splendid! We shall send Ford after them when they are done."

"Yes, he said he would fetch them, and"—seemingly of its own accord, Chelsea's gaze again darted toward the gentlemen—"post them for us," she added absently. Suddenly, she wondered why Mr. Wainwright had said nothing about the portrait? *What could it mean?* Something, she feared, was amiss. Unaware of her actions, Chelsea began to nervously twist her hands together in her lap.

"Alayna, dear?"

Feeling a cool hand lightly touch her arm, Chelsea's head whirled back around. "Excuse me, Aunt Millicent, did you say something?"

"I was merely inquiring if you and Ford had given any thought to your wedding trip. And who you might be planning to take along?"

"Oh, our wedding trip. Uh—no"—Chelsea shook her head—"we've not yet discussed it."

"Alayna!" Lord Rathbone's booming voice commandeered her attention. Her eyes large and round, Chelsea sprang to her feet at once. "Would you step over here again, please, darling?"

Feeling her nails digging into the palms of her hands, Chelsea was across the room in a flash. Yet, upon reaching

Ford's side, the reassuring smile he bent on her alleviated some of the tension building within her.

"Mr. Wainwright needs to ask you one last question, my dear. It seems a loose end is still dangling." Lord Rathbone glanced down at Chelsea, and apparently noting the anguished look in her eyes, said, "You have nothing to fear, Alayna, I promise you Sully is tucked safely away behind bars."

Chelsea tried valiantly to calm herself, and forcing a deep breath of air into her lungs, turned toward the magistrate. But, noting tiny beads of perspiration popping out across his brow, she thought that gentleman seemed a bit overwrought.

"I uh, do not know where to begin with this, Miss Marchmont," the red-faced gentleman said hesitantly, "but . . . you understand I would not be doing my job properly if I did not uncover all the pertinent facts in the matter."

Fear pushed at the back of Chelsea's throat. After waiting for what seemed an eternity for the man to proceed, she finally said, "If it is about the—about my portrait, Mr. Wainwright, I already know that—"

"Why, that is it exactly, Miss Marchmont!" The magistrate exhaled a relieved breath. "It seems, well, uh—" Once again the magistrate appeared at a loss.

Lord Rathbone came to the rescue this time. "Alayna darling, it seems Sully has made certain accusations—ridiculous accusations, I might add—regarding your identity."

Chelsea's heart plunged to her feet.

"The prisoner, Miss Marchmont . . . well, he . . . he maintains that you are *not* Alayna Marchmont, which of course, is not to say that I believe a word of it—"

"Good God, man!" Lord Rathbone exploded. "Anyone can see that the idea is pure rubbish! Sully is obviously trying to divert the blame for his perfidious activity onto someone else's shoulders. It is nothing more than a ruse. And, a transparent one at that."

"Well, of course, I agree with you wholeheartedly, your lordship," Mr. Wainwright said. "Still, at the outset, Sully did present a fairly convincing case."

Chelsea felt all color drain from her face.

"Nonsense!" Lord Rathbone sputtered. "What could the reprobate possibly base such an accusation upon?"

"Well, uh . . . like Miss Marchmont said, it was her portrait, which *Sully* said—"

"We all know about the missing portrait, Wainwright. I fail to see where Alayna's likeness has anything to say to Sully's accusation."

"Well, according to Sully, and of course, you understand, it is his word against that of Miss Marchmont—"

"So, there you have it," Lord Rathbone cut in again. "If it is Sully's word against Alayna's, no man in his right mind would side with Sully."

"Well, uh . . . ." The magistrate seemed unconvinced.

"Where is the portrait now?" Chelsea managed to ask in a fairly even voice.

"Well, you see, that's where the problem lies, Miss Marchmont. It seems—"

"Did you not bring it with you?" Lord Rathbone asked impatiently. "All one need do is take a look at it. Alayna said it was the best likeness of her yet."

The magistrate's head jerked up. "That so, Miss Marchmont?"

Attempting to swallow the sharp terror that threatened to choke off every ounce of air in her lungs, Chelsea nodded thinly.

Rathbone turned another smile upon her. "My cousin would never tell a falsehood, Wainwright. Though I daresay there is not an artist alive who could do her beauty proper justice."

"Why, that is precisely what my clerk's wife said," Mr. Wainwright chimed in, his voice suddenly sounding quite relieved. "Seems his wife saw Miss Marchmont at services a fortnight ago, at the first reading of the banns, and according to her, the portrait did not favor the young lady in the least. She said you were much prettier than your portrait, Miss Marchmont."

"There, you have it," Lord Rathbone concluded. "Apparently this artist fell as far short of the mark as every one before him has."

Fighting to keep her quavering voice from breaking altogether, Chelsea asked, "Does your clerk have the portrait now?"

"Well, uh"—Mr. Wainwright scratched his head again—"that is, he *did* have it, but the thing is, Miss Marchmont, the portrait seems to have vanished into thin air. Dreadfully sorry. I had intended to deliver it to Lord Rathbone when I came to call today, would have made matters much easier, you understand. But—"

"No harm done," Rathbone put in, pleasantly. "I shouldn't think I'd even want the miniature now that Sully's had his . . . well—" he paused. "We have plans to commission a new one, a much *better* one, don't we, Alayna, darling?"

Her brown eyes still round with fear, Chelsea nodded weakly.

"Well, thank you for your help, Miss Marchmont," Mr. Wainwright said roundly. "So sorry to have put you through this. I can see now that the notion was indeed quite ridiculous, but a man in my position cannot take chances, you understand."

"No, o-of course, not," Chelsea murmured, directing a shaky smile up at Rutherford. "W-will that be all? Aunt Millicent and I were discussing our . . . our wedding trip . . . darling."

"Then go along with you, sweetheart. Wainwright and I still have the matter of my charges to consider."

Feeling a flood of blessed relief wash over her, Chelsea hurried away. How on earth the gentlemen had arrived at the conclusion that she was indeed Alayna Marchmont, in the face of such blatant evidence to the contrary, was beyond her comprehension? Only one thing stood out clearly in her mind. This had been the absolute worst experience of her entire life.

Lying abed that night, Chelsea could not thrust aside the horrendous feeling of guilt that had settled about her shoulders like a cocoon this morning. This havey-cavey nonsense had gone too far. Attending church while pretending to be Alayna Marchmont had been bad enough, though the second time, she realized, had been a bit easier, perhaps due to the pleasant sense of 'togetherness' she had felt with Lord Rathbone. But, today. Today was the worst discomfort she had ever experienced. She had broken the law! And, unbeknownst to him, she had dragged Lord Rathbone along with her, actually pulled him into her perfidy! Lord Rathbone was the most honorable man she had ever met. He would *never* break the law. He was all that was good and right and honest.

And, she . . . she was no better than Sully. And, though she feared for her very life when her awful treachery came to light, she could not live a day longer with herself if she did not confess the whole truth to Lord Rathbone at once. Her trickery had already caused him a great deal of grief, but today's episode with Mr. Wainwright had been too much. Chelsea had to come forward with the truth. When Alayna returned next week, her explanation of the unfortunate affair would surely save Chelsea from the gallows.

Of course, she reasoned further, thereafter, her good name would be ruined beyond repair—for who would hire a young lady who had spent time in jail—but, that did not matter now. What mattered was, she was deceiving Lord and Lady Rathbone shamelessly and it had to stop. The agony of it had become unbearable. Not even the thought of living without the constant threat of Alayna's interference in her life was enough to balance this torment. It had to end. She had to tell the truth.

Having at last reached a decision in the matter, Chelsea turned over and, at length, fell into a fitful slumber.

The following morning she entered the dining room determined to draw Lord Rathbone aside and confess the awful truth to him. But, she was startled to discover that that gentleman was not at the castle!

"Ford decided to make an early start for London," Lady Rathbone said. Then, at the crestfallen look on Chelsea's face, she added, "He will return in plenty of time for the ball, dear girl. In fact, I expect him back within the week."

When Chelsea could not manage any sort of reply, Lady Rathbone continued, "I know you will miss him frightfully, my dear, but I assure you the time will pass quickly. We've plenty to keep us busy."

Despite the truth of that, Chelsea was so overwrought she could not eat a bite of breakfast that morning. She had awakened poised and ready to make her confession speech today, and to bravely suffer the consequences, whatever they might be. And now . . . this. Dear God, how was she to go on until Lord Rathbone returned?

By the third day, she had grown so pale and wan that even Lady Rathbone commented on her inability to eat and lack of focus on the plans they were making for the fair and the ball.

"Alayna, my girl, you mustn't take on so. Rutherford will most certainly have returned to the castle by tomorrow. What do you say we take our tea out-of-doors this afternoon?" she suggested brightly. "Perhaps the fresh air will serve to stimulate your appetite. You must eat, my dear, how else will you be fit to dance the night away at our lovely ball?"

Chelsea smiled feebly as she rose from the sofa in the drawing room to wheel Lady Rathbone's chair into the corridor. In the hallway, they met Jared. Lady Rathbone gave him instructions regarding their afternoon repast, then she and Chelsea continued toward the garden.

Once outdoors, they skirted 'round the side yard and headed toward a neat grassy lawn. There, a small army of servants were busy trimming the overgrown hedges and pruning back several rows of wild roses. Chelsea pushed Lady Rathbone's chair up to a stone table standing beneath an ancient old oak, then settled herself on a small bench nearby. At their feet, a sea of blood-red poppies nodded their approval of the company. Though the air smelled crisp and fresh outdoors, the peaceful setting did nothing to lessen the sharp turmoil roiling inside Chelsea.

In moments, Jared appeared with the tea things and after laying out the meal, Chelsea made a valiant attempt to nibble on a cucumber sandwich, more to appease Lady Rathbone than to fill her own empty stomach. But, it was no use. After only a cursory bite, she laid the sandwich aside.

"Alayna, dear," Lady Rathbone began, her alert gray eyes still fixed on Chelsea, "it saddens me to see you wasting away so. You simply must eat, my girl." She paused, then said, "Though, it quite pleases me to know that you have come to care so deeply for my son."

Chelsea lifted an alarmed gaze. "E-excuse, me?"

"Oh, do not play the innocent with me," the older woman chided affectionately. "Your actions these past few days have been quite tell-tale. You are as in love with Rutherford as any young lady could be."

Chelsea blanched, but that did not deter Lady Rathbone from her course. "It is nothing to be ashamed of, Alayna. On the contrary, it is to be commended. Despite the fact that you and Rutherford's match was not engineered for love, I am quite pleased to see that it is happening anyway. A harmonious union is quite difficult to maintain without affection. And, now," she reached to pat Chelsea's hand warmly, "the two of you have such a great deal of joy ahead of you. I am quite pleased, my dear."

Chelsea managed a somewhat uneven smile, then dropped her gaze to her lap. Perhaps Lady Rathbone was the tiniest bit correct in her assessment. Chelsea had indeed come to care for Lord Rathbone. In fact, she had quite possibly fallen in love with him the moment she laid eyes on him. He had, after all, just saved her life. But, of course, *her* feelings for the gentleman did not signify, and even so, they were certainly a long way from . . . *real* love. Weren't they?

"There, there, dear," Lady Rathbone said, still gazing intently at Chelsea. "If it is any comfort to you, my dear, I am quite certain Ford shares your sentiments. I have seen the way he looks at you."

Chelsea's eyes widened with fresh alarm. "Looks at me?"

Lady Rathbone laughed. "Indeed. And just look at the way he prolonged making this trip to London. He would not have gone a'tall if it were not absolutely necessary. He did not want to be away from you, Alayna. Surely, in light of the way you feel about him now, you intend to return to Honduras with him once the pair of you are married." She paused, then added quietly, "One wonders how you would survive a really long absence, my dear."

Having grown more uncomfortable by the minute, Chelsea wanted only to bolt from the garden and lock herself in her bedchamber. She was *not* Alayna Marchmont and she was *not* to marry Rutherford Campbell!

"Can you say nothing for yourself, Alayna?," Lady Rathbone's tone was a bit sad. "You have become so very dear to me. I should not want to see you unhappy for the rest of your days. Happiness is not so very easy to come by in this world. One would be foolhardy indeed to walk away from it."

Chelsea fought the impulse to run from it. "I am certain

you are right, Aunt Millicent," she murmured. "But, I-I . . . but, you see, there is something I . . . I . . ."

"What is it, my dear? What is troubling you?"

Chelsea bit her lower lip to keep from blurting out the horrible truth in a rush. If only she could be certain what to do. She gazed at Lady Rathbone imploringly.

"Yes?" Lady Rathbone's expression was expectant.

Lowering her lashes, Chelsea considered how to begin. She suddenly felt so very confused and alone, as if she could not fully trust herself to know what was right anymore. It was true, she *had* missed Ford. She had missed him fiercely. Without him, the castle had seemed empty and forlorn. And in spite of her resolve to confess the whole truth to him, the thought of being jerked from his side and never to see him again was almost more than she could bear. Perhaps . . . was it possible, she did not need to tell him the truth? Perhaps, if . . . oh, it was all so confusing.

"What is it, Alayna, dear? I can see that you are quite distressed. I am sure you will feel much better if you tell me what the trouble is."

Chelsea felt a rush of confused tears begin to swim in her eyes. "Oh, Aunt Millicent, I—" She feared she would burst if she did not tell someone! "I-I . . . you see, I have a friend, Aunt Millicent, who finds herself in a . . . a rather difficult situation. It seems this friend gave her word to another friend to do a certain thing, and my friend has quite tried her best to do it, but the doing—that is, you see, when the doing of the deed is uncovered—it may cause others, whom my friend has also come to care a great deal for, a . . . a certain amount of grief. My friend's problem, Aunt Millicent, is"—she turned round brown eyes upon Lady Rathbone—"to whom does my friend owe her allegiance? To the friend to whom she gave her word, or to those for whom she has come to care?"

Lady Rathbone drew in a long breath. "Well," she pursed her lips. "Your friend indeed has a problem."

Her hands clenched tightly in her lap, Chelsea waited breathlessly for the answer.

"I should think," Lady Rathbone began, "that to remain entirely honorable, your friend should endeavor to keep her word."

Chelsea could hardly believe her ears.

"That is," Lady Rathbone continued, "if the doing of the deed does not go against the law, or is in any way dishonorable."

Chelsea's eyes squeezed shut. It was just as she feared. She *had* to tell Lord Rathbone the truth. But could she? Now. Now, that . . . oh, how had her sense of right and wrong become so hopelessly entangled with her feelings for Lord Rathbone?

Ten

Upon entering the dining room the next morning, Chelsea was thrilled beyond measure to find Lord Rathbone himself seated at the head of the table. The smile that lifted the corners of her mouth was both spontaneous and brilliant.

"Rutherford!" she cried, "you have returned!" Then upon hearing the sound of Lady Rathbone's indulgent laughter, she felt more than a trifle embarrassed by her uncharacteristic show of exuberance.

"Did I not tell you he would?" the older woman said, amusement still evident in her voice. "Alayna and I have both missed you, Ford."

"And I you, Mother," Lord Rathbone said, his tone oddly terse. He flicked a gaze at Chelsea as she slid into her place at the table.

But the gentleman's cool demeanor was lost on her, so overjoyed was she to see him again. Drinking in the glorious sight of his handsome face, it was as if in the past three days she had lost all recollection of it. The vivid impressions she had so carefully tucked into her heart had somehow vanished and now she was breathless to fill up the void again with new and precious images of him.

Her eyes travelled over his face as if she were beholding it for the first time. The breadth of his tanned brow, his straight nose, and the gentle flare of his nostrils seemed to fascinate her. The resolute set of his jaw and the slight, but delicious curve of his full lower lip intrigued her.

He looked especially attractive this morning in a forest green brocade waistcoat and buff-coloured jacket. His snowy white cravat contrasted sharply with the deeply tanned skin of his neck and face.

As Chelsea's eyes travelled upward once more, she noted that while in London, he had had his hair trimmed, for the dark, thick locks were now styled in a manner that she recognized as being very much in vogue with the Corinthian set.

Suddenly the gentleman turned a quizzical gaze on Chelsea and her stomach did a funny flip-flop.

"As soon as you have eaten your breakfast, Alayna, there is a matter I should like to take up with you . . . in private," he said quietly.

The smile on Chelsea's lips widened. "Of course, Rutherford."

Her gaze cut to Lady Rathbone, whose lips were still twitching as she watched Chelsea. "You'd best eat, my dear," she said.

Chelsea smiled nervously. "As it happens, I feel quite famished, Aunt Millicent." She turned to the servant hovering at her elbow. "If you'd fill a plate from the sideboard for me, please."

The servant hastened to do her bidding. "The eggs, too, miss?"

Chelsea nodded eagerly. "And some of the custard and a wedge of the meat pie. Why, I declare," she said to no one in particular, "I am absolutely ravenous!"

Only Lady Rathbone seemed to find the comment amusing.

Minutes later, Lord Rathbone laid aside his napkin and gazed directly at his cousin, who, at the moment, was giving full attention to the food on her plate. It had rather surprised him to realize that he had truly missed her. He had thought that being away from her, and from the castle, would feel much the same as it always did, that having left those concerns behind, he would be able to carry on in his normal detached fashion, his mind firmly fixed on the business at hand. But, that had not been the case this time. Thoughts of Alayna had constantly surfaced, making concentration when he was away from her as difficult as it had been when she was near. Which, he realized, made the troublesome rumors he had heard circulating about her in London that much more difficult to bear.

His mouth firmed into a thin line as images of her and . . . *no!* He would not think on that again until he had heard her confirm, or deny, the truth of the matter to him with her own lips.

The story was a sordid one and he had not enjoyed hearing it bandied about in the clubs and drawing rooms he had frequented. But being a fair man, he would not judge a person on the basis of hearsay alone. He would give Alayna the opportunity to confess the whole truth to him, or to assure him that the vile rumors were nothing more than gossipmonger's tongues run amuck. In Alayna's defense, he did not believe she would fabricate a falsehood in order to protect herself. He was quite certain she would tell him the truth.

Leaning back in his chair now, he continued to watch her devour the food on her plate. Watching her, he could not suppress a small smile. She was gobbling her food in much the same way as the hungry children of newly purchased slaves eat, scooping the food into their mouths as if they had not eaten in a week.

In many ways, Alayna was as guileless as a child. It was one of the many things that endeared her to him. Despite her continued obstinance about returning to Honduras with him, he was certain she found his talk of the plantation fascinating. A sort of child-like hunger for adventure shone from her eyes as he talked and as she hung tenaciously on to his every word. And, just a moment ago, he smiled with inward satisfaction, she had been every bit as happy to see him as he was to see her.

But, his jaw firmed again, he would not let his true feelings for her show just yet. Not until he heard what he wanted to hear, nay, *needed* to hear from her own lips. He had to know if she cared for him, and . . . equally as important, that there had been no other man before him.

He pushed away from the table. "I shall await you in the library, Alayna."

She lifted her gaze. "I shall only be a moment."

"Take your time." Moving away from the table, he felt her eyes following him as he exited the room.

When Lord Rathbone heard her gentle rap at the library door, he rose from his position before the rent table.

"Come in, Alayna."

Stepping into the room, he noted that she had taken the time to change her gown. At the breakfast table, she had looked charming. Now, dressed in a primrose sprigged muslin with a wide blue sash tied beneath her breasts, she looked . . . breathtaking. Her butter gold hair seemed to sparkle and her dark brown eyes were as bright as dew drops glistening in the meadow. His pulse quickened as he watched her glide toward him, the soft folds of her gown outlining the gentle curves of her lithe body.

Dragging his eyes to her face, he was suddenly struck by the enormous difference there also. In place of her unmasked joy at seeing him, she now wore a fixed look of . . . resolute determination. His eyes narrowed with disgust. Unless he completely missed the mark, Alayna knew exactly what this interview was about.

With a cool nod, he indicated a chair where she might sit. But she surprised him by saying, "Thank you, I prefer to stand."

"Very well." He positioned himself before the large desk in the center of the room and folded both arms across his chest. After a pause, he said, "Is there something you wish to confess to me?"

He was not prepared for the look of shock that transformed her face again, as if the very life were being sucked from her body.

So, he had *not* missed the mark.

"I am waiting," he said, realizing that in a perverse way he was actually enjoying her discomfort.

The sharp rise and fall of her breasts momentarily distracted him, but he managed to push the delightful image from his mind. She had grasped the back of a nearby chair, apparently for additional support.

"Y-you know?" she murmured faintly.

"I know enough. But, in all fairness to you, I am willing to hear your side of the story."

"M-my side?"

"That is correct." He waited, but when she seemed loath, or perhaps, unwilling, to begin, he said, "Perhaps I should tell you what I have heard and then allow you the opportunity to confirm, or refute, it."

Since she still looked as if for the moment speech was impossible, he surged ahead. "It seems that your . . . shall we say, blatant indiscretions . . . are on the lips of everyone in Town, my dear."

"M-my indiscretions?" Her lovely brows drew together with puzzlement.

Rathbone nodded coolly. "You are being linked with a man by the name of Mr. Harry Hill. An *actor*, Alayna. *A common actor!*" Feeling rage begin to pulse through his veins, he tried valiantly to contain it. Despite the guilt written all over her face, Alayna had not yet had her say in the matter.

He watched while a variety of other incriminating emotions appeared on her flushed countenance, then he fairly exploded. "I *demand* to know the meaning of this, Alayna!"

In an effort to calm himself, he began to pace back and forth before the huge desk. Still, she said nothing.

He stopped pacing to glare at her. "Either you are acquainted with the man, or you are not! And, if you are, I demand to know to what lengths the . . . er . . . the association has progressed."

Suddenly, her flushed cheeks became the color of new fallen snow. "P-progressed?"

"Dammit, Alayna! Can you do nothing but stutter and stammer in your own defense? It is enough that my future wife has consorted with such . . . such low-lifes! It would be the outside of enough to learn that she had . . . that she is carrying on a . . . that she means to . . ." He parked both fists on his hips. "You know very well to what I am alluding, Alayna. I *demand* to know the truth at once!"

Suddenly the dam of his betrothed's silence seemed to break. Replacing the fearful reticence in her gaze was a new level of determination. Her dark eyes flashed as she cried, "Then I shall tell you the truth! I shall tell you the whole truth, as ugly and horrible as it is!" Her pretty nostrils flared as she spat out the words. "I am not the person you think I am! I am someone entirely different. *I* would never consort with the sort of person you mentioned. *I* do not know an actor, or any theatrical people. *I* would never do anything to bring dishonor to *my* name . . . *or to yours.* The truth is, I lov—" Abruptly, she halted.

Stunned, Lord Rathbone just stood there. He watched her dark eyes begin to brim with moisture and her chin to tremble. The anger raging within him melted away. He had heard, that is, he had *nearly* heard, exactly what he wanted to hear. She loved him. And, the plain truth is, he loved her. He exhaled a long breath. He was satisfied.

Two strides closed the distance between them. "Alayna,

darling . . ." he said, his arms reaching to clasp her by the shoulders.

"I never meant this to happen," she murmured faintly through her tears.

"Nor did I," he echoed thickly.

"Please believe me, Rutherford, I am so sorry. I never meant to hurt you . . . I never meant to . . ."

"Sh-h-h. It is all right, my darling. You need say no more."

She lifted imploring eyes to his. "But . . . you do not understand, I am not—"

He reached to put a finger to her lips. "Not another word, my sweet. I know that you love me and that is all that matters."

"Oh-h," she whimpered.

In one swift motion, he gathered her into his arms and gently pressed her trembling body to his. "Ah, my dearest Alayna, I do love you. I love you with all my heart. I never meant it to happen either. I never so much as contemplated the possibility. Life is so much simpler without love to complicate it, but the truth of the matter is, you have stolen my heart."

When at last he pulled back, it was to lower his mouth to hers.

Chelsea hadn't the will to resist him. With his arms wrapped tightly about her, his moist lips pressed to hers, she seemed to lose what little grasp she had left on rational thought. A moment ago, she had meant to tell him everything, to confess her true identity to him, to reveal her awful treachery. She would leave nothing out. But now . . . clinging desperately to the man she loved, she could no more tell him the truth than she could fly.

When his lips at last left hers and began instead to drop feathery light caresses on her bare neck and throat, Chelsea reveled in the shivery current that raced through her. She'd never been held by a man before, had never even imagined what a kiss might feel like. But, now, with her arms twined up around his neck, her back arched against the length of his hard body, she knew imagination could never come close to the delicious truth of this reality.

"Ah, Alayna," he murmured, his breath warm against her ear. "How shall I wait til we are married to make you mine?"

Suddenly, Chelsea's eyes sprang open. *"Wait?* But . . . you *must!* That is . . . *we* must! Oh-h!"

She felt the low rumble of his laugher bubbling up from his throat as he hugged her close to him again. "Of course, we shall wait, my darling. I may be head over ears in love, but I am still a gentleman. I would never compromise you."

Chelsea did not hear him. Forming her hands into fists, she pushed hard against the solid wall of his chest. "Please, let me go. I should never . . . we mustn't . . . *please!"*

His lips twitching, Rutherford moved a small step backward. "I was a fool to ever doubt you, Alayna. You are as pure as . . . allow me to beg your forgiveness, my dear." His tone was both solemn and sincere.

Still lost in her own mortification over the scandalousness of her behaviour, Chelsea could only repeat, "Please forgive me, sir, I should never have—"

"Forgive you!" Laughing aloud, Lord Rathbone released her completely. "You have done nothing wrong, sweetheart. We are to be married. It is perfectly acceptable that a gentleman and his betrothed should"—his eyes twinkled merrily as he gazed down upon her—"indulge a bit."

"Oh!"

Rathbone laughed again. "You a perfectly proper young lady, Alayna. And you were entirely within the bounds to call a halt to my forwardness"—he grinned rakishly—"that is, for now."

Chelsea was too overset to speak. Stricken, she turned and bolted from the room. *She was anything but a perfect young lady!* She had taken this horrid perfidy to new depths of degradation. Dear God, how was she to climb out of it now?

Eleven

When Lady Rathbone retired to her chamber following dinner that evening, Chelsea was left alone again in the company of Lord Rathbone. Turning a shy gaze on him as he relaxed before the fire, she experienced the selfsame breathless reaction that she had felt this morning following his kiss. This afternoon, she had finally realized that not even the sick feeling that lay perpetually in the pit of her stomach was enough to deter her heart from the course it had chosen. She simply couldn't help herself. No man had ever affected her as Lord Rathbone.

At length, he turned toward her. "I meant to say no more on the subject, Alayna, but I thought you'd like to know that while in London, I took the liberty of setting the record straight regarding your whereabouts these last weeks."

Chelsea schooled herself to stay calm. There was, after all, no further need to be frightened of him. Both he and his mother were firmly convinced that she was indeed Alayna Marchmont. "My whereabouts?" she returned quietly.

Rathbone nodded. "The word in Town is that"—he shook his head as if he could not put down the oddity of it—"you are currently travelling about the countryside in the company of this Mr. Harry Hill."

"Oh, my." Chelsea smiled feebly.

Rathbone rose from the wing chair he had occupied near the fire to fetch himself a snifter of brandy from the sideboard. "Apparently the man has got up a troupe of players—you being among them," he added, grinning at Chelsea as he recrossed the room to stand before the fire, absently twirling the amber liquid around in the goblet. "I actually heard something about your smashing debut on the boards in Bristol." He chuckled again as he continued to contemplate the absurdity of the notion. "Can you imagine the like?"

"Um . . . no." Chelsea managed a weak laugh. "I cannot."

"Of course, I knew that part to be a complete fabrication, for how could you possibly be two places at once?"

Chelsea chose not to comment. She had no idea where Alayna was at present, but, surely, she was not touring about the countryside playacting on the stage! Not even Alayna would do something so caperwitted as that.

"You know, my dear," Rathbone began afresh, his tone now solemn, "we are very fortunate in that by choosing to live abroad, we shall escape London's vicious gossip mill. I can assure you that, on the whole, the women of my community have far better things to occupy their time than fabricating vile rumors about one another."

Chelsea lowered her gaze from Lord Rathbone's handsome face to her lap. Apparently, he was assuming from her actions this morning that she meant now to fall in with his plan for their future. Their future together. In Honduras. She could not stop the low sigh of longing that escaped her at the thought. Despite the near overwhelming guilt she felt for deceiving the gentleman so shamelessly, another part of her heart sang with joy at the prospect of marrying Lord Rathbone and beginning a glorious new life with him. For that to actually come true would be nothing short of a miracle for Chelsea.

A small but sad smile lifted the corners of her mouth. "We are indeed fortunate, Rutherford. To say truth, I can hardly fathom it."

* * *

At table the next morning, Lord Rathbone's countenance was again all smiles and good humor.

"I had thought that today, Alayna, we might drive into Chester. I have yet to meet with the gentleman the land agent there recommended to me. As I do not expect the interview to take overlong, I thought the two of us might take a leisurely stroll through the shops together."

Chelsea could not help but feel exhilarated by his suggestion. "Why, I should enjoy that very much, Rutherford."

"A capital idea!" Lady Rathbone chimed in. "As soon as the mist lifts this morning, the day should turn off quite sunny. If I were not so old and decrepit, I admit I would greatly enjoy such an excursion myself," she added with a laugh.

"Then you must come with us, Aunt Millicent," Chelsea said, turning a concern-filled gaze upon the feeble old woman.

"No, no." She laughed. "You children run along. I shall sit by the window and enjoy the sunshine right here."

"Are you quite certain, Aunt Millicent?"

"Indeed! I am certain."

Lord Rathbone began afresh. "I should warn you, Alayna, we've nothing like the Rows in Honduras. If you feel you have need of anything—feminine fripperies or such—I would advise you to make your purchases now while you've the opportunity."

"Oh, well, I"—Chelsea shot another glance at Lady Rathbone—"I can't think of anything I especially need. Perhaps I could purchase something for you, Aunt Millicent. Once Rutherford . . . and I . . . are gone, there will be only Jared and Mrs. Phipps to give a thought to your comfort."

"You are very thoughtful, Alayna," Lady Rathbone said smiling, her tone sincere.

"Yes, she is, very, isn't she, Mother," Lord Rathbone put

in agreeably. He turned another warm smile on Chelsea. "I must admit, Alayna, that your good nature and sweet temperament has quite taken me by surprise. As I recall, you were a bit of a terror as a little girl." His lips twitched as he gazed fondly at Chelsea.

"Indeed, she was!" Lady Rathbone added. "Why, I never saw a more selfish and willful little girl, and—"

"And you and our other aunts spoiled her shamelessly!" Rathbone sputtered accusingly, though affection was still evident in his tone.

"Well, she was a darling child nonetheless, all golden curls and"—Lady Rathbone cast a gaze at Chelsea, who held her breath while awaiting the conclusion of this sentence—"and dimples."

Exhaling a relieved breath, Chelsea hurriedly put in, "As I recall, you were positively horrid, Rutherford. You used to tease me incessantly simply because I was a girl and too little to defend myself."

"Well, we are both grown up now"—he reached for his coffee cup and sat back in his chair to sip it—"and I should like to take you into Chester and buy you a gift."

"A gift?" Chelsea's brown eyes became round with delight. "But . . . why?"

"Because I've not yet bought you a betrothal present, and I should like it to be something special."

"Oh-h-h," Chelsea drew the word out tremulously. She had never received a gift from a gentleman before.

Dressing for their outing, Chelsea could not put down the feeling of breathless anticipation that had assailed her yesterday morning when she saw Lord Rathbone at table again and that continued to beset her every time she found herself in his delightful company. She had hardly slept for thinking about him, reliving again and again the wondrous feel of his lips on hers, and going over and over in her mind all that he had said to her since. Uppermost in her thoughts was the fact that he had said he loved her. But, of course, she told herself, he did not really love *her.* He loved Alayna. A pang of sadness stabbed her. If only she could remember that.

Last evening, she had thoroughly enjoyed sitting by the fire with him as they continued to talk far into the night about the wonderful life that awaited them in Honduras. Chelsea sat enthralled as Lord Rathbone spoke at length about the plantation. She learned that a portion of his land was given over to the growing of sugar cane and that he was experimenting with a new type of irrigation pump, as well as, the rotation of various crops.

In spite of the niggling anxiety in the back of her mind that she was showing far too much interest in affairs that did not really concern her, she asked question after question of him, knowing all the while that her questions pleasured him. And, pleasing Lord Rathbone, she found, gave her the greatest joy she had ever experienced in her life.

Now, as Dulcie helped her into another of Alayna's lovely frocks—this one a pretty blue and white striped round gown with a tiny blue velvet spencer jacket—she greatly looked forward to spending the entire day with him. After settling the matching blue toque bonnet onto her curls, she drew on a pair of long kid gloves and hurried belowstairs.

In the hall she caught sight of Lord Rathbone imparting instructions to one of the liveried footmen. Not even trying to squelch the tingling sensation that pulsed through her veins as her eyes raked over his attractive form, she openly admired his rugged masculinity. He looked as handsome as ever this morning in a cut-away coat of dark brown superfine with a pair of thigh-hugging beige breeches tucked into polished brown top boots.

Upon hearing her clipped footfalls on the bare stone floor behind him, he turned to face her. Chelsea at once returned the smile of greeting on his face, then noticing the canary yellow waistcoat he wore, her smile became a laugh.

"How very fetching you look!" she said, reaching a gloved finger to flirtatiously tap his broad chest, brilliant in the yellow silk brocade affair.

Rathbone laughed a bit sheepishly. "A bit showy, I expect. I confess it is not my usual style."

"Nonetheless, I like it very much. It makes you look like a . . . a—"

"Swangra buckra?"

Chelsea laughed merrily. "A what?"

"Swangra buckra," Rathbone said again, as he curled her hand over the crook of his arm and escorted her into the sunny courtyard. "It's a term the Negroes use when referring to an elegantly dressed white man. I believe the literal meaning has something to do with a powerful or superior being."

"Then they are exactly right," Chelsea returned gaily.

"I daresay you flatter me, my dear."

"No, I don't," Chelsea returned quietly, then blushed to her toes when his answering smile sent waves of pleasure coursing through her.

As the small curricle jounced along the sun-dappled countryside, Chelsea thought she'd never felt so happy and content in all her life. Even the blood red poppies and sky-blue cornflowers dancing in the fields they passed seemed to nod gay greetings to them. Overhead she was aware of birds chirping and trilling in the tree-tops and when a butterfly, looking much like a flying splash of color, whizzed past her nose, she felt as giddy as a child being let out of doors after a long cold winter of confinement.

Without considering what she was doing, she snuggled a bit closer to Lord Rathbone on the cushioned bench, enjoying to the hilt the warm feel of his hard thigh pressed to her softer one.

Apparently feeling every bit as contented as she, he edged closer to her. "You feel nice, Alayna," he murmured.

Her heart fairly bursting with joy, Chelsea smiled up at him. "I've never been so happy, my lord," she whispered, gazing at him through mist-filled eyes.

"Nor have I," he returned gravely. "To say truth, I am very pleased with the way things have turned out between us. I admit, when Mother and our aunts Lettie and Eudora first began to push for the match, I was against it." He paused, as if considering whether or not to proceed. "If you must know, it was your letters, Alayna, or rather, what I perceived from your letters—as infrequent as they were," he added, his tone growing hard. "At any rate, they were quite full of . . . well, your *ton* activities, new ball gowns, your various jaunts here and there, riding in Bath—" He halted abruptly. "By the by, you never did tell me why you ceased to ride. As I recall, you were quite an accomplished horsewoman." He turned a questioning gaze on Chelsea.

The moment he had begun to speak of Alayna had been so jarring to Chelsea, she had fairly reeled from the blow. "I . . . I simply gave it up," was all she could manage now.

"Hmmm, I see. Well, in any event, you seem to have also given up many of your former undesirable traits. And, I daresay, I am glad enough for the change in you. Mother is quite right, you have become a very charming and selfless young lady. I confess I feel privileged to make you my wife."

Chelsea felt like dead weight on the bench. How quickly she had forgotten that she was, indeed, only playing a part.

The sickening feeling in her stomach had not left her by the time they arrived at the famed Rows in Chester. Before they even reached the land agent's office, several townsfolk recognized the pair of them and remarked gaily upon the forthcoming fair to be held on the castle grounds.

"I expect in my absence, you and Mother have finalized your plans for the upcoming festivities," Lord Rathbone remarked to Chelsea, after yet another person had commented upon it.

"Yes." She nodded. "All is readiness now. The placards were posted near a week ago."

"Ah, yes. I quite forgot I had promised to do that for you. But, I see that in your usual competent fashion, you handled it quite well without me. You are a marvel, Alayna." He smiled down upon her.

Chelsea made no comment, though the compliment warmed her.

After spending a few moments at the land agent's office, the two set out to browse through the many interesting shops. To appease the gentleman, Chelsea felt forced to make a few small purchases—a half dozen pairs of kid gloves, a box of linen handkerchiefs and two lengths of plain white muslin suitable for light summer gowns.

"You will be glad enough for it," Lord Rathbone said as they exited the shop. "Summers can be quite warm in the tropics. More often than not, I return to the house at the end of a long day in the sun with my shirt sleeves rolled up and perspiration dripping from my brow."

Chelsea found it difficult to imagine that the elegantly attired gentleman striding along beside her could ever appear so disheveled as all that.

Apparently divining her thoughts, he grinned. "I doubt you will refer to me as a swangra buckra then. In fact, I wonder if you will admire me at all when my trousers are splattered with mud and my once white shirt is soiled, or torn beyond repair."

In an effort to keep from saying that she would admire him no matter what, Chelsea turned her face away, biting her lower lip so hard she feared it might bleed.

They strolled in silence for a spell, then at length, Lord Rathbone said, "I daresay the time has come for me to select a gift for you, sweetheart."

They were approaching a small shop with a window full

of sparkling jewels. Pausing before it, Lord Rathbone slipped an arm about Chelsea's slim waist and drew her closer to his side. "Just there," he said, pointing a gloved finger at some item displayed in the window. "What do you think? I spotted it a week ago and almost purchased it then, but decided to wait 'til we came into town together. Do you like it?"

"I-I'm not sure which piece you mean," Chelsea said quietly, realizing that even if she wanted to, she would be unable to stop him from purchasing a gift for her. Of course, whatever he bought, she would turn it over to Alayna the minute she returned to the castle.

"Just there. The heart-shaped locket with the tiny diamond in the center. I realize it isn't a'tall showy, but upon our marriage, you will, of course, inherit a good many lovely pieces from Mother. In the meantime, I have not seen you wear even one piece of jewelry, Alayna, and I should like to give you something that you might wear every day." His voice grew hoarse. "To remind you how very much I love you," he concluded, his final words just above a whisper.

"Oh-h," Chelsea breathed, longing with all her soul to echo the sentiment. "It's . . . beautiful, Ford. I shall be very proud to wear it . . . always," she added sincerely.

Lord Rathbone's chest expanded proudly. "Then, it's yours. Come, we shall purchase it straightaway."

On the return trip back to the castle, Chelsea could not help reaching up at intervals to finger the golden locket clasped around her neck. The warm metal against the bare skin of her throat felt rich and smooth. She had not worn jewelry these last weeks for the simple reason that she did not own any, and apparently thinking that jewelry or accessories were unnecessary in the country, Alayna had not included any of her own when she had packed the two trunks that had accompanied Chelsea to Chester. Though, of course, Chelsea knew that Alayna did have quite an extensive collection of very costly pieces—diamond brooches, pearl necklaces, ruby earrings and a number of expensive bracelets to match. And, Chelsea knew, Alayna wore them often. Chelsea again fingered the locket. Alayna, she feared, would find this little trinket quite plain, perhaps even, too plain to wear.

Chelsea tried to show a cheerful face that evening and again when she came down to breakfast the next morning. She knew her time with Lord, and Lady Rathbone, was growing short. Alayna would be returning to the castle any day now. What would happen to Chelsea then was anybody's guess.

Twelve

"We shall take an excursion to Pemberton Keep this afternoon," Lord Rathbone declared, turning a smile upon Chelsea as she slid into her place that day for luncheon. "I sent word to the Pembertons last evening that we would be calling. It's been an age since I visited them. I 'collect, you were once a favorite of Lady Pemberton, Alayna."

"Why, you are quite right, Rutherford," Lady Rathbone put in. "I completely forgot how fond Eleanor was of Alayna. We should have sent a note 'round telling her you were here. I am sure she would have come to tea."

"Indeed, we should have," Chelsea murmured, at a loss as to who the woman was, and unable to summon the least bit of enthusiasm for yet one more trial she must endure before this hated charade was behind her.

"You are welcome to come with us, Mother," Lord Rathbone said, his eager tone a direct contrast to Chelsea's flat one. "You and Alayna could visit Lady Pemberton while I consult privately with Arthur. It seems Mr. Osgood, whom I am thinking of hiring as your new steward, was once employed by Arthur. I mean to quiz Pemberton thoroughly about the man."

"Well, you may go right ahead and do so," Lady Rathbone said with a laugh. "I shall be content to stay right here. Give them both my regards and tell Eleanor that I am greatly looking forward to seeing her at our ball come the end of the week. Alayna, you must remember to show

Eleanor your new locket. She has such an appreciation for lovely things."

"Indeed, I will," Chelsea murmured, reaching to finger the pretty necklace, which she had not taken off since Rutherford clasped it around her neck.

Lord Rathbone directed another smile at Chelsea. "Alayna has promised to wear the locket always."

"That was very sweet of you, my dear," Lady Rathbone said.

"Well, then," his lordship concluded, reaching to help himself to yet another serving of roast beef and asparagus. "We shall leave just as soon as I have gone over last week's accounts. Shouldn't take overlong."

Chelsea nodded in silent agreement and in spite of the gnawing anxiety she felt over being put to yet another test, found herself quite looking forward to spending the long afternoon in Lord Rathbone's agreeable company.

Abovestairs, she took her time leisurely donning another of Alayna's lovely gowns—a lavender sprigged dimity trimmed with blond lace at the neck and sleeves. She finished off the picture perfect outfit with a wide-brimmed leghorn bonnet that tied beneath her chin with a lavender satin ribbon.

"You look as charming as ever, Alayna," Lord Rathbone said, a flick of his wrist setting the horses drawing the small carriage into motion.

During the half-hour ride to Pemberton Keep, Chelsea nearly forgot her growing unease as once again she lost herself listening to Rutherford talk about his upcoming plans for the plantation.

"Did I mention that I mean to petition Parliament on behalf of myself and the other planters in regard to more equitable taxation on the exporting of mahogany and sugar?" he remarked to Chelsea, as they jostled across the new bridge. "I had hoped to have time to attend a session when I was up to London last week, but I regret that all my days were filled with other matters, arranging for supplies to be sent on ahead of us and obtaining the necessary legal papers for the release of my inheritance."

Chelsea's heart swelled with pride at the thought of Rutherford actually addressing parliament. "You did not mention that to me," she said, her tone full of the interest she felt. "Perhaps you will still have a chance to deliver your speech before we leave England for good," she added, ignoring the prick of guilt she felt for again bringing up the subject of returning to Honduras with him.

"I have every intention of doing precisely that, my dear."

Chelsea thought a moment longer on his idea for lowering exportation taxes, then she said, "If the products that the planters export to England benefit everyone here, I should think Parliament would want to comply with the planter's requests."

A sly look crossed Lord Rathbone's face. "My thoughts exactly. You do, indeed, have a keen eye for business, Alayna. To say truth, I grow more amazed each day at how like-minded we are." He seemed to edge a bit closer to her on the bench. "I have no doubt that we shall get on very well together as man and wife."

Chelsea's heart felt near to bursting. For her part, there was no denying she fell more and more in love with Lord Rathbone as each day passed. But, as usual, her glorious feeling of elation was short lived.

"I wonder what became of the Pemberton's youngest son, William?" Rathbone asked suddenly. "Surely Lady Pemberton has mentioned him in her letters to you, Alayna?"

Chelsea squirmed uncomfortably. "No, I—I don't recall that she has."

"Hmmm. That quite takes me by surprise. Considering."

Chelsea turned a look of bewilderment on her companion. "Considering?" Perhaps she would be wise to forget her pleasure for a bit and use this time instead to learn more about the woman whom she, or rather, whom Alayna, had so favorably impressed as a child.

Rathbone glanced her way again, this time his brows pulled together in a decided frown. "You still manage to astonish me at times, Alayna. You seem to easily recall some of the most inconsequential things, and then, out of a clear blue, be completely ignorant of others."

Chelsea exhaled a huge sigh of dismay as once again, the weight of deception bore down upon her. But, suddenly on impulse, she tilted her chin upward and turned a saucy gaze on Lord Rathbone. "That is because I have decided to put the past completely behind me," she said gaily, scooting even closer to him, "and concentrate on nothing but the future. *Our* future. Together." Wearing a sweet smile, she curled both gloved hands around his strong forearm and thrilled with delight when the sudden action caused his upper arm to unexpectedly graze her breast.

Apparently the intimate contact caught his attention as well, for his gaze turned rakish. "May I say I applaud your decision wholeheartedly, my dear. And if you continue to behave in such a brazen fashion toward me while we are at the Keep, I doubt that Lady Pemberton will have a single word to say in regard to the *tendre* young William developed for you last Season in London."

The smile that curved Chelsea's lips froze in place. If Lord and Lady Pemberton had been in London last year, they would surely know that she was not Alayna. Chelsea bit back the terror that gripped her. Still, she reasoned, Alayna had not cautioned her against seeing the Pembertons while in the country. And, furthermore, Chelsea was fairly certain that Alayna had been in Brighton during the Season last year. Chelsea had been there, too. And she had never once heard Alayna mention a *tendre* with a gentleman named William. She fought to hold her fear at bay, but, as usual, her efforts met with little to no success.

At length, the small curricle wheeled into a wide drive

lined on either side with tall poplar trees, the column of deep green leaves making a rustling sound as the carriage breezed past. If Chelsea had not been so preoccupied with her churning stomach, she would have noticed that Pemberton Keep, situated atop a green grassy knoll dotted with clumps of scrub oak and ash trees, was indeed grand. The cotswold-grey stone building, Lord Rathbone said, as they drove up, had been erected several centuries back, and in size was the only estate in the county to compare with Castle Rathbone.

"Certainly you recall coming here as a child, Alayna," he added, as they stepped into the elegantly appointed entrance hall on the ground floor.

Chelsea gazed about with cursory interest, but before she had a chance to reply, both Lord and Lady Pemberton appeared in the hall to greet them.

Chelsea forced a smile to her face as a tall, white haired woman with brilliant blue eyes rushed toward her.

"Alayna, my dear!" she exclaimed. "How lovely you look!" Chelsea could not halt the enormous sigh of relief that escaped her as the woman reached to embrace her. Beside the ladies, Lord Pemberton was enthusiastically pumping Rutherford's outstretched hand.

"Will you just look at her, Arthur! William was right, Alayna has become a veritable beauty!"

"Indeed, she has," the angular Lord Pemberton said, a smile of welcome softening his once handsome features. "I daresay if William could see you now, Miss Marchmont, he would be sorry he settled on another bride."

Chelsea seized the moment, realizing before she could stop herself that her voice sounded a bit shrill. "I say, how long has it been since William married?"

"Nearly a year now," Lady Pemberton said proudly. "Do come in and sit down, my dears. I was so happy to receive word that you were coming." She ushered her guests into a spacious room situated off the main hall and toward a matching pair of Egyptian sofas before the hearth.

"Why, these are lovely!" Chelsea enthused, feeling almost giddy now as she ran a hand over the figured silk arm. "You have such exquisite taste, Lady Pemberton."

"Thank you, Alayna. As I recall, you used to admire so many of my things. I believe I wrote to you when I acquired these pieces on our last trip abroad." A blue-veined hand lovingly stroked the green silk cushion on the sofa as she took a seat beside Chelsea. Lord Rathbone settled into a straight-backed chair near her, while Pemberton reclined opposite the threesome in a large wing chair.

"The sofas came directly from Rome," Lady Pemberton continued, "Arthur and I were visiting there while William attended the congress in Vienna."

"Ah yes, that was only last year, was it not?" Chelsea said, mentally calculating the months the gentleman would have been on the Continent.

"Indeed. Which is why you saw so little of William last Season," Lady Pemberton concluded.

"Fortunately we were still in Rome when the war broke out again at Waterloo," Lord Pemberton put in.

"I do hope William was not—" Lord Rathbone began, his brows pulled together with concern.

"Perfectly safe!" Lady Pemberton enthused. "I declare William is the luckiest young man in the world. Escaped every conflict he was involved in without a scratch. Not a scratch!"

"I expect he and his wife are very happy now," Chelsea said, clinging tenaciously to the one subject she had uncovered that gave her a venue to speak upon.

"Oh, indeed, they are. But you and Felicia were . . . no—no, perhaps I am thinking of that lovely Miss Martinson. Dear me, I fear my memory has a tendency to fade in and out these days. At any rate, William and Felicia are . . . well, you know . . ." she gave Chelsea a speaking look.

Across from them, Lord Pemberton laughed aloud. "Our new daughter-in-law is increasing," he said matter-of-factly. "William couldn't wait to start his nursery, and from the look of things, I expect they could be having twins!"

"Arthur!" Lady Pemberton exclaimed with outrage. "There is a young lady present!"

"Rubbish! These two will be at it themselves before long!"

Feeling her cheeks begin to burn with fire, Chelsea demurely lowered her lashes. And, a moment later, was pleased beyond measure when Lord Rathbone reached to cover her hand with his large warm one.

"Do forgive my husband," Lady Pemberton said, "he is as plain spoken as he ever was."

Chelsea glanced up in time to see the warm look still on Lord Rathbone's face. Basking beneath the glow of it, she realized she felt as close to him in that moment as she had the day he returned from London and kissed her.

A brief pause ensued, then Lord Rathbone and his host took up the conversation again, and a moment later, the gentlemen both stood and Lord Pemberton showed Rutherford into the library.

Left alone with Lady Pemberton, that woman suggested the ladies take a turn about the room.

"I've a score of new treasures to show you," she said to Chelsea.

Chelsea was surprised at how very soon she managed to relax completely as she listened to the older woman go on and on about each of her prized possessions. In great detail, she told Chelsea where and how she had acquired most of them.

Chelsea grew enthralled with a lovely collection of miniature marble statues and a unique silver inkstand that dated all the way back to Cromwell's day.

As the tour of the large room drew to an end, Lady Pemberton said, "I have decided to give you and Rutherford something."

"Oh, no," Chelsea demurred. "That is not necessary."

"Nonsense. If you had married William, much of it would have fallen to you anyhow. You must choose something you like. Perhaps the Severs vase, or the crystal goblets. They're from Austria, you know. Oh!" Suddenly, the woman's eyes lit up. "I know the very thing! You admired it greatly as a child. Come."

She led the way up a winding staircase to a landing that overlooked the foyer and picture gallery below. Heading down a wide corridor, her blue eyes began to twinkle. "I expect you know exactly where I am going, do you not, Alayna?"

"Ummm, I . . . think so."

"Well, you are absolutely right! And, I insist that you indulge me on this."

Chelsea fixed what she hoped was a knowing look to her face as she walked alongside Lady Pemberton. Presently, they entered a lovely sitting room, done entirely in blue and white. The furniture gracing this room was unlike any Chelsea had ever seen before. Every piece was of rich dark wood and ornately carved. All of the high-backed chairs and bench seats were covered with a beautiful shade of delft blue velvet. Even the tiles surrounding the fireplace were blue and white, each one intricately painted with detailed pastoral scenes.

"My Flemish collection," Lady Pemberton said proudly. She quickly crossed the room. "I want you to have this pretty worktable you always admired, Alayna."

"Oh-h." Chelsea's eyes widened as she took in the lovely piece. She had often wished for just such a sewing table. The deep well and pouch would be perfect for all her sewing implements, with plenty of room for additional thread and ribbons. "Oh, but I couldn't—"

"Nonsense! I shall have it refurbished with a new silk pouch in whatever colour you choose." She turned an indulgent smile on Chelsea. "It will bring you hours of pleasure as you sit at your needlework in . . . oh, dear, I fear I have quite forgot where it is Rutherford is taking you."

"Honduras," Chelsea murmured quietly, still looking with longing at the delicate table.

Lady Pemberton's smile widened. "And you have decided to accompany him, after all. I am very proud of you, Alayna. I must say, I was not happy when you wrote to me that you did not mean to travel abroad with your husband. What changed your mind, if I may be so bold?"

Again, Chelsea felt a rush of guilt grip her middle. But before she could formulate a reply, Lady Pemberton spoke up.

"Why, I can see the reason in your eyes, Alayna. You have fallen in love with Rutherford!" She clapped her hands together with glee. "That explains the heartfelt looks he bestowed upon you downstairs." She moved to embrace Chelsea again. "I am so happy for you. I admit I had wanted nothing more than for you and my William . . . but, that no longer signifies, does it? The important thing is that you and Rutherford are to be very happy. I am sure Millicent is beside herself with joy."

Suddenly Chelsea felt sick to her stomach. Lady Pemberton was a dear person, and it was quite clear that she sincerely cared for Alayna, or at any rate, had cared for her at one time. And the fact that Alayna had actually written to the woman must mean that Alayna felt warmly toward her. Fighting the remorse that engulfed her, Chelsea wished only to hide her face in shame.

"I—suddenly, I-I am not feeling at all well, Lady Pemberton. Perhaps we might . . . ?"

"Oh, dear. You do look quite pale, Alayna. Come, we shall send for Rutherford at once. You mustn't get sick only days away from your wedding! And the ball! Oh, my!"

On the return trip to Castle Rathbone, Chelsea remained unusually silent. Try as she might, she could not put down the feeling that she shouldn't have accompanied Rutherford to Pemberton Keep. The more innocent people she drew into this circle of deception, the worse she felt. If only Alayna had told her exactly when she would be returning to the castle. With the ball only two days away, and the fair and the wedding to follow, Chelsea should be making plans to leave the castle, not courting disaster by traipsing about the countryside on Lord Rathbone's arm.

Chelsea's feeling of dread increased the minute she and Rutherford stepped into the drawing room at the castle.

Except for Jared, who was busy near the hearth with the tea things, the room was empty.

"Do you feel well enough to take tea, Alayna?" Lord Rathbone asked, his voice full of concern as he dropped his hat and gloves onto a chair, then strode toward the tea table where Jared stood.

"Miss Marchmont and I shall require tea this afternoon, after all," he told Jared. "That is, if Miss Marchmont feels up to it."

The butler glanced up from his work. "Very good, sir. Her ladyship has already taken her tea. I expect you and Miss Marchmont will require a fresh pot."

Lord Rathbone directed another questioning gaze at Chelsea, who was hovering just inside the door. She answered with a nervous shake of her head.

"A fresh pot will not be necessary, Jared. And on second thought, I should like only a bit of brandy, if you please," Lord Rathbone said crisply.

"Very good, sir." The butler moved to the sideboard, on the way directing a glance at Chelsea. "Something arrived for you today, Miss Marchmont."

Chelsea took a few small steps into the room. "For me?"

Jared picked up a silver salver from the sideboard and carried it forward.

On it lay a single letter. Chelsea blanched when she recognized Alayna's elaborate script on the front side.

"What is it?" Lord Rathbone asked curiously.

Chelsea could barely speak. "It appears to be a . . . letter from a friend. If you will excuse me, Rutherford."

Watching her, Lord Rathbone's brows pulled together. "Are you quite certain you are feeling all right, Alayna? Perhaps I should send for the doctor."

"No, no. I should simply like to rest a bit."

Lord Rathbone continued to gaze at Chelsea with concern as she exited the room and hastened to her own chamber.

Flinging her bonnet onto the bed, she tore into the letter. It did not escape her that Alayna had deviously written Chelsea's name on the backside, which to prying eyes would indicate that the letter had been written by a 'Miss Chelsea Grant.'

Chelsea's eyes anxiously scanned the note inside, which was short, almost terse. It merely confirmed that Alayna would, indeed, be returning to the castle as planned, in plenty of time for the wedding ceremony. Fortunately, the actual day designated for the event had not been altered. The ceremony was to be held in the castle chapel at noon, on Saturday. Only three days away.

Thirteen

Chelsea elected to remain in her bedchamber the remainder of the day. Dulcie brought up a tray for their dinner that evening, and as they ate she expressed her concern for Chelsea's distress.

"Shouldn't be overlong before Miss Marchmont returns to the castle now, miss."

"I hope so," Chelsea murmured.

"W'ot do you think . . . he'll do?" Dulcie asked, a bit fearfully.

Chelsea smiled sadly. "I haven't a clue, Dulcie. I try not to think about it."

"W'ot did Miss Marchmont say, I mean, in her letter?"

Chelsea glanced up from the crust of bread she was nibbling on. "You know about the letter?"

Dulcie nodded. "Don't nothin' escape the household staff, miss. Her ladyship got a letter and a package today."

"Hmmm."

They continued to eat the small meal in silence. At length, Chelsea pushed away from the table.

"You done, miss?"

Chelsea nodded. "You may have my pudding, and the biscuit, if you like."

Dulcie's eyes lit up. "Thank you, miss."

After Dulcie had quitted the room, carrying the supper tray with her, Chelsea walked absently to the narrow slit of window in her suite and peered out. It was already dark outdoors. Save for the few stars twinkling in the night sky, nothing was visible. She wondered what Lord and Lady Rathbone were doing?

Over the weeks she had come to greatly enjoy their evenings spent together in the sitting room. Sharing the cozy setting with them at the end of a long day made Chelsea feel like she was part of a real family. She missed having a family of her own. Evenings spent all alone at her room in London were often quite dreary, as were holidays and other special times of the year when families enjoyed being together. An infinite pang of sadness gripped her. How very much she would miss Lord, and Lady Rathbone, once Alayna returned and she was back in London.

Unable to shake the acute sense of loss that had settled about her, she moved as if compelled toward the door of her chamber. Perhaps if she hurried, she might find her host and hostess lingering still in the sitting room.

But upon reaching the small, now achingly familiar chamber, she was dismayed to find it empty. Re-entering the corridor, though, an unfamiliar sound caught her attention. Music? Coming from . . . somewhere.

Thus far, having not seen a pianoforte, or a harpsichord, anywhere in the castle, she was at a loss as to where the pretty sound was coming from. Attempting to follow the haunting melody to its origin, she rounded a corner only to come face to face with Dulcie.

"Oh! It's you, miss! The playin' sounds real nice, don't it, miss?"

"Yes," Chelsea murmured, then up ahead, she noticed a group of twittering housemaids clustered together in the corridor.

Dulcie's gaze followed Chelsea's. "Ever'one wished to hear it close up," the little maid murmured. "You won't tell will you, miss?"

Chelsea smiled. "No, of course, not. But, why are you standing apart from the others, Dulcie? I expect you could hear a good deal better if you were also stationed near the door."

"Oh . . ." Dulcie shrugged. "The others . . . they don't like me much, miss."

"Why ever not?"

Dulcie lowered her gaze. "They say I'm . . . above myself. On account of not staying in the servants wing, and . . . living up in London, and all."

"I see." Chelsea smiled ruefully. "And I expect taking a meal with me now and again doesn't help matters either, does it?"

Once again, Dulcie's shoulders lifted and fell. "It don't really signify, miss. We'll be gone in a day or two."

Another pang of remorse gripped Chelsea. "I expect you are right. Not a bit of it signifies. Not really."

With a sigh, she proceeded down the corridor toward the shuttered chamber where she found both Lord and Lady Rathbone ensconced. By castle standards, this room was a smallish one, apparently little used for it was only partially furnished. A tattered sofa, a few chairs and a tea table were scattered about. In the center of the room stood an ancient, wing-tipped harpsichord. Chelsea had never seen a musical instrument quite like this one before, but more intriguing than that was the fact that Lord Rathbone himself sat before the keyboard.

Her brown eyes round with wonder, Chelsea quietly entered the room, unable to pull her gaze from the handsome gentleman whose fingers were flying over the yellowed ivory keys. Chelsea had no idea the gentleman was so very talented, so very proficient.

"Ah, there you are, my dear," Rathbone said, glancing up as she drew near. Even with his eyes focused on Chelsea, his long fingers continued to produce the lovely strains of music.

From the corner of her eye, Chelsea noted Lady Rathbone seated in her Bath chair near the fire. But, instead of speaking to the woman, she headed straight for the harpsichord and Rutherford's side. Presently, he concluded the tune and turned a smiling countenance upward. "I hope you are feeling better, my dear, and this noise I am making did not disturb your rest."

Chelsea did not respond to the comment. "I had no idea you were so musically talented, my lord!" she exclaimed.

Across the room, one of Lady Rathbone's gray eyebrows lifted.

Rathbone laughed. "I expect you were much too young to remember the many hours I used to spend right here as a boy, Alayna. Though, I seem to recall you later making sport of my absorbing interest in music," he concluded wryly.

"Oh, but I—" Having committed yet another blunder, she felt her cheeks redden. She flung a nervous glaze toward Lady Rathbone. "But, you play beautifully now!"

Lord Rathbone stood. "Perhaps you would be so good as to entertain me now."

"Oh, no. Please, play something else."

"Perhaps later. It is your turn now." A hand indicated the worn cushion on the wooden bench.

With a shrug, Chelsea smiled agreeably and slid onto the bench, not the least concerned that she could perform something credibly well. Even Alayna played the pianoforte, so she had nothing to fear on that score.

After skimming through a short minuet by Mozart, she directed a look at Lord Rathbone. He stood facing her, an elbow resting on the square edge of the ancient instrument. "I wonder if you are familiar with this tune," Chelsea asked pleasantly, then launched into a popular London song called "Reason Kneels to Love."

When Rathbone began to hum along, Chelsea felt relaxed enough to join him, her sweet treble soon harmonizing perfectly with his deep baritone. Toward the end of the song, they were singing lustily, then when Chelsea began the second verse and Ford skipped to the third, they both dissolved into a gale of merry laughter.

"After a bit more practice," Ford ventured, still smiling, "we might be fit to perform for our friends! What do you think, Mother?" He turned toward the older woman, who had sat quietly through the impromptu recital without uttering a single word.

For the first time since coming into the room, Chelsea also gazed fully at Lady Rathbone. But, the cold look she found on the older woman's face startled her. She had seen nothing to compare to that look since the day Sully abducted her from the castle. Involuntarily, she shuddered.

"Well," Ford went on, oblivious to his mother's state of mind as he strode toward the small pie-crust tea table upon which rested a bottle of port and several glasses, "what do you think, Mother, are we accomplished enough to perform at the fair, or not?"

"Oh, dear me, no!" Chelsea exclaimed, managing to regain herself and turn her attention again to Ford.

"Nonsense," he protested. He poured himself a drink and began to fill a second glass. "Your musical talent is quite exceptional, Alayna. Which," he added, teasingly, "I find rather extraordinary considering how very much you hated to practice your scales as a child." Without looking at her, he said, "Would you care for a drink, darling?"

"No, thank you." Chelsea shook her head as she tentatively moved to take a seat on the faded old carmine sofa opposite where Lady Rathbone sat near the low-burning fire.

Lord Rathbone handed his mother the second glass of the wine and sat down on the sofa next to Chelsea. "So," he began afresh, the relaxed smile still on his lips, "what did you think of our little song, Mother? Alayna and I sing quite a fine duet, do we not?"

Lady Rathbone's gaze remained fixed on Chelsea. "Indeed. Though, I seem to recall our Alayna insisting that one of her school chums was far more accomplished at the piano than she. A Miss Chelsea Grant."

Chelsea's jaw dropped clean to the floor as every last drop of blood drained from her face.

Beside her, Rutherford said lightly, "Well, what of it? Alayna is quite talented in her own right. Aren't you, darling?"

Chelsea swallowed hard. "Per-haps I will have that drink, if you don't mind, Ford."

"Certainly." He rose to his feet again.

Chelsea kept her nervous gaze glued to her lap. Why had Lady Rathbone mentioned her name just now? *What could it mean?*

"A toast!" Lord Rathbone declared, returning to the sofa and handing Chelsea a goblet brimming full of wine. "To my two favorite women in all the world!"

Reaching for the glass, Chelsea downed a generous gulp of the warm liquid, not noticing that across from her, Lady Rathbone did not.

"I understand you received a letter today, Alayna," the older woman said, still eyeing Chelsea closely. "From your friend, Miss Grant."

Chelsea nearly choked on the gulp of wine in her mouth. "Indeed," she mumbled, fighting desperately for control.

"Was she not the young lady they named the Brighton Beauty your last term at school?" Rathbone asked casually.

Chelsea coughed.

"Are you all right, darling?" Rutherford's brow furrowed with concern.

Chelsea nodded vigorously, as yet still unable to speak.

"I also seem to recall," Ford went on blithely, completely unaware of the discomfort he was causing her, "that you were frightfully jealous of Miss Grant."

Chelsea stared at him. *Alayna jealous of her?*

"Your letters to me, while you were at Miss Farringdon's, and for several months afterward, were full of 'Miss Grant did this and Miss Grant did that.' " He cast a bemused gaze on Chelsea. "You girls must have had quite a rivalry going."

Not that Chelsea was aware of! "Well—uh—perhaps, we did. Just a bit."

"Far more than a bit, I should think!" Ford exclaimed. "That is, if what you said following Miss Grant being named Brighton Beauty is true."

"W-what . . . did I say?"

"That you wished her banished from school for the rest of the term!"

"Why, I most certainly did not! Beside, Alay—I mean, I got to play Juliet! And, if I do say so myself, my performance was far superior to hers . . . I mean . . ." Suddenly Chelsea felt inordinately hot and flustered. Her ridiculous outburst had confused even her! She concluded by downing another generous sip of the wine.

After a pause, Lady Rathbone said, "Alayna always was very good at play-acting. Though, I expect Miss Grant is quite an accomplished actress, as well, wouldn't you say so . . . Alayna?"

Chelsea felt near to collapsing. Lady Rathbone had most certainly learned the truth and was trying now to bait her.

"Where is Miss Grant these days?" Ford asked innocently.

Chelsea lifted a nervous gaze upward, but hadn't the least idea what to say.

Across from her, Lady Rathbone commented dryly, "I admit, I have wondered about that myself. Where is Miss Grant, Alayna?"

Chelsea went rigid with fear.

Ford gazed at her expectantly. "Well, where is she living now, darling?"

"Ummm . . . perhaps you should ask her yourself," Chelsea fought to toss the reply off tartly. "After all, she is coming to the castle for a visit."

"Ah . . . in time for the ball? Splendid!" Ford returned

brightly. "I daresay I should quite like to meet the young lady."

"You would?" Chelsea's eyes were round.

"Indeed. You have told me so very much about her, I feel I am already acquainted with her."

Chelsea downed the last of her wine in a greedy gulp and instantly feeling its numbing effects, turned a crooked smile on her companions. "Well, I hope neither of you will be disappointed."

In spite of the unusual quantity of spirits she had consumed earlier, Chelsea had a difficult time falling asleep once she returned to her bedchamber that night. She couldn't thrust the fear from her mind that Lady Rathbone had learned something, nor cease wondering why the woman had not confronted her just now and demanded an explanation? None of it made any sense.

After lying awake for several fitful hours, she sat straight up in bed. Springing to the floor, she snatched up a candle and flew to the door that connected her chamber with the dressing room where Dulcie slept.

"Dulcie!" she mouthed, "let me in! I must speak with you at once!"

An instant later, the door creaked open and Dulcie, clad in a loose-fitting nightrail, stood rubbing the sleep from her eyes. "W'ot is it, miss?"

Chelsea breezed past the girl to set the flickering candle down on a table. "I am certain Lady Rathbone has somehow learned the truth. I need your help, Dulcie."

"W'ot do you want me to do, miss?"

"Before I tell you, I must have your word of honor that you will not speak of this to anyone. No matter what! Will you give me your word, Dulcie?"

Her glazed eyes round, Dulcie nodded quickly. "Yes, miss."

"Good. Here's what I'd like you to do . . ." In whispered tones, Chelsea outlined her thoughts to the sleepy abigail. Once she had secured Dulcie's acceptance of the plan, she tiptoed back to her own chamber and climbed into bed. In no time at all, she fell fast asleep.

The next morning, Chelsea became aware of the disturbance in the corridor outside her bedchamber before she was fully awake.

"I tell you, the girl was seen skulking from her ladyship's chamber!" exclaimed an irate female voice, who Chelsea recognized as being Mrs. Phipps, the housekeeper.

On her feet in an instant, Chelsea grabbed her wrapper and flung it about her shoulders. Throwing open the door of her chamber, she spotted not only Mrs. Phipps, but a stern-faced Jared, and an assortment of maids, who with their noses stuck in the air, were staring with disdain at Dulcie.

"What is the meaning of this?" Chelsea demanded of Jared.

Bending a slight nod Chelsea's way, the butler replied, "It appears, miss, that your girl was caught . . . meddling."

Her own heart hammering wildly, Chelsea threw a startled gaze at Dulcie, whose face, she noticed now, was decidedly ashen. "Is this true, Dulcie?"

Dulcie thrust her chin up. "I didn't take nothing, miss! Honest, I didn't! I was just—"

"Here, here, what's this?" came a deep voice from the far end of the corridor.

Everyone watched as determined strides carried Lord Rathbone forward. "What seems to be the trouble, Jared?" he asked coolly.

Jared's nod of greeting to his lordship was almost imperceptible. "It seems Miss Marchmont's abigail was observed leaving her ladyship's bedchamber a moment ago."

Lord Rathbone cast a gaze at Dulcie. "I take it this is not customary behavior?"

"Indeed, it is not!" Mrs. Phipps cried. "The girl's only duties are to attend Miss Marchmont. She don't have no business whatsoever in—"

"That will be enough, Mrs. Phipps," Lord Rathbone said sternly. He turned to Chelsea, a dark gaze flicking over her person. Chelsea tightened the wrapper about herself. "What do you have to say to this, Miss Marchmont?"

Before Chelsea could reply, Dulcie cried out again, "I didn't take nothing, sir! Honest, I didn't!"

"No one has accused you of taking anything, girl," Lord Rathbone said, then he glanced at Jared, "have they?"

"No sir; not yet, sir."

"I see." His gaze reverted again to Chelsea. "May I suggest we resume this investigation downstairs. The library will suit. You will join us, Miss Marchmont, when you have . . . that is, when you are properly clothed." He turned away. "You will fetch her ladyship, Jared. Mrs. Phipps, Dulcie, you will come with me."

The party dispersed.

Ten minutes later, Chelsea breathlessly joined the small group already assembled in the library.

A cool glance from Lady Rathbone, who was seated in her Bath chair a bit apart from her son, was enough to set Chelsea's heart pounding again in her breast.

"Perhaps you will be good enough to explain your abigail's odd behavior to all of us," Lady Rathbone said, as soon as Chelsea had taken up a position just inside the doorway.

Chelsea had no idea what had already transpired. In an effort to determine if Dulcie had been forced to divulge anything, anything at all, she flung a glance at the trembling girl. Though the maid's eyes were wide with fright, something in them told Chelsea she had indeed kept her word and said nothing incriminating.

Chelsea turned to address Lord Rathbone. "Dulcie was merely carrying out my orders this morning, sir. I had sent her to inquire if Lady Rathbone wished me to read to her today."

A snort from Mrs. Phipps said she did not believe that for a minute. Then, apparently unable to contain herself, the stout woman cried, "The girl was hidin' somethin' in her skirts! Them London gels ain't to be trusted, I tell 'ye! They's no better than they have to be!"

"Mrs. Phipps, you will kindly hold your tongue," Lord Rathbone said sternly. He glanced at Dulcie, a shuttered look obviously trying to determine whether or not some sort of article might still be concealed beneath the girl's apron, or perhaps in a pocket. "Has . . . er . . . has anyone determined precisely what the missing article might be?" he asked.

Apparently believing that he was being addressed, Jared replied, "No sir; not yet, sir."

"Then it appears there is nothing for it but to conduct a thorough search of the girl—"

Chelsea cut in sharply. "If Dulcie said she did not take anything, then she did not take anything!"

"Thank you, Miss Marchmont," Lord Rathbone said, his tone a bit patronizing. "Nonetheless, it appears a search of the girl's person is in order."

Mrs. Phipps made a lunge for poor Dulcie.

"Owa-oh!" she cried, with an indignant jerk gathering her skirts about her.

"Mrs. Phipps!" Lord Rathbone bellowed. "Leave the girl be."

"Leave me be!" Dulcie chimed in. "You's nothing but a old busybody!"

Lord Rathbone folded his arms across his chest, his lips pressed together with disgust. "Miss Marchmont, you will please take Dulcie aside and determine the contents of her pockets." When Chelsea seemed to hesitate in carrying out his orders, he said, "Now!"

Deciding that perhaps it was best to remove Dulcie from the library altogether, Chelsea signaled to the girl, then froze in place when Lord Rathbone said, "Mrs. Phipps will assist."

Chelsea's head jerked up. "Are you saying you do not trust *me* to tell the truth?" Her tone revealed her outrage at being thought a liar.

"I am saying nothing of the sort, Miss Marchmont." He paused, then said, "Perhaps a search of Mother's room is also in order. Mrs. Phipps, you and Jared will undertake that office. If it is determined that anything is missing, you will report your findings to me at once. I take it that arrangement is satisfactory with you, Mother?"

Lady Rathbone flung a glance at Chelsea. "Indeed."

"Very well. Everyone, save Miss Marchmont and her abigail, have leave to go."

Chelsea chewed on her lower lip as Jared, Mrs. Phipps and Lady Rathbone quitted the room. She had no idea what a search of Lady Rathbone's chamber would reveal. She hoped nothing. She had never asked poor Dulcie to rifle through Lady Rathbone's belongings, she had merely asked the girl to keep an ear open, and an eye out, for any sort of evidence or incriminating murmurings amongst the servants. If it was true that nothing escaped them, it was likely they might have an idea where, how, or from whom, Lady Rathbone had learned the truth about Chelsea.

She turned what she hoped was a reassuring smile on Dulcie. If the girl was, indeed, concealing something on her person, it was likely not to be discovered now by anyone but herself.

When Chelsea heard the heavy oaken door to the library click shut behind Jared, she directed an expectant gaze at Lord Rathbone. He stood with legs planted wide apart, a stern gaze fixed on Dulcie. After drawing a breath, he announced, "Under the circumstances, Dulcie, Miss Marchmont will no longer require your services."

Both Chelsea and the girl gasped.

"No!" Chelsea cried, "you, cannot—!"

Rathbone turned a cool gaze on her. "I cannot," he mouthed with disbelief. "Indeed, I can, Miss Marchmont, and I have. The girl will quit the premises at once."

"But—" Chelsea's bosom rose and fell as she fought to contain her rage. "Dulcie, you will please await me upstairs."

A stricken look on her face, Dulcie scampered from the room.

When the door had clicked shut once again, Chelsea whirled on Ford. "I forbid you to dismiss that poor girl. She has done nothing wrong and I will not have it!" She knew she was overstepping the bounds, but she could not, *would* not, be responsible for causing Dulcie to lose her position.

"You *forbid* me?" Lord Rathbone stared at her, his eyes wide with shock and disbelief. "It appears I am seeing your true colors once again, Alayna." He moved to take a seat behind the massive desk. "I refuse to retain a servant who cannot be trusted. Apparently you have forgotten our recent experience with Sully."

"This is hardly the same thing!"

"It is precisely the same thing!" He flung open a drawer and withdrew what appeared to be an account book. Chelsea watched with horror as he deliberately reached for a pen.

"But, Dulcie was merely carrying out my orders this morning! That is the whole truth, I tell you. There is nothing more to the matter, save the fact that the castle servants do not like the girl."

Dipping the pen in the inkwell, Rathbone did not glance up from his scribbling. "The girl goes, Alayna." He blotted the bank draft he had written and held it out to Chelsea. "Here is sufficient money to pay what is owed of her wages and to see her back to London, or wherever else she wishes to go."

Chelsea folded her arms across her bosom. "No! I will not turn her out! You've no idea how difficult it is to find employment."

Rathbone snorted. "You sound as if you have had experience at that yourself, Alayna, which, of course, is quite ridiculous." He waved the draft at her. "Take it. The matter is concluded. I will hear no more of it."

Her nostrils flaring with each breath she drew, Chelsea stood her ground. At length, she said, "If you insist on turning Dulcie out, then you leave me with no choice but to refuse to return with you to Honduras."

Rathbone stood. "Very well." His eyes on her were cold as he let the bank draft flutter to the desktop. "Perhaps I have been wrong about you, Alayna. Perhaps we would not get on well together, after all." His tone was firm as he went on. "Where I live in the tropics, it is very often superstition and magical beliefs that guide men's lives. There, it is imperative to guard against insurrection, rebellion, or disloyalty, of any sort. Orders given by the master must be followed to the letter. I have seen danger of the worst sort, to say nothing of costly disorder, caused by a single untrustworthy servant. What type of example would be set if even a planter's wife refused to obey him? It is not to be tolerated, Alayna."

With her heart in her throat, Chelsea listened closely to his words. She knew he spoke the truth, but, in this case, the decision she had made in the matter could not be reversed. Through the fine mist that was gathering in her eyes, she returned his steady gaze. "Dulcie and I will leave immediately for London once you and I have recited our marriage vows, my lord," she said quietly.

With her head high, she turned and swept from the room.

* * *

In bleak silence, Rathbone watched her go. In a word, in one small word, she had made a mockery of all that he stood for. No. She had said, no. She had flatly refused to obey him and had done so in the presence of others. Though it broke his very heart to do so, he could not back down.

Fourteen

Despite the tears of sadness gathering in her eyes as she made her way back to her bedchamber, Chelsea decided that the sudden turn of events would in all likelihood prove a blessing in disguise. Now, when Alayna returned to the castle she could decide for herself if she wished to accompany her husband to a foreign clime. After all, what the pair of them did after they were married was none of Chelsea's concern. For her part, she was simply glad to have preserved Dulcie's living.

Discovering the little maid hugging her knees like a frightened child in a corner chair in her room, Chelsea cried, "Dulcie, assure me that you did, indeed, take nothing from Lady Rathbone's chamber!"

Dulcie sprang to her feet, her eyes wide. "I meant to return it, miss, right after I showed it to you, but—"

"Oh, Dulcie," Chelsea groaned, her eyes rolling skyward. "Give it over this instant! Whatever it is, I must return it at once."

"You mightn't want to do that, Miss." So saying, Chelsea watched horror-struck, as Dulcie twisted about to lift the hem of her skirt. In seconds she had produced the stolen article and thrust it at her mistress.

Staring at a perfect likeness of Alayna Marchmont, Chelsea moaned. "Oh-h-h. Where did you find it, Dulcie? And why were you in her ladyship's room?"

"In the top drawer of the commode next to her ladyship's

bed. Her own maid said there was a picture of a yellow haired beauty in the package the post delivered up yesterday, and I was worried it was Miss Alayna's."

Still gaping with disbelief at the miniature, which without being told, Chelsea knew to be the missing portrait of Alayna, she murmured, "But, who could have sent it?"

"Don't know, miss. Perhaps that foul man w'ot kidnapped you done it."

"Sully," Chelsea breathed, thinking that if the man were indeed still trying to disprove her identity, it made sense that he would try to elicit Lady Rathbone's help. Yet Lady Rathbone had heard all about Sully's accusations and as well the conclusion drawn by Ford and Mr. Wainwright. Therefore, the portrait alone should not be enough to convict her, should it? "Did you find anything else, Dulcie?"

"No, miss. I looked for the letter, but when I heard Mrs. Phipps approaching, I froze up. That's when I slipped the picture in my pocket and I—"

"I know, you skulked from the room." Chelsea shook her head with dismay. "Oh, Dulcie, you should never have entered Lady Rathbone's bedchamber. That was never my intent when I solicited your help in the matter."

Dulcie hung her head. "I'm sorry, miss. I only meant to help."

"Well"—Chelsea sighed heavily—"I shall have to return the portrait before it is discovered missing." She turned to go, pausing only long enough to say, "By the by, there is no need for you to leave the castle, Dulcie. Lord Rathbone regrets his . . . er . . . hasty decision. Your position with Miss Marchmont is safe."

"Oh! miss!" Dulcie dropped a grateful curtsy. "Thank you ever so!"

Chelsea didn't hear the girl, she was already hurrying toward Lady Rathbone's suite.

Upon reaching the nearly hidden chamber, she spotted the heavy oaken door standing wide open and marched inside as if she had every right to be there. Mrs. Phipps and two housemaids were roaming about, sifting through the piles of dusty books and yellowed newspapers. Without a word to either of them, Chelsea made a bee line for the little cabinet that stood next to the old woman's bed. There, she turned completely around, her body shielding the cabinet from view. Palmed in her hand behind her back lay the tiny miniature, which she skillfully tucked into the top drawer, all the while gazing calmly at the distracted women who were too intent on their work to notice what Chelsea was about.

After a pause, she said, "I take it neither of you has yet to discover anything amiss?"

"Nothing as yet, Miss Marchmont," the housekeeper replied coolly.

"Very well . . ." Chelsea made a move toward the door, "if you should come across anything out of place, I will thank you to report the matter to me straightaway." Holding her chin aloft, she breezed past the women into the corridor. Then, with an immense sigh of relief, she quickly retraced her steps back to her own suite, confident that she had, indeed, saved the day for Dulcie. She only hoped when all was said and done, she would fare as well.

She decided it best to stay close to her own chamber for the remainder of the day, and spent the long hours going over and over all that had transpired between herself and Lord Rathbone since his appearance at the castle. She recalled their trips into Chester, the visit to Pemberton Keep, the many long talks they shared each evening in the sitting room, and the pleasant musical interlude they had enjoyed just last night. And of course, the memory of his kiss in the library burned like a perpetual flame in her mind. It would be a lie to say she did not care deeply for the gentleman, which made the rift that had sprung up between them that much harder to bear.

Still, she knew the breach was for the best. With both

his lordship and Lady Rathbone angry with her, they might be more inclined to forgive Alayna her part in the subterfuge. And that, Chelsea told herself sadly, was of far greater import than her own feelings in the matter.

She reached upward to curl her fingers around the golden locket that Ford had presented to her as a token of his love. Caressing the warm metal caused tears of sadness to spill onto her cheeks. That Lord Rathbone had selected the betrothal present especially for her had been a fleeting dream. At the time, it had not mattered to Chelsea that the dream would soon splinter to pieces. For a time, it had been real; for time, it had been hers.

But, now . . . now that she had come to her senses, she knew she had no right to wear the locket. It did not belong to her. It belonged to Alayna. She reached behind her neck to unclasp it when a sudden rap at the door alarmed her.

"Alayna!"

Recognizing the deep timbre of Lord Rathbone's voice, Chelsea froze.

"Alayna, open the door."

Springing from the sofa where she sat, the necklace slipped from Chelsea's fingertips and disappeared between the worn velvet cushions of the couch.

Pressing her cheek against the oak paneled door, Chelsea longed to do as Lord Rathbone requested, but if she did, she feared she would not have the strength to keep from hurtling herself into the gentleman's arms and declaring how very much she loved him and that she missed him greatly.

"Alayna," Lord Rathbone said again, his tone growing insistent. "Open the door. I must speak with you."

"I . . . I do not feel well, sir," Chelsea stammered.

A pause followed. When next the gentleman spoke, his tone had altered considerably. "Nor do I. Will you please open the door?"

Chelsea bit back the rush of hot tears that threatened to

erupt and betray her feelings. "I . . . cannot, sir." She felt her throat tighten painfully. "Please . . . leave me to my rest."

"Alayna, I must speak with you. I cannot bear it that we . . . please . . . darling . . ." his plaintive tone trailed off.

Chelsea's eyes squeezed shut. "I . . . do not wish to see you just now, sir," she lied.

There was another pause. "Very well, Alayna."

The next sound Chelsea heard was the echoing of his receding footfalls on the bare stone floor of the corridor.

Stumbling toward her bed, she slumped onto it. Her dream had indeed come to an end. A sudden stab of longing made her double over in pain, then with horror she realized that if Alayna were to return to the castle this evening, or perhaps early tomorrow, she might *never* see Lord Rathbone again. That thought filled her with the most horrific anguish she had ever experienced in her life. It was so overwhelming, she feared she might perish from it.

By six of the clock on the following evening, Alayna had not yet returned to the castle. Chelsea received a short but terse note from Lady Rathbone informing her that she *must* attend the ball being held that evening in her own honor. More a command than an invitation, Chelsea knew that once again, she had no choice but to comply. To not attend, would cause both Lord and Lady Rathbone undue embarrassment.

Chelsea had again spent that day alone in her room. From her narrow window overlooking the mews, she had whiled away the long hours watching the endless stream of activity below as guests arrived at the castle for the ball and the wedding. Any moment she had expected to see Alayna's face among those emerging from a coach or landau, but she did not.

At luncheon and again at tea time, Dulcie brought up a tray for her meals. In excited tones, she kept Chelsea abreast of all the preparations underway for the upcoming festivities.

Though, Chelsea had looked forward to the ball and the fair with longing, wishing more than anything that she might be on hand to share in the fun, that had been before . . . before she and Lord Rathbone had come to daggers drawn. Now, her greatest fear was, how to get through this evening in his presence?

After removing the tea tray, Dulcie quickly reappeared in Chelsea's chamber, this time carrying one of Alayna's beautiful ball gowns draped over her arm. With great care, she gently laid the dress across the foot of Chelsea's bed.

"I took the liberty of gettin' it pressed for you, miss. Didn't know which of you'd be wearin' it"—she grinned crookedly—"but, at any rate, the packin' wrinkles is gone."

Chelsea eyed the lovely gown. She did not own anything half so grand, and had never in her life expected to have occasion to wear such a garment.

"You'd best be gettin' ready, miss," Dulcie urged. "Orchestra is already settin' up in the ballroom." She darted across the room to drag forth a copper tub from behind a painted screen. Then, with Chelsea looking on, she reached for the bell rope and gave it a hearty tug.

"Dulcie, you know none of the bell pulls are operable."

Dulcie grinned wisely. "They are now. His lordship put a engineer fellow to work this mornin' afixin' 'em. Wouldn't do for the guests to be shoutin' for a maid or a footman when they's in need of somethin', 'e said."

Chelsea managed a sad smile.

"Footmen should be bringin' up hot water for your bath any minute. You'll see, miss."

Chelsea pulled herself to her feet and headed for the dressing room to remove her clothing.

And, just as Dulcie predicted, a parade of footmen soon

appeared in the corridor, each carrying a pitcher full of steaming hot water which they carefully poured into the small tub in Chelsea's room.

"You'll have a grand time at the ball tonight, miss," Dulcie said as she busied herself laying out fresh undergarments for Chelsea. "Even her ladyship is in high alt. The old ba . . . I mean, her ladyship even smiled at me once. Can you imagine the like? I mean, after yesterday and all." Dulcie shook her head in wonder as she prattled on.

Chelsea barely heard, so overset was she about what lay before her.

"Kitchen's full of delicious smells," Dulcie said. "There's plum duffs and Charlotte's, and raspberry tarts. And puddins' for tonight's supper and the weddin' breakfast tomorrow."

At the mention of the wedding, Chelsea groaned aloud. "Oh, Dulcie, what am I to do if Alayna has not returned by tomorrow morning? I cannot possibly stand in for her at the wedding ceremony."

Helping Chelsea into the lovely ball gown, Dulcie laughed gaily. "Don't you worry none, miss. She'll be here. Miss Marchmont won't want to miss wearin' her new weddin' finery."

Chelsea thought of the beautiful new wedding gown hanging in the clothespress. How very like Alayna to insist upon outfitting herself properly even though her bridegroom would be absent from the wedding.

With her own elaborate toilette at last complete, Chelsea anxiously appraised her image in the looking glass.

"You look beautiful, miss!"

Chelsea smiled wryly at her own reflection. She did look pretty. The rose silk gown was a perfect fit, as were all of Alayna's frocks. Turning slowly to one side, she watched the whisper-soft folds float gently about her body. Her golden hair, swept into a cloud of curls, was finished off with a pearl encrusted head dress and a deeper rose-colored feather. Would Ford think she looked pretty tonight, she wondered? At the thought of seeing him again, her heart began to hammer fitfully in her breast.

"You'd best go now, miss. His lordship will be awaitin' you. 'E said to tell you 'e'd be in the withdrawin' room."

"Thank you, Dulcie."

Moving through the castle, Chelsea was aware of the bustle of activity about her. Servants scurried thither and yon, hardly a one of them noticing her as she lightly trod upon the narrow, red carpet runner that had been especially laid for this evening through the main passageways of the castle, all of which led to the grand ballroom.

Upon reaching her destination, a liveried footman stationed just outside that room, sprang forward to fling open the door for her. Chelsea caught sight of Lord Rathbone before he turned from where he stood before the hearth to see her.

Taking in his lean muscular form, smartly attired this evening in an elegant black cut-away coat, black pantaloons and polished black pumps, an almost suffocating sensation threatened to overtake her. But, she must remain aloof toward him, she told herself. Exhibiting any warmth toward the gentleman tonight would serve only to destroy the distance inadvertently established between them by yesterday's breach.

She was nearly upon him before he, at last, turned to face her. When he did, Chelsea was stunned by the naked look of hurt and longing in his eyes. But, in an instant, the look disappeared and his face once again became a mask of cool indifference.

"Good evening, Alayna," he said, a dark gaze raking over her slender form. "You look . . . tolerably well."

A tremulous smile wavered across Chelsea's lips. "I am feeling much better, sir."

"Well, then . . ." A brow lifted cryptically as he extended

an elbow. "I expect the ballroom is full of people who are eager to greet the happy couple."

Chelsea bit back the stab of raw grief she feared would destroy the composure she was working so hard to maintain. Despite the anguish they both felt, she knew they had no choice but to see this evening through.

"I am certain we shall manage somehow, Rutherford," she murmured softly. She did not see the look of surprise that flickered across his face.

Moments later, when every eye in the glittering hall was turned on them, Chelsea took strength from the mere presence of the tall gentleman by her side. This being the first real ball she had ever attended in her life, she was not prepared for the additional nervousness she felt for being thrust also into the limelight. Yet, somehow, it was comforting to know that, despite his cool exterior, Lord Rathbone felt every bit as miserable as she.

At odd moments during the evening, Chelsea considered the possibility that Alayna might return to the castle while the ball was in progress. But, she dismissed the notion. Unaware that any festivities had been planned to celebrate her nuptials, Alayna would not think it necessary to arrive at the castle shielded by darkness. More than likely, she would simply stroll into the castle the following morning, prepared to change into her wedding gown, repeat her vows and depart again for London within the hour.

Still, as the crush of smiling guests crowded about Chelsea and Lord Rathbone to express their well-wishes and accolades, her anxious gaze darted regularly to one or another of the many entrances leading into the brilliantly lit hall.

At length, Lord and Lady Pemberton stood before them.

"At last, it is our turn to greet you, my darlings!" Lady Pemberton exclaimed, alternately kissing the air beside Chelsea's cheeks. "How very pretty you look! Doesn't

Alayna look pretty?" she asked her husband, who was occupied pumping Ford's outstretched hand.

"They both look dashed handsome!"

"I was talking earlier with Millicent," Lady Pemberton told Chelsea. "I cannot think when I have seen her looking so fit. I know she will miss you frightfully when your husband whisks you off to Bombay, or . . ." she turned a quizzical gaze on Rutherford.

"Honduras," he supplied firmly. "Alayna and I shall reside in Honduras after we are wed."

Chelsea grimaced and when they were once again alone, turned toward him. "I have not changed face on the subject of accompanying you across the sea, Rutherford."

His jaws ground together and he refused to look at her when he spoke. "We are to become man and wife, Alayna. And, as you so aptly reminded me a moment ago, we shall manage somehow. In spite of the fact that one of us finds the living arrangements distasteful," he added curtly.

At the mention of their being together again, Chelsea's spirits rose the veriest mite, only to be crushed once more when she reminded herself that *she* was not the young lady who would be living with the gentleman.

With reluctance, she turned her attention to the colorful blur of couples spinning through a contredanse in the center of the room. Though she and Rutherford had been busy greeting the guests during the first set, he now put a hand to her back and guided her to the floor for the second. Though the pressure of his warm hand at her waist caused a fluttering sensation in her stomach, she nonetheless succeeded quite well in maintaining her cool demeanor toward him.

When the dance had concluded, however, she was grateful when Lord Rathbone relinquished her hand to Lord Pemberton, and then to another gentleman who had stepped forward, requesting that she stand up with him.

To her immense delight, this gentleman, whom Ford had

addressed as Mr. Brownlea, kept up a running discourse throughout the entire number, his lighthearted comments giving Chelsea occasion to smile and, at times, even to laugh.

Upon returning her to Lord Rathbone's side, Mr. Brownlea remarked, "Your betrothed is a rare flower, your lordship. Perhaps I might be granted a second dance with her following supper. Since she is already spoke for, shouldn't think it would garner notice, what?"

A glare from Lord Rathbone sent Mr. Brownlea packing and a hand at Chelsea's back guided her to the fringe of the crowd. "It appears you had plenty of smiles for Lord Pemberton," he remarked dryly. "And I could not help but notice that the fortunate Mr. Brownlea was the object of what could only be termed a coquettish attitude on your part. To say truth, I did not enjoy watching you with either gentleman."

Because it hardly signified, Chelsea elected to say nothing in defense of her actions.

After a lengthy spell of silence, however, Lord Rathbone asked, "Would you care for a glass of rataffia, or perhaps champagne? I admit I could use a drink."

"As could I," Chelsea murmured.

"Well . . . which?"

"Either will suffice."

With a huff, Lord Rathbone moved from her side to fetch the drinks.

But a split second after he had returned with them, Chelsea was startled to distraction by the shrill sound of a familiar voice to her left.

"Now I recollect! It was in Brighton!" As one, both she and Ford turned toward a plump matron, whose flushed face was now beaming up at them.

Recognizing the woman as a close friend of her former employer, Lady Hennessey, Chelsea's heart fell to her feet.

She had completely forgot that Mrs. Forsythe lived near Chester!

"I am sorry I do not recall your name, madam," Ford was saying.

"But, certainly *you* remember me, young lady!" The woman gazed expectantly up at Chelsea, who stood nearly a head taller than she.

"Umm . . . I am so sorry, my lady, but I—"

The woman's lips pressed into a thin line. "Do not pretend you do not know me, Miss Grant. I was two weeks in Brighton with Lady Hennessey and was actually present in the drawing room the day you were . . ." she paused, the speaking look on her face aptly concluding the sentence, for Chelsea anyway.

Although she winced, she still managed to say, quite evenly, "Apparently you have me confused with Miss Grant, madam. It is true we do favor one another, and in Brighton, were quite often mistaken for one another."

Hearing Miss Grant's name mentioned, Lord Rathbone directed a remark to Chelsea. "I understood Miss Grant was to be in attendance this evening, Alayna. Has she not yet arrived?"

"No," Chelsea said quickly, aware that Mrs. Forsythe was still regarding her curiously, "she has not." She turned a steady gaze on the woman. "When Miss Grant does arrive, I shall bring her to you straightaway."

Mrs. Forsythe's brow furrowed as she reluctantly backed away.

"A bit odd, that," Ford mused, his eyes following the woman's departure.

"Indeed," Chelsea murmured. "But, it is quite true, you know. People often mistook C-chelsea for me. We grew quite accustomed to it, actually."

"Hmm. Can't say as I recall you mentioning a marked resemblance to that young lady. I am doubly anxious to meet her now."

Chelsea declined a direct response to that, but a second later, she was doubly chagrined when Mrs. Forsythe approached them once more.

"Now that I think on it, Miss Marchmont, you are quite right. *You* were the pretty one. And as for you, young man, you have made the right choice, indeed. It would never do to align yourself with *her* sort!"

Chelsea cringed.

"Her sort?" He directed a puzzled gaze at Chelsea.

One of Mrs. Forsythe's eyebrows lifted knowingly. "I don't mind saying that Lady Hennessey and I were quite shocked to learn of the unfortunate scandal associated with Miss Grant. You were quite right to apprise her of the details, Miss Marchmont. Indeed, we were both immensely grateful. One cannot be too careful these days." She smiled agreeably at the betrothed pair standing mute before her. "I wish you both every happiness."

As the woman strolled away again, Chelsea schooled herself to remain calm. Not wishing to show Alayna in a bad light, she had no intention of explaining anything to Lord Rathbone regarding the incident to which the woman had referred.

It did not surprise her, however, when almost at once, Ford asked, "What on earth was that silly woman alluding to?"

Chelsea affixed a smile to her lips and employed a particularly annoying habit of Alayna's. Changing the subject. "Did you notice the stunning brooch she had pinned to her turban? I declare it was the most lavishly cut emerald I have ever seen. And with a ring and bracelet to match! But, the necklace was a bit much, don't you agree?"

Lord Rathbone's gaze fell to Chelsea's neck, which was decidedly bare. "Speaking of jewelry, may I inquire why you are not wearing the locket I gave to you, Alayna? I seem to recall you saying that you would never take it off."

Chelsea flinched. "I did not think it flattered my gown,"

she replied airily. But, catching the fleeting look of hurt that darkened Lord Rathbone's eyes, she longed to retract her hastily spoken words. Instead, she said, "You refine too much on it, sir."

She was not prepared for the sudden flash of anger that twisted his mouth. "Confound it, Alayna! I refuse to countenance this nonsense a second longer!" With that, his fingers curled around her upper arm and he fairly dragged her from the ballroom.

Advancing to a dimly lit area on the balcony just beyond a pair of opened French doors, he whirled to face her. "I intend to have it out with you this minute, Alayna."

Chelsea recoiled from the anger blazing in his eyes. "Please, Ford. It is quite chilly out here, I much prefer to remain indo—"

"We shall return to the ballroom once we have arrived at an amiable pass! You are behaving precisely as you used to do as a petulant child. You've no idea how disagreeable I found you then!"

"Well, this is a fine time to tell me!" she sputtered. "On the eve of our marriage!"

"I would have said as much earlier, if I had seen signs of it earlier. But, I did not. For all intents and purposes, during our last weeks together, it appeared to me you had outgrown your insufferable obstinacy. And, I don't mind saying, I was glad enough for it. Now, once and for all, you will return to Honduras with me and I will tolerate no further rebellion from you on the matter. Do I make myself clear, Alayna?"

Staring evenly at the angry man, Chelsea tried to think of an ugly retort. But, she could not. Suddenly, all she could think of were the last delightful weeks they had spent together. Gazing up at him, she further realized that *she* had no genuine fight with the gentleman. It was he and Alayna who had differences to settle. *She* would gladly go to the ends of the earth with him. And beyond if he so desired.

"Have you nothing to say for yourself, Alayna?"

Watching his jaws grind together and his nostrils flare with fury, Chelsea wondered if even Alayna could continue to be so very cruel to him?

"Very well," he spat out. "I will detain you no longer, nor will I try to repair the damage done to our friendship." He continued to stare at her, then a moment later, in a considerably softened tone, he said, "I . . . regret the rift that has sprung up between us."

Chelsea felt her lower lip begin to tremble. Suddenly the emotion filling her breast felt near to bursting. She worked valiantly to push it down, but it was no use. "I . . . too, regret it, sir," she said softly.

Ford registered his surprise at her admission. "Oh, Alayna." He reached for one of her gloved hands and nestled the palm of it against his smooth cheek. "These past weeks with you have been the happiest of my life. I cannot abide the thought of not having you with me in Honduras. Please, my darling, say you will come with me."

Tears swam in Chelsea's eyes. "Dear, Ford . . ." she barely whispered, "I would go with you anywhere."

"Oh-h-h, Alayna . . ." He reached to draw her into his arms.

Not resisting him a whit, Chelsea arched her back as he gathered her close, molding her to the length of him. *Dear God, how she loved him!* But . . . it was not to be. It could never be. Suddenly, a rush of painful tears brimmed in her eyes.

Apparently feeling the sob that rose within her breast, Ford drew back. "Why are you weeping, little one?" A gloved finger gently brushed a sparkling droplet of moisture from her lashes. "I love you so very much, Alayna. And though you have never quite repeated the words back to me, I am certain that you love me, as well. What can be troubling you now? You do love me, do you not?"

Through her tears, Chelsea managed a tight nod. "Yes," she mouthed, "I do love you. More than life itself."

He joyously hugged her to him again. "I am the happiest man alive, Alayna."

Hearing 'Alayna's' name on his lips, Chelsea stiffened again in his arms. She should not have said what she did. Alayna did not love him. "Please, Ford—" she made a weak effort to pull away. "I-I should never have told you how I feel. Please, sir, forgive me."

A puzzled look on his face, Ford drew back once again to gaze into her eyes. "Why ever should you not tell me how you feel, peagoose?"

Chelsea bit her lower lip. Then, with no resistance whatever, she let Lord Rathbone, Alayna's betrothed, enfold her once again in his strong embrace. When his warm lips found hers, she gave herself up to the delicious shower of sparks that exploded in her brain. Yet, when the kiss drew to an end, a wave of profound sadness replaced her immense pleasure. For a long moment, she nestled against him.

If she could not be wed to Lord Rathbone, her life may as well end, for she knew she would never again feel so very safe, so very protected, so very loved by a man.

Fifteen

"She ain't here, miss!" Dulcie announced the following morning when she brought up Chelsea's breakfast tray.

Chelsea barely heard her. She had awakened especially early this morning and stationed herself by the window, partly to catch a glimpse of the festivities on the castle grounds below, mostly to watch for Alayna. "Oh, Dulcie." She turned toward the little maid, who was busy setting a plate of scones onto a table. "Whatever shall I do?"

Dulcie lifted a worried gaze and shook her head. "I dunno', miss."

"It simply wouldn't do for me to stand in for Alayna at the wedding."

Considering that, Dulcie's face screwed up. "Why not, miss? If 'is lordship was set to 'ave a . . . a . . ."

"Proxy," Chelsea supplied absently, then she cried, "No! No, I couldn't! I simply couldn't! Still . . . if Lord Rathbone were set to have a proxy stand in for him, then perhaps Alayna could have one, as well."

" 'Course she could, miss!"

"But I . . . I would have to divulge the whole truth to everyone before . . . that is . . ." Her throat tightened convulsively as she thought about what Lord Rathbone would expect *after* the wedding. "I mean, I couldn't let . . . oh, dear!" She hastened again to the window and peered out. "Alayna *must* arrive soon, she simply *must!*"

Her eyes anxiously scanned the crowd of merry-makers

cavorting on the castle grounds. From her vantage point, she could see several colorful booths, triangular scraps of red and yellow cloth snapping in the breeze from each corner of the wooden stalls. In front of them, criers loudly hawked toys, dolls and Bartholomew babies, the prizes to be awarded should anyone win the toss of the ball. She spotted a pair of jugglers throwing pins between them and a man on stilts, tossing boiled sweets to a group of eager children. What she did not see, was Alayna.

"Oh, Dulcie." She turned dejectedly from the window again. "What are we to do?"

"Perhaps you should eat your breakfast, miss."

Suddenly struck with an idea, Chelsea cried, "I should like you to deliver a note to Lord Rathbone first." She hastened to a small writing desk in the corner of the room and withdrew a crisp sheet of linen paper. After scribbling a few words across it, she held it aloft to study it, then staring at it horror-struck, she ripped the page to pieces.

"W'ot is it, miss?" Dulcie asked wide-eyed.

"Lord Rathbone has never seen a sample of my handwriting before. He would surely recognize it as not being Alayna's! You must simply tell him for me, Dulcie, that Miss Marchmont is not feeling well, and that . . . that the wedding ceremony must be delayed a bit." She paused. "Yes; yes, that should do nicely," she concluded, a bit out of breath.

Near eleven of the clock that morning, however, a note was delivered to Chelsea from Lady Rathbone. She and the older woman had exchanged only a few words last evening at the ball. But, the discourse had been later, much later, after she and Ford had successfully patched up their differences. Earlier in the evening, Chelsea had been painfully aware of Lady Rathbone watching her closely. After supper, however, when Chelsea had eyes for no one save Ford, Lady

Rathbone's attitude had undergone a miraculous change as well. No longer did Chelsea feel the woman's sharp gaze upon her, albeit behind thick spectacles, instead she experienced once again the frail old lady's warmth and acceptance.

"You look as pretty as a picture tonight, my dear," Lady Rathbone had said, a smile on her lips as a footman wheeled her chair to where Chelsea and Ford sat, a bit apart from the others as they ate their midnight supper.

"Thank you, Aunt Millicent," Chelsea had murmured, barely able to pull her eyes from Lord Rathbone's handsome face.

"I cannot stay angry with my darling Alayna for long," he had replied, also gazing with love at Chelsea.

The older woman had smiled at them, then she said, "For both your sakes, I hope that is always the case."

Chelsea hadn't thought much about Lady Rathbone's parting comment then, but with a fresh sense of foreboding, it burned into her mind now. Once Lord Rathbone discovered she was *not* his cousin, Alayna Marchmont, she hoped his charitable attitude would extend also to her.

Her eyes quickly scanned the message from Lady Rathbone. In short order, it said that a delay in the proceedings this morning would not be tolerated and that the wedding ceremony would begin promptly at noon in the castle chapel.

"Oh-h-h," Chelsea said on a sigh, letting the scrap of paper drift from her fingertips to the bed. *Whatever was she to do?*

She glanced toward the clothespress where Alayna's lovely wedding gown hung in plain sight. The white lawn bridal costume was, by far, the most beautiful of all the many gowns Alayna had sent along with Chelsea. The empire-waisted dress was fashioned with long sleeves that ended in points just above the wrists. A pattern of seed pearls and silver threads were stitched onto the low-cut bodice, and the skirt was decorated with a garland of sculptured white roses, their leaf tips outlined in silver. Completing the ensemble was a close-fitting bridal cap with a sheer net veil, and tiny silver slippers, the toes of which were embroidered with white rosebuds.

Chelsea exhaled a long sigh, then with fresh insight, decided that perhaps it would behoove her to pack up her few belongings now in readiness to depart the minute Alayna arrived. Energized by the idea, she raced to the wardrobe and dragged her small, well-worn valise from behind the many garments hanging there. Reaching back in, past all of Alayna's lovely gowns, she withdrew her own few frocks. Next to the more elegant creations, her dresses looked quite shabby, but that did not signify now. She flung her clothes into the valise and was rifling through the cupboard near the clothespress for her boots and bonnet, when a rap at the door startled her.

"Alayna!"

Recognizing Lady Rathbone's angry bellow, Chelsea froze in place. She hadn't heard that tone of voice from the old woman since her early days at the castle. When Chelsea did not answer the summons at once, Lady Rathbone began to loudly thump her cane against the door. "Alayna, open this door at once!"

The noisy ruckus brought Dulcie scurrying from her chamber. "Shall I answer the door for you, miss?"

"In a moment, Dulcie." Chelsea hastily slid her hastily packed valise beneath the bed. "Now," she mouthed.

In seconds, a silent footman pushed Lady Rathbone's chair into the room. Waving the man away with her cane, she pinned Chelsea with a hard look.

"You don't appear the least bit sick to me, gel! Are you planning to marry my son today, or not?"

Chelsea struggled for the courage to speak. "I—"

"Speak up, gel! If you are not sick, then pray what is the trouble?" Narrowed eyes behind thick spectacles scrutinized her. "By now, you should be dressed in flowers and lace, and fluttering about like a nervous Nellie!"

Chelsea swallowed a gulp of much-needed air. "I-I . . . was just about to get dressed, ma'am."

"Good." Lady Rathbone bellowed for the footman, then turned again to Chelsea. "I expect you to be ready for the parson's mousetrap within the hour, young lady. In the meantime, I shall summon Mr. Stephens. I expect he is enjoying himself at the fair. Jolly monstrous crowd there . . ." she grinned crookedly. "Once you and Rutherford are wed, you will be obliged to put in an appearance yourselves."

With that, she allowed herself to be wheeled from the room.

Chelsea turned a tremulous gaze on Dulcie. "The white frock will do nicely, Dulcie."

Nearly an hour later, Dulcie handed Chelsea a beribboned bouquet of pink-tipped daisies surrounding a perfect amethyst rose in the center. The flowers had been sent up by a footman from Rutherford.

Chelsea brought the fragrant blossoms to her nose as Dulcie secured the bridal veil to the tiny lace cap that fit snugly against Chelsea's honey-colored curls. When the veil had floated into place before her face, Chelsea gazed at her image reflected in the looking glass. Oddly enough, hidden behind the veil, she could, indeed, pass for Alayna Marchmont.

Just outside the castle chapel, which was located at the far end of the top floor of the ancient stone relic, Chelsea met up once again with Lady Rathbone.

"You are a picture of loveliness, my dear." The woman's grey eyes behind her thick lenses were a bit sad. "I trust you will make my son very happy."

Suddenly realizing the enormity of what she was about

to do, Chelsea choked back the high emotion that swelled within her breast. "Oh, Aunt Millicent," she murmured, "if only I could; if only I could."

"Well, a'course ye can! Let's get on with it!" She waved to Jared, who had been standing a bit apart from them, to wheel her Bath chair down the aisle. As the butler drew near Chelsea, she was certain she saw in his stoic gaze a slight softening around the stern lines of his mouth.

Blinking through the moisture in her own eyes, she gave the man dressed in black a small answering smile.

Having never attended a wedding ceremony before, Chelsea wasn't at all sure what was expected of her. Poised just beneath the arched doorway of the chapel, her eyes behind the gauzy veil scanned the dimly-lit interior of the small room. Only a few people were assembled there. The rest of the guests who had been invited for the ball, and who had stayed overnight, were very likely enjoying themselves now at the fair. Chelsea caught a glimpse of Lord and Lady Pemberton, and a few other people whom she knew now to be close friends of Lady Rathbone. But, the face she did not see was that of Rutherford Campbell.

Her gaze travelled the length of the aisle to the altar. It was draped with a white cloth over a wine velvet runner. A profusion of lit candles stood at attention in an ornate silver candelabra, their tiny blue flames flickering in the stillness.

Then, from behind the altar, she saw an invisible door open and Mr. Stephens stepped forward. Close behind him came Lord Rathbone. At the sight of the tall, handsome gentleman, Chelsea's breath lodged fitfully in her throat. Lord Rathbone looked more dashing today than ever. Spilling down the front of his dark blue coat was a froth of twisted white linen. He had on an elegant pair of white satin pantaloons that ended just below the knees, his lower limbs encased in white silk hose with silver buckles gleaming atop a pair of dark blue pumps.

When he caught sight of her standing at the top of the aisle, he leaned over to whisper something to Mr. Stephens, then headed up the aisle toward her. Chelsea felt her breasts expand against the tight-fitting bodice of her gown. *She was about to marry Lord Rathbone!*

"You look beautiful beyond words, my dear," he whispered, his dark eyes smiling as he reached to drape one of her hands, encased in soft white kid, over his arm.

As she moved beside him down the aisle, a hush fell over the assembled guests. No music accompanied them. The only audible sounds were their muffled footfalls on the worn carpet runner trailing down the center of the narrow aisle.

The couple took up a position before the parson and a moment later, Chelsea became aware of Lord Pemberton stepping forward to give her away.

"Dearly beloved," the vicar began.

Her brown eyes round, Chelsea listened to the vicar speak the solemn words. In due course, Lord Pemberton moved away and Lord Rathbone stepped again to her side.

After what seemed an eternity the clergyman's liturgy was still droning on. When he, at last, seemed near to winding down, Chelsea breathed a low sigh of relief. In a few moments, Alayna Marchmont, wherever she was, would become a married woman.

"—and do you, take Rutherford Charles to be your wedded husband?"

"Um . . ." she cast a wide-eyed glance at Ford.

"Well," he whispered, his tone urging her onward. "You do mean to marry me, don't you, darling?"

Chelsea's tongue suddenly became too thick to speak. All she could manage was a tight nod.

"Then . . . tell him."

Chelsea turned toward the vicar.

"It is quite all right, my dear," Mr. Steven's voice was low, low enough that only she and Ford could hear him.

"Hesitancy in a young lady only proves to me that she takes her marriage vows seriously. I think that quite a good sign." He nodded solemnly as he awaited Chelsea's reply.

She swallowed hard. "I do."

The vicar smiled as Ford breathed a sigh of relief and she heard, as well, a collective breath escape the congregation.

"And, do you, Rutherford Charles take Alayna Alice, to be your wedded wife?"

"I do," Ford proclaimed at once, his voice sure and bold, its deep timbre resonating through the chapel, and through Chelsea.

"Very good, son." The vicar beamed. "Now, then, may I have the ring, please, your lordship?"

Chelsea turned an anxious gaze on Ford as he fumbled in his waistcoat pocket for the ring.

Then, suddenly, from the rear of the chapel, a shrill feminine voice rang out. *"Stop! Stop this at once, I say!"*

Every head in the room spun about.

"I insist you halt these proceedings at once!" cried the young lady, her blond hair flying loose behind her as she ran pell-mell toward the pair standing before the altar.

Everyone, save Mr. Stephens, seemed unable to utter a single word. "I fear you are a trifle late, miss," he said. "We have already got past the part where I ask if anyone has any objection to this—"

"That does not signify! I demand you cease these proceedings at once!" Alayna Marchmont glared first at the vicar, then whirled toward Chelsea. "How dare you attempt to steal my husband!"

"Steal?" Chelsea murmured, her tone incredulous.

"Excuse me," Lord Rathbone put in, "but just exactly who are you, miss?"

Alayna's blue eyes rolled skyward as she turned toward him. "You always were a dolt, Rutherford!"

"He is not a dolt!" Chelsea snapped, flinging the veil aside so she could better see what was taking place.

"Thank you, my dear," Lord Rathbone said calmly. "Now, if you will please tell me who this young lady is."

"I am your cous—" Alayna began, but was interrupted by a bellow from the congregation.

"Enough!" Every head whirled toward Lady Rathbone, who had risen unsteadily to her feet from her chair parked near the front pew. She turned to address the now very rapt assembly. "Those of you who are not involved in this contretemps will kindly leave the chapel while the rest of us attempt to sort it out."

With no further urging whatsoever, the wedding guests—flinging furtive glances over their shoulders as they did so—filed down the aisle and disappeared into the corridor.

"Now, then," Lady Rathbone began afresh, turning her attention to the stunned group assembled before the altar.

"Why, Aunt Millicent!" Alayna cried, "You are wearing spectacles!"

"Aunt Millicent?" Ford repeated numbly. "Who is this young lady?"

"She is your cousin, Alayna," his mother said evenly.

"Alayna?" Ford muttered, flinging a befuddled gaze from one pretty blond woman to the other. "But, who is—? Who are—?"

"She is Miss Chelsea Grant!" Alayna exclaimed with high triumph. "She is here under false prete—"

"Chelsea Grant?" Ford repeated incredulously. "The Brighton Beauty?"

Chelsea gave a helpless little shrug. "You said you wanted to meet me."

"I did not say I wanted to marry you!" he spat out, his eyes blazing with fury. "I demand to know the meaning of this!"

"Miss Grant had me kidnapped!" Alayna declared hotly.

"Kidnapped?" Ford directed a scowl at Chelsea. "So, Sully elicited your help in this, did he?"

"Sully? Who is Sully?" Alayna demanded. "I tell you it was Miss Grant who had me kidnapped. She wanted a hundred pounds for me!"

"Only a hundred pounds?" Ford muttered. "But, I was given to understand that Sully wanted—"

"Who is Sully?" Alayna stamped her foot impatiently. "I tell you, it was Miss Grant who had me—"

"Alayna!" Chelsea cut her off snappishly. "Why are you saying that I had you kidnapped? I have been here at the castle the entire time, just as you asked me to be. I would never have you—"

"How very like you to deny it, Chelsea." Alayna folded her arms across her bosom and glared at her friend.

At this juncture, Lord Rathbone cut in again. "I demand to know whether or not you and Sully were working together on this, Alan . . . I mean, Miss Grant."

"We most certainly were not!" Chelsea cried. "I had never met Sully until the day he appeared at the cast—"

"Who is Sully!"

Lord Rathbone continued to ignore Alayna's pleas. "Well, if you were not working with that reprobate, then pray tell what were you doing in the carriage that night, impersonating my—my cousin? If indeed, that is who this young lady is."

"How dare you question my veracity!" Alayna sputtered afresh. "I tell you she had me kidnapped! I insist you send for the constable at once!"

"Alayna." Chelsea spun around, a hurt look in her eyes. "Why are you fabricating this nonsense? Why can you not simply tell Rutherford the truth?"

Alayna thrust her chin up. "I *am* telling the truth. And, I shall prove it." She dove into her reticule and began to rifle through it looking for something.

"I do not want the money you promised me," Chelsea

said quickly. "The fact is, I refuse to take a farthing for my part in the deed."

"You refuse to take the money?" Lord Rathbone said, staring wide-eyed at Chelsea. "That does seem a bit irregular, for a kidnapper." He directed another look at Alayna. "Are you certain you are who you say you are, miss?"

"Of course, I am!" Alayna's blond head jerked up. Apparently unsuccessful in locating what she had been looking for, she cried, "I insist you have Miss Grant arrested at once!"

Chelsea gasped with fresh alarm.

"I prefer instead to see some proof of *your* identity, young lady," Ford countered.

"Don't you recognize me?" Alayna asked digging again in her reticule. "But, I tell you, *she* is the impostor!" She whirled again toward the bride. "You have always been jealous of me, Chelsea Grant! You have always wanted what I have! But, you shan't have my husband, you shan't!"

"May I remind both of you young ladies," Ford sputtered anew, "that thus far in these proceedings, I have been declared no one's husband!"

At that moment, an insistent thumping sound interrupted them. They all turned toward Lady Rathbone, who was angrily rapping her cane against the stone floor. "I have the young lady's proof right here," she said, pressing her lips together with seeming disgust as she handed Ford an item wrapped in brown paper.

Lord Rathbone's brow furrowed as he unwrapped the package. Cupping the small object in his palm, he glanced from one pretty blond to the other.

Alayna, having at once recognized the object as being the miniature of herself, cried, "So! There. You have it! That is the very portrait of myself that I had painted for you when our betrothal was announced. It is the best likeness of me yet!"

"I seem to recall several persons mentioning that fact to me," Rathbone muttered, still staring hard at the object.

"But, why did you not already have it, Ford? And, what are you doing in England? You are supposed to be in—"

Again, Lord Rathbone ignored his cousin's pleas, and instead directed a question at his mother. "Why did you not show this to me earlier, Mother? And how did you come to possess it?"

Chelsea was highly interested in the answers to those questions herself.

"To say truth," Lady Rathbone began, "I haven't a clue who sent the portrait to me. Perhaps it was Sully. As to why I did not show the painting to you before now, which, of course, would have served to expose Miss Grant's perfidious activity, I expect I was waiting for the opportune moment. This, it appears, is it."

Silence descended for a spell, then Mr. Stephens, whom apparently everyone had forgotten was still standing there, said, perhaps a bit too brightly, considering, "Well, then, now that we have established which one of these lovely young ladies is the real Miss Marchmont, may I suggest we get on with the ceremony?"

"I think that a splendid idea," Alayna said, elbowing her way into position beside Ford.

"Not so fast!" he snapped. "We still have not ascertained why Miss Grant has been at the castle these last weeks, purporting to be my cousin. If it were not for the money, then what—"

"I told you," Alayna interrupted, her tone impatient, "she had me kidnapped so she could marry you herself! I cannot think why you have not yet sent for the constable. Miss Grant should be locked up!"

"Alayna!" Chelsea sputtered aghast.

"Well, you should be!" She turned to Ford. "I expect the constable is just outside, along with the rest of the county." She glared at Chelsea. "My companion and I . . . I mean,

I found it the outside of enough that there was a fair in progress—"

"You have a companion?" Ford said icily. "Pray tell, who might that party be?" His gaze on Alayna was frosty.

"Well, uh . . ." For the first time, she appeared at a loss. "You see, I-I was rescued, that is, my maid and I were rescued."

"Rescued?" Ford repeated flatly.

"That is correct. The experience was quite harrowing actually. But my . . . my knight was very brave. Very brave, indeed."

"Your knight?" Ford echoed.

"Indeed." Alayna tilted her chin up. "The gentleman is quite dashing. He is an acquaintance of mine from London. If it had not been for him," she struck a tragic pose, "there is no saying what would have happened to me, or to my maid, Jane Ann."

"Very commendable," Rathbone muttered acerbically. "Now, if you will please tell me this paragon's name?"

"Would you like to meet him?" Alayna seemed pleased.

"Indeed, I would," Ford replied, his tone calculated. He turned to the vicar. "Would you kindly fetch Miss Marchmont's escort for me, please? The gentleman's name, Alayna?"

"Mr. Harry Hill."

Chelsea's eyes widened as Ford's dark orbs narrowed with fury.

"Are you acquainted with him?" Alayna asked innocently.

Lord Rathbone's nostrils flared with rage. "Suffice to say, I have heard the name bandied about."

"Oh!" Alayna brightened. "I had no idea his talent as an actor was so wide spread! I am thrilled you want to meet him, Rutherford. If you please, Mr. Stephens, Mr. Hill is awaiting me belowstairs in the foyer."

The vicar hurried from the chapel while before the altar,

Lord Rathbone's chest heaved up and down with each breath he drew.

"I can assure you," Alayna said, "Harry will explain the entire affair—I mean, the entire episode to everyone's satisfaction."

"I am counting on that," Ford said icily.

"Well, I must say," Alayna prattled on, "I felt very fortunate that Mr. Hill happened along when he did. I cannot think what possessed you to do such a vile thing, Chelsea. She has always been jealous of me," she told Ford again. "Since we were girls at Miss Farringdon's Academy in Brighton. I recall telling you about the time she—"

Suddenly Chelsea could stand it no longer. "Alayna, this is unconscionable! You know very well I was only doing what you asked me to do! I would never do anything to harm you!"

"Oh, Chelsea, if only that were true. But, you've simply no idea where I have been, or what I've been through these last weeks."

"I should like to know where you have been these last weeks," Ford said frostily.

An uncomfortable silence ensued. Then, with a grunt, Lady Rathbone rose from her chair and hobbled forward. "Perhaps this will shed additional light on the matter." She cast a disgruntled look at Alayna as she handed her son a folded up piece of paper.

Both young ladies held their breaths as Rutherford unfolded the letter and scanned the words on the page. When, he glanced up again, his eyes were a shade darker than midnight.

"What is it, cousin Ford?" Alayna asked sweetly.

As usual, Rathbone ignored his cousin and spoke instead to his mother, who stood leaning on her cane. "This does indeed clear things up, Mother."

"Splendid!" Alayna cried. "Then shall we resume the ceremony?"

Lord Rathbone directed an icy glare from one young lady to the other. "We shall resume nothing. The only vow I intend to make today is to remain *un*legshackled to anyone for the remainder of my natural life!" With that, he flung the letter aside and charged up the aisle.

"Now, look what you've done!" Alayna cried, flinging a hurt look at Chelsea.

"Miss Grant has done nothing," Lady Rathbone said evenly, "beyond fall in love with my son."

Sixteen

"How could you, Chelsea?" Alayna cried, angrily pacing between the window and the bed in Chelsea's room where the two young ladies had adjourned following Lord Rathbone's exit from the chapel. "You knew very well that Rutherford was set to marry me!"

Chelsea slipped out of the lovely wedding gown she had been wearing and handed it to Dulcie who dutifully returned it to the clothespress. "You should have told Rutherford the truth just now, Alayna," she remarked.

"Why did *you* not tell him a month ago? If Rutherford were at the castle, there was no longer a need for *me* to be here. His presence alone would have satisfied the parish residency requirement."

"If I had confessed to Lord Rathbone then that I was not you, he'd have had me hanged!" Chelsea struggled with the hooks on the back of her own gown until Dulcie reached to help.

"Oh, Chelsea, you cannot expect me to believe that! Rutherford may have a short temper, but to have you hanged for such a minor transgression is doing it up a bit, don't you think?"

Chelsea parked both hands on her hips. "I was merely trying to protect you, Alayna, and myself, by continuing with the charade. Under the circumstances, it would not have been a great leap for your cousin to link me with Sully."

"Who is Sully?" Alayna cried impatiently.

"He is the real kidnapper."

Alayna's brow puckered.

"Sully was the primary reason Lord Rathbone came to England in the first place." In short order, Chelsea explained the former overseer's plot to steal Lord Rathbone's inheritance and the abduction that resulted from it. "Surely you can see why I felt the need to continue with the ruse," she concluded in a somewhat defensive tone, then turning to Dulcie, who had just completed the task of doing up her gown, she said, "Thank you Dulcie."

The little maid then set to work on Chelsea's hair, undoing the elaborate coiffure she had created in order to set off the bridal veil.

"If you must know, Alayna," Chelsea added self-righteously, "this has been the absolute worst experience of my entire life."

Alayna's eyes rolled skyward. "Do spare me, Chelsea." She pranced to the window again and looked out. "You have obviously quite enjoyed pretending to be me. From the look of it, you meant to carry the pretense far beyond anything I intended." She whirled around to glare again at Chelsea. "I never gave you leave to marry him!"

"I was merely standing in for you!"

"Then, how do you account for the fact that he knew nothing of it? When did you mean to tell him?"

Chelsea heaved an exasperated sigh. "If you had returned to the castle yesterday, this would never have happened. You could have attended your own betrothal ball and—"

"There was a ball?"

Chelsea nodded angrily.

"Oh!" Alayna pouted. "Well, I should have been here in plenty of time if you had not had me kidnapped so that you might attend the ball yourself and marry Rutherford today in my place!"

"I did not have you kidnapped, Alayna!"

"Of course, it was you! Who else could it have been?"

Chelsea shook her head with dismay. "I haven't the slightest notion," she breathed. Nothing made any sense anymore.

Alayna plopped onto the bed. "Thank Heaven, Harry happened along when he did. And, thank Heaven he was able to overcome that . . . that frightful rustic who commandeered the coach and took us on a wild ride through the woods this morning. You can imagine my surprise, Chelsea, when we finally reached the castle and I saw the grounds full of people! *They* must have reached the castle by crossing the bridge."

"The bridge? What does the bridge have to say to anything?"

"Why do you continue to play the innocent with me, Chelsea? The man you hired to kidnap me used the excuse that the bridge was out to take us on the roundaboutation!"

Chelsea stared at Alayna as if she'd gone daft. "I swear to you, Alayna, I haven't the slightest notion what you are talking about." On impulse, she turned to Dulcie. "Do you know anything of this, Dulcie?"

Dulcie shrugged. "N-no, miss. Perhaps her ladyship could answer."

"Lady Rathbone? But, why would she—"

"Rubbish! Aunt Millicent would never set kidnappers on me," Alayna declared firmly. "I still say it was you, Chelsea Grant. I should have known better than to trust you."

Chelsea swallowed an angry retort as she impatiently snatched the hairbrush from Dulcie's hand and began to yank it through her own hair. When the curls had been brushed out and her hair again hung smooth down her back, she jerked up her old flat chip bonnet and jammed it onto her head. With intermittent glares at Alayna, she hastily tied the ribbons beneath her chin. "I shall be on my way now. Dulcie, if you will please retrieve my bag for me."

Dulcie dove under the bed and dragged the worn valise forward. "Here you are, miss."

To forestall her departure, Alayna flounced to the door and positioned herself before it. "Before you go, I should like to know precisely how you and my cousin passed the time while I was away? A month is quite a long time to spend in a gentleman's company. I cannot help but notice that my doltish cousin has . . . well, changed a bit since last I saw him."

"Changed?" Chelsea murmured.

"He is . . . taller, and a good deal more . . ."

"Dashing."

"There!" Alayna's blue eyes snapped with fire. "I knew you were trying to steal him from me! Admit it, Chelsea, you were!"

"I will admit to nothing of the sort. I was merely doing what you asked of me, Alayna. And now that you have returned to the castle"—she shifted her valise to her other hand—"I shall be on my way."

Alayna reluctantly stepped aside. "With no parting word to Ford?" she chided.

Her free hand now on the doorlatch, Chelsea paused. "I hardly think your cousin is in a frame to receive me," she replied evenly. "Though I do intend to extend my apologies to Lady Rathbone before I depart."

A sudden scratch at the door made both young ladies jump.

"Who is it?" Alayna called out, whereupon a maid stuck her head around the doorjamb to announce that Lady Rathbone desired a private word with Miss Grant. "In her chamber, miss," the housemaid said.

"So," Alayna cast a triumphant look at Chelsea, "it appears my aunt has a good deal more to say to you before you go. Aunt Millicent can be quite foul tempered, Chelsea." With a gloating look, she headed for the looking glass to pat her own blond curls into place. "I intend to go to the fair. Perhaps I shall find my handsome cousin Ford on the grounds."

With no further comment to Alayna, Chelsea hurried to Lady Rathbone's suite. Encountering a solemn-faced Jared stationed outside the door, Chelsea smiled a bit wryly at the man.

"Her ladyship is expecting me," she said.

His features as impassive as ever, Jared replied, "Indeed, miss."

Advancing into the achingly familiar chamber, Chelsea spotted the older woman seated in her customary place on the worn sofa as she had so many times before while waiting for Chelsea to come and read to her. Suddenly, Chelsea collected the first time she had stepped into this room. The anxiety she felt now was not unlike what she had experienced then. "You wished to see me, Lady Rathbone?" she said quietly.

The woman glanced up. "Ah. There you are, Miss Grant." A hand indicated Chelsea's usual place across from her.

Instead of complying with the woman's wishes, however, Chelsea said, "I shan't be staying, ma'am. I am prepared to leave the castle straightaway." She set her valise down at her feet, and moved only a few steps closer. "I should like to say how very sorry I am for—"

"Please, do sit down, Miss Grant. I shall have Jared bring us a nice pot of tea."

Chelsea shook her head. "I have taken advantage of your hospitality far too long as it is, ma'am. I merely wanted you to know how terribly sorry I am for the mischief I have caused. I . . . should never have let the . . . deception get to such a state. I am frightfully sorry, my lady."

"Do sit down, Miss Grant," the old woman insisted. When at last Chelsea complied, she went on. "I am not angry with you, my dear. I understand that you were merely endeavoring to keep your word to Alayna. I take it she wanted you to pretend to be her for the month preceding the wedding in order to satisfy the parish residency requirement. Was that not the case?"

Her lashes lowered, Chelsea nodded. "I suspected that you knew something was afoot."

"True. I did unravel the coil . . . eventually. Though, by the time I recalled that my niece's eye were as blue as the sky and your's, gel, are nut brown, I admit I was enjoying your company far too much to turn you out." She smiled sadly. "It was not until Eudora's letter arrived a few days ago, the day you received one from 'Miss Grant', that I put the last of the pieces together."

"But"—Chelsea lifted her eyes—"you said nothing. Why did you not?"

"If you recall, I came close to exposing you that evening in the music room. My son's happiness means a great deal to me, Miss Grant. I was quite angry over the idea that you might be pretending an affection for him in order to further the deception. But, last evening, at the ball, I could see that you do, indeed, care for him. And, today, I fully intended to allow the pair of you to marry." She paused. "It was I who had my niece waylaid at the inn this morning."

"Oh," Chelsea breathed. Believing that Lady Rathbone was now sympathetic to her plight, she felt her chin begin to tremble. "You must believe me, Lady Rathbone, I wanted to tell him the truth. But, in the beginning, I feared he would think me a criminal, and that I would have to answer to charges along with Sully. I felt *dreadful* about deceiving you, and Mr. Wainwright and of course, Mr. Stephens. I never meant any of this to happen. Not any of it!"

"I believe you, my dear."

"But . . . do you think *he* will? Will Rutherford ever be able to forgive me?"

Lady Rathbone's wrinkled cheeks softened. "I expect he will. In time. Ford's pride is hurt right now, but he will not stay angry forever. To your credit, Miss Grant, you did a splendid job of portraying Alayna. Lord Pemberton was set to have the young lady who interrupted the wedding forcibly removed from the castle." She laughed. "To say truth, Miss Grant, I haven't had such a grand time in years."

Through the moisture that was clouding her vision, Chelsea smiled sadly.

Lady Rathbone reached to pat her hand.

"I know you love my son, Miss Grant. And if it's any consolation to you, I am certain he loves you equally as much. I just wish my little scheme to detain Alayna had been successful. If she did not return to the castle in time for her own wedding, I felt it would serve her right to lose him. They do not love one another as you and Rutherford do."

Chelsea's hopes rose the veriest mite. *Did Lady Rathbone think there was still a chance?*

"But," the old woman continued, "now that Alayna is here, Rutherford is honor-bound to marry her. I have attempted to make light of her prank to deceive us, but the truth is, by travelling about the countryside with a troupe of vagrant play-actors, Alayna has disgraced herself. Eudora said word is already out in London, that Alayna's stage debut is the *on-dit* of the Season. Apparently she attempted to disguise herself, but the subterfuge failed miserably, she has fooled no one. If Alayna has any hope for respectability now, she no choice but to marry Rutherford and leave England straightaway."

Her hopes dashed to the ground, Chelsea fought the anguish building inside her. The thought of Rutherford married to another was almost more than she could bear.

"And what of you, Miss Grant? What are you to do now?"

Chelsea struggled to reply. "I . . . shall return to London, ma'am."

"Ah, London. And what will you do there?"

"I design bonnets for my living. Although this past month, I have been frightfully remiss in my promise to my employer, Mr. Merribone. I had every intention of sending along new designs for the others to make up in my absence."

"And you've not sent along even one, have you?"

Chelsea shook her head. "I have let everyone down."

"You have done nothing of the sort, Miss Grant. You have been a great comfort to me. And you have accomplished far more here at the castle than my niece would have had she been here." She gazed with renewed sadness upon Chelsea. "It is a frightful shame that you and Rutherford . . . well, we mustn't think on that."

Chelsea bit her lower lip to keep from sobbing aloud.

"I should like you to stay on a bit longer at the castle, Miss Grant."

Chelsea looked alarmed. "Oh, no, I couldn't!"

"But, with all the servants occupied with the fair and our guests indoors, there is no one to take you to London, or to Chester to catch the mail coach. You must stay, at least for a day or two."

Chelsea did not know what to say. She had not expected anyone at the castle to come to her aid. She had meant to set out on foot. Chester was not so very far away. She would manage. She gazed tearfully at Lady Rathbone.

"I shall have Mrs. Phipps prepare a chamber for you There must be several available now. I understand news of the aborted wedding caused quite an exodus among the guests." Her eyes twinkled with high amusement. "I look forward to seeing you this evening at supper, Miss Grant. *Jared!*"

At the sound of Lady Rathbone's familiar bellow, Chelsea smiled ruefully. Despite the bell-pulls being newly repaired, apparently the woman still preferred shouting when she required something.

"Miss Grant will be staying," she told Jared, when he appeared in the doorway. "You will have Mrs. Phipps see to her accommodations."

She smiled up at Chelsea, who had risen to her feet to fetch her valise. "You may wait in our little sitting room. I expect no one will disturb you there."

As instructed, Chelsea settled herself in the sitting room to wait. On the one hand, she had no desire to remain any longer at the castle, on the other, she was finding it more difficult than she'd imagined to drag herself from Lord Rathbone's side.

Seventeen

Chelsea would have sooner died that evening than take her place at table alongside Lord Rathbone and Alayna. Apart from the fact that she was now forced to appear in Polite Company dressed in one of her own gowns, frocks that were far more suited to the workroom of Mr. Merribone's shop than the dinner hour at a castle, she was consumed with fear over how Lord Rathbone would react toward her now that her treachery had come to light.

Slowly descending the stairwell that evening, the muffled sounds of people talking and laughing in the drawing room drifted upward toward her. Judging from Lady Rathbone's comments earlier, she had expected that only the immediate family would be present for the meal. Yet, the noisy hub-bub below sounded rather like a party in progress. Which, of course, had been the original intent, a gala celebration of the wedding that had taken place that day. But there had been no wedding today.

A knot of anxiety formed in Chelsea's stomach as she drew near the entrance to the cavernous room. Hesitating in the doorway, she noted that apart from Alayna and Lord and Lady Rathbone, there were, indeed, a number of unfamiliar faces present tonight.

One gentlemen, she noticed in particular, not because she recognized him or because he was unusually attractive, but because he was attired in a wildly absurd fashion. Not a tall man, he wore bright red pantaloons, a pea-green waistcoat and a dotted black and yellow shirt. His light-colored hair was slick with pomade and his cravat was wound with a flourish. His collar rose so high about his neck as to make turning his head nigh on impossible. Yet, while conversing with Alayna, he still managed to illustrate every single word with an exaggerated pose or posture. Was this the infamous Mr. Hill, the man who had rescued Alayna from Lady Rathbone's feeble attempt to kidnap her? The oddly dressed man may be a splendid actor, but beyond that, Chelsea could only wonder what Alayna found so captivating about him.

Her reverie on the dandy was cut short by a greeting from Lady Rathbone.

"Do come in, Miss Grant!" the woman called from her place near an intimate grouping of sofas and comfortable looking chairs.

Flinging only a furtive glance toward the imposing figure of Lord Rathbone, who stood at the far end of the room, engaged in conversation with another gentleman whom Chelsea had never seen before, she headed with some relief toward Lady Rathbone.

"You look very pretty tonight, Miss Grant," the older woman said, her voice loud enough to be heard by a tall, angular gentleman who stood but a few feet away, holding a goblet of claret in his hand.

With a rather lopsided grin on his face, the gentleman ambled over.

"Ah, Lord Weymouth," Lady Rathbone said, "may I present Miss Grant? Weymouth and his sister, Lady Anne, only just arrived," she told Chelsea. "Weymouth is one of Rutherford's chums from his days at the university."

"How'd you do, Miss Grant," the likeable gentleman said, his words a trifle slurred. "This is my sister, Lady Anne." He gestured toward a young lady, who greatly resembled him, in that they both had wide brows and rather longish, pinched noses.

But the young woman was beautifully dressed in a lavender silk creation with ropes of sparkling jewels around her neck. She strolled over, and after acknowledging Chelsea with a cool nod, took a seat in a brocade wing chair near Lady Rathbone. Chelsea slipped onto the sofa nearest Lady Rathbone's chair, while Weymouth lowered his lanky frame into what was appropriately called a drunkard's chair.

Fixing a languid gaze on Chelsea, Lady Anne said, "I was unaware there were small children in the household, Lady Rathbone."

The old woman's wrinkled face registered some surprise at that, while Chelsea, pinned beneath Lady Anne's condescending look, squirmed a bit. She supposed that in her dowdy gray frock with the high-neckline and simple white collar, she did look rather like a governess.

Upon catching the haughty young lady's drift, Lady Rathbone bristled. "Miss Grant is not a governess. On the contrary," she said shrilly, "she is a dear friend of mine. Her grandfather, Sir George Andover, was a prominent benefactor to a fashionable academy for young ladies in Brighton that she and my niece attended together. In fact, in that part of England, Miss Grant is known as the Brighton Beauty."

"Hmmn." One of Lady Anne's arched brows lifted.

"Say what?" spouted her brother, springing suddenly to life. "Demme! How like Rutherford not to let us know we had a celebrity in our midst!"

Chelsea blushed as Lord Weymouth jumped to his feet and honored her with an elaborate leg. "Privileged to meet you, Miss Grant? Demme! A real celebrity!"

Chelsea laughed sheepishly. "It was quite a long time ago, sir."

"Nonsense!" Weymouth headed for Lord Rathbone. "I say there, old man, why did you not tell us we've a celebrity with us tonight?"

A bored look on her face, Lady Anne rose languidly to her feet and strolled toward Alayna and the flashily dressed man, who was still posturing before the hearth.

Following her departure, Lady Rathbone turned to Chelsea. "Weymouth and his sister know nothing," she said in a whispered tone. "As I said, they only just arrived this evening. On their way to London to finish out the Season, I understand. Mustn't pay Miss Priss any mind." She winked at Chelsea. "And, of course, Weymouth is quite harmless. He obviously spent the day tippling and is now deep in his cups." She grinned, then added in a conspiratorial tone, "I took the liberty of placing you near me at table."

Moments later, Chelsea did, indeed, find herself seated at the bottom of the long mahogany dining table next to Lady Rathbone. Lord Rathbone sat at the top, with the unknown gentleman, who Lady Rathbone told her was the new steward, Mr. Osgood, seated near him.

For the most part, Chelsea ate her dinner in relative silence, managing to keep her eyes fixed on her plate lest they travel, of their own accord, the length of the table in an anxious quest to mate with Lord Rathbone's dark orbs.

When the uncomfortable meal had finally drawn to a close, the entire party, gentlemen included, headed again for the drawing room. Coffee was served to those who desired it, then during a brief lull in the proceedings, Lady Rathbone addressed her niece.

"Perhaps you and Mr. Hill would consent to entertain us with a scene from one of your stage productions, Alayna."

That the woman would suggest such a thing seemed quite extraordinary to Chelsea.

Alayna didn't seem to think so. "We'd be delighted, Aunt Millicent!" she squealed, turning to consult with Mr. Hill, who hadn't left her side for so much as a second since long before dinner.

"To my knowledge," Lady Rathbone continued, twisting about in her chair in an effort to address her son, who stood near the sideboard, "theatrical productions are not at all common in the tropics. Is that not true, Rutherford?"

A dark brow lifted cryptically. "That is correct, Mother."

"My niece fancies herself somewhat an actress," Lady Rathbone told the Weymouths and Mr. Osgood. "Perhaps you will want to get up a company of players once you have removed to Honduras, Alayna."

Alayna looked aghast. "Absolutely not!" Her tone registered supreme distaste at the idea. "You know I have no intention of actually living in the tropics, Aunt Millicent!"

The sudden clatter of Lord Rathbone's coffee cup being slammed to the sideboard claimed everyone's attention. "When you become my wife, Alayna," he sputtered, "you will live where I say you will live!" Turning his back on the company, he angrily reached for a decanter of brandy and splashed a generous portion of it into a snifter.

Momentarily silenced by her cousin's loud outburst, Alayna said nothing further.

But, Lady Anne was undeterred. "I quite agree with you on that head, Alayna," she drawled. "The jungle is no place for a lady." She turned a disapproving look on the dark-haired gentleman who was angrily twirling amber-colored liquid around in his glass and scowling at anyone whose eyes chanced to meet his. "You are being quite boorish, Rutherford."

He favored the outspoken young lady with a snort.

"I say, old man, believe I shall have one of those!" Weymouth said brightly. He rose unsteadily to his feet and toddled to the sideboard to help himself.

His jaws grinding together, Lord Rathbone turned to pour a drink for Mr.Osgood, politely handed it to the man, then stalked to the hearth.

Seated near Lady Rathbone, Chelsea kept her lashes lowered, yet she remained as vitally aware of Lord Rathbone as if the gentleman were perched in her pocket.

"Which scene would you prefer we do, Cousin Ford?" Alayna asked, having apparently decided her betrothed's state of mind was of no consequence. *"A Midsummer*

Night's Dream, the balcony scene from *Romeo and Juliet,* or *All's Well That Ends Well?"*

For the first time all evening, Lord Rathbone turned a dark glare on Chelsea, who, despite her best efforts to the contrary, was now gazing innocently up at him. "I daresay the last will serve," he said, his measured tone deliberate.

Chelsea felt her cheeks grow as pink as Mr. Hill's pantaloons, then suddenly she was aware of Alayna standing in front of her, dangling a bright object before her downcast eyes.

"I found this in my room earlier, Miss Grant. It must be yours, for I own nothing quite so plain." She carelessly dropped the heart-shaped locket into Chelsea's lap then whirled about. "We shall use the hearth as the stage!" she called gaily. "Everyone will please remove to the opposite end of the room!"

Lady Rathbone was closely watching Chelsea. "Allow me to help you with that, dear." She retrieved the locket from Chelsea's trembling fingers and made short work of clasping it around her neck. "There. It looks lovely." She smiled warmly. "You must wear it always."

Far too overset to speak, Chelsea dared not lift her eyes upward, lest she once again encounter Lord Rathbone's angry glare.

The scene Alayna and Mr. Hill performed was surprisingly well done. When the young lady's final speech had concluded, everyone—save Chelsea, who could summon only a modicum of enthusiasm, and Lord Rathbone, who could summon none at all—cheered loudly.

Apparently noticing her betrothed's lack of appreciation for her acting ability, Alayna cried, "Must you be such a down-pin, Rutherford? Most gentlemen would be pleased beyond measure that their future bride was as wildly accomplished as I! Your attitude is quite unnatural, don't you agree, Aunt Millicent?"

"Agree about what, dear? I fear I wasn't listening."

"I said, that if I am to be forced to live in that uncivilized jungle where Rutherford resides, I should be allowed to do something to entertain myself. I think your idea of forming a theatrical company quite a good one. Harry would come along, wouldn't you Harry?"

"Eh? Come along where?" Harry struck a pose.

"To Honduras. With me."

"Honduras, eh? That the new theater just went up in Glasgow, what? Or was it Edinburgh?"

Alayna giggled. "There, you see, Ford! Civilized people haven't an inkling as to what Honduras is! I cannot think you'd expect me to even consider living in that insect-laden swamp on the other side of the world." She flounced toward Harry. "We shall now perform the balcony scene from *Romeo and Juliet.* Positively my most favorite of all!"

Chelsea watched Ford's eyes narrow as his betrothed and Mr. Hill commenced to posture once again. Neither of the actors noticed when the seething gentleman moved to refill his brandy glass, then charge through the double French doors, seeking refuge on a balcony of his own choosing.

Apparently Lady Rathbone noticed. When Chelsea felt a cool hand on her arm, she glanced at the older woman, whose speaking eyes urged Chelsea to follow her son outdoors.

The questioning look on Chelsea's face became a hurt smile. But summoning what little courage she had left, she rose noiselessly to her feet and slipped through the doors after Lord Rathbone. The crisp air outside felt cool against her flushed skin.

Because it was also quite dark outdoors, only a thin sliver of moon was visible in the night sky, she paused for a moment in order to get her bearings.

"What do you want?" came a brusque voice behind her.

Chelsea suddenly went icy with apprehension. She turned to see Lord Rathbone leaning against the high stone railing that encompassed the narrow passageway, his eyes dark sockets in his bronzed face.

"I was . . . looking for you," she said, fighting the tremor of fear that shook her.

"Well, now that you have found me, Miss Grant, what do you intend saying to me?"

Chelsea had no speech planned, but suddenly she realized that for the first time ever, she was free to speak the whole truth to the gentleman. No longer was she playing a part! She could be herself. The startling revelation served to considerably lessen the fear that was gripping her middle. Drawing a deep breath, she approached Lord Rathbone with her head held high. "Your mother has seen fit to forgive me for my part in Alayna's scheme to deceive you. I had hoped you might do likewise. I am deeply sorry for—"

He snorted with derision. " 'Wherefore was I to this keen mockery born?' "

Momentarily confused, Chelsea blinked, then she murmured, *"A Midsummer Night's Dream."* A small smile found its way to her lips. She hadn't known what to expect from the gentleman, but lines from Shakespeare were definitely not it.

She moved a step closer to the stone railing and resting an elbow on the waist-high balustrade, she lifted a finger to her chin and gazed up at him with wonder. That he'd have ordered her from his sight would have been far more likely than reciting poetry to her.

" 'See how she leans her cheek upon her hand! O! that I were a glove upon that hand . . . that I might touch that cheek.' " His tone was low, to the point of being seductive.

Chelsea's breath lodged in her throat. *Was he making love to her?*

She was startled afresh when, suddenly, Rathbone flung his brandy snifter to the ground and caught Chelsea up in his arms. The moist lips he pressed to hers were rough and savage. Yet, despite the swiftness of the action, Chelsea welcomed the heady sensations that raced through her veins. Winding her arms tightly around his neck, her answering passion surprised even herself as she eagerly returned his ardor, breath for breath, kiss for hungry kiss.

Low moans of pleasure escaped her. Feeling his arms at her back molding her to him, the intensity of her desire increased, and when one hand slid to cup her buttocks, pressing the soft flesh of her thighs against the lean, hardness of his, she could feel the heat of his need through the thin fabric of her skirt, straining against the tight confines of his breeches.

Only then, did the throbbing urgency she sensed in him, and in herself, alarm her. She attempted to pull away, but Ford's strong arms refused to release her. Instead he deepened the kiss, bending her body backward over the railing. When she felt his knee working to pry apart her legs, she stiffened with terror and cried out.

"No!"

But he did not hear her.

"Stop!" she cried, her balled-up fists pushing hard against his chest. "Please Ford, I beg of you! Stop!"

With a growl, he thrust her from him, his chest heaving with pent-up passion. "So," he spat out, "there is a limit to what a hundred pounds will purchase."

Hurt brown eyes regarded him with shock and disbelief. "I refused to take the money!" When he made a fresh lunge for her, she raised a hand to fend him off, but he was too quick.

Strong fingers curled around her delicate wrist. " 'Tempt not too much the hatred of my spirit,' " he ground out, his black eyes smoldering. "Also from *A Midsummer Night's Dream,* my dear."

Wrenching from him, Chelsea cried, "How dare you insult me! You are vile and reprehensible, and I hate you!"

With loathing in her eyes, she turned and fled from him. Escaping through the double doors, she raced through the drawing room and did not stop running until she reached the safe haven of her own bedchamber. Upon latching the door behind her, however, her anger dissolved at once into tears. Flinging herself across the bed, she sobbed into the pillow. Her heart had been broken in two and it would never, *ever* mend.

Far, far into the night, she awoke with a start. Dream figures swam crazily in her head. Ford and Alayna, their laughing faces distorted, were taunting her with poetry from Shakespeare. The dramas were all mixed up, a line from this play, a sonnet from that.

One couplet rang loudly in Chelsea's ears:

> "The King's a beggar, now the play is done;
> All is well-ended, if this suit be won."

Her breath coming in fits and starts, Chelsea sat bolt upright in bed. It was true. The play was done, and Alayna had won. Angrily, she tossed the coverlet aside.

If she left the castle now, no one would be the wiser.

Eighteen

Stealing from the castle in the dead of night, without so much as a parting word to Lady Rathbone, was not what she wanted to do, Chelsea thought, as she tramped through the damp grass, picking her way around the deserted stalls on her way toward the bridge and the main byway to Chester. But, she had no choice. She could not bear to spend another day in Lord Rathbone's presence. He and Alayna would soon be wed and she must forget she'd ever met the man.

She darted across the bridge and skirted around the stand of trees that shielded the castle from the outside world. So far as she could see, only one good thing had come of this entire wretched month. If Alayna's scandalous behavior were, indeed, on the lips of everyone in Town, then Chelsea need no longer live in fear of Alayna Marchmont's interference in her life.

How very clever it had been of Alayna to *not* apprise Chelsea of her whereabouts for the month, otherwise, Chelsea would have recognized the impropriety of the action and refuse to be coerced. A fitful sigh escaped her. She was free from Alayna, but would she *ever* be free of the claim Alayna's cousin now had on her heart?

The dilemma plagued her all the way to London. Along with it rang one last line from the mighty Bard. 'We cannot fight for love as men may do.' How true the sentiment was. As a woman, and as a lady, she could not fight for the man she loved. She had no choice but to accept the inevitable and go on. With decision, she vowed to never again think about either Alayna Marchmont or Rutherford Campbell.

Disembarking from the Royal Mail Coach at the White Horse Cellar near Piccadilly, she retrieved her valise from the driver who had stacked it atop the coach when they departed Chester. Though she felt a bit peckish now as she set out on foot, she decided it would be far wiser to use her last shillings to secure decent lodgings for the night than to spend the money now on a hot meal.

Approaching busy Oxford Street, she had to fight for space on the crowded flagway. A stream of carriages and lacquered coaches clattered noisily on the nearby cobblestones. Suddenly, from out of nowhere, a pack of stray dogs ran barking and yelping into the street, chasing the wheels of a speeding four-in-hand. Clutching her valise to her, Chelsea heaved a weary sigh. She'd been back in Town less than a quarter hour and already she longed for the fragrant air and peaceful tranquility of the country.

After trying at several boarding establishments to secure a room, she at last found a suitable-enough one on the top floor of a narrow three-story house, not far from Mr. Merribone's millinery shop. Tomorrow, she would seek out her former employer in the hopes that he'd see fit to take her on again.

The following morning, Chelsea took up a position across the square from Mr. Merribone's millinery shop, her heart in her throat as she waited for signs of life about the place. Mere moments after he'd let up the blinds and opened the front door, she squared her shoulders and approached the tiny shop.

Though it was still quite early, the cobblestone street around the square was not entirely deserted. A few fruit and vegetable carts rumbled past, the horses hooves ringing like chimes on the crisp cool air. She spotted a black cat nosing through a pile of rubbish, and in front of her, two matrons with baskets slung over their arms, were headed briskly toward the open-air market at the far end of the street.

Stepping furtively into Mr. Merribone's establishment, Chelsea spotted the proprietor behind the counter, busily arranging some colored ribbons on a shelf.

The round-faced man glanced up, then blinked with surprise when he saw who stood poised on the threshold. "I say, is that you, Miss Grant?"

Chelsea nodded. "Indeed, it is, Mr. Merribone." She cast a gaze about the shop. Though quite thin of customers this time of morning, there were an inordinate number of bonnets displayed for sale. Had Mr. Merribone hired a new designer in her absence, she wondered? Yet, if he had, the newly designed bonnets did not appear to be selling quite as rapidly as her creations had. Quite often, hers sold the very day she completed them, consequently the tables were quite often bare this early in the day.

"How are you this morning, Mr. Merribone?" She asked, trying for a lighthearted tone that she didn't feel.

"How am *I*? How is your aunt?" he asked, a bit tersely.

Chelsea looked puzzled. "My aunt?"

"The one who was ill."

"Ah, yes; my aunt. She is feeling much better, thank you." Her gaze continued to flit about the shop.

"Are you shopping for a new bonnet today, Miss Grant, or . . . ?"

Chelsea decided to keep her business to herself for the moment. She bent to inspect a rather plain-looking Rutland poke displayed on a table, fully aware that Mr. Merribone's hawk-like gaze was following her every move. Holding the poke aloft, she said, "It is a bit plain, don't you agree, Mr. Merribone?"

One of the proprietor's bushy brows shot upward.

Chelsea turned the bonnet this way and that. It felt good to be thinking in a creative vein again. She smiled, then said simply. "Feathers. It needs feathers, Mr. Merribone."

Without a word, Mr. Merribone turned and disappeared through the curtained partition into the workroom. When he reappeared a moment later, he was carrying a handful of feathery plumes. "I'd be much obliged if you'd dress that one up a bit, Miss Grant."

It was then that Chelsea noticed the sheen of perspiration glistening on the man's brow.

Laying the poke bonnet aside, she looked her former employer square in the eye. "Mr. Merribone, I am not being entirely honest with you this morning. Truth to tell, I came to the shop today to ask if I might have my position as chief designer back. I admit, I reneged on the promise I made to you to send along new designs this past month, but . . . as it turned out, my time was not my own. I am truly sorry for the slight, Mr. Merribone."

The tense look on Mr. Merribone's face instantly dissolved. "You may start today, Miss Grant. Indeed, it is good to have you back in London, Miss Grant."

Chelsea held up a hand. "I shall return to work for you on one condition, Mr. Merribone."

"You've only to name it, Miss Grant!"

"I must have your word, that under no circumstances, will you ever again allow me to take tea with a customer. I insist on remaining at my post the entire day, Mr. Merribone. If a customer requests to see me, or my designs, she shall have to view them right here in the shop. I insist on it, Mr. Merribone! I insist on it!" she concluded fervently.

"Very well, Miss Grant. I shall institute the new policy at once."

Chelsea smiled broadly, then she removed her own bonnet and set to work.

* * *

Two weeks later, on a particularly gloomy Tuesday afternoon, Chelsea had just finished stitching a bunch of bright red cherries to the brim of a Minerva, and was carrying the pretty confection to the front of the shop, when she chanced to overhear a snatch of conversation between two Quality customers, who were passing the time in idle gossip while they browsed in the shop.

"I have it on good authority," one of the women declared hotly, as she set the *Angouleme* that Chelsea had decorated only that morning atop her light brown hair, "that the little hoyden eloped with that actor friend of hers!"

Chelsea halted dead in her tracks.

"No-o!" the second lady exclaimed, her mouth gaping open with delicious interest. "But can you be certain of it, Lydia?"

The first woman smiled smugly. "Word came straight from Lady Anne. She and her brother, Lord Weymouth, actually spent time at the castle."

Chelsea's heart began to pound feverishly in her breast. She edged closer to the women, pretending to have urgent business in that corner of the shop.

"Rumor has it that Mr. Kean turned them out of his company, and now the pair of them are getting up a troupe of actors of their own and are planing to travel about the countryside like a band of Gypsies." The woman's lips pursed with scorn.

"Why, I can hardly fathom the like!" her friend declared.

The first woman untied the pink ribbons of the *Angouleme,* lifted it from her head and reached for a blue silk Babet.

"That looks divine with your coloring, Lydia," her companion said, then in the same breath, asked, "but, how will they get on? I hear the gentleman hasn't a feather to fly with."

"Does now." Lydia preened in front of the glass. "Lady Anne said A. M.'s cousin, who, according to Lady Anne, is a frightfully disagreeable chap, settled quite a generous allowance on the girl. Word is, the cousin was buying her off. Seems the two were once betrothed and he was outraged to learn that the"—her tone became almost inaudible— "*lovers* had spent upwards of a fortnight together!"

"Oh, my stars!" The second lady's eyes widened. "And, to think, my Penelope attended Miss Marchmont's come-out ball! Oh, dear me!" She clapped a hand over her mouth. "I did not mean to utter the young lady's name aloud!"

"Pishaw! Everyone knows who she is."

Having each selected new bonnets, the women sailed past a dazed Chelsea. "If the hoyden has a shred of decency left in her," added Lydia, "she will never show her face in this city again!"

That night, Chelsea hardly slept a wink for thinking about what she'd overheard in the shop that day. If Alayna had indeed married Mr. Hill, did that mean Lord Rathbone had returned to Honduras as he had threatened to do, *un*legshackled to anyone? Or was it possible he might still be in England?

Chelsea's pulse quickened at that thought.

If Ford were still in Britain, was it possible he might come to London, perhaps to testify at Sully's trial, which from an account Chelsea had read in *The Times,* was set to begin soon. Or, perhaps, he'd be coming to London to address Parliament. She knew he meant to present his petition on behalf of the planters before he left England. Would he try to find her if he came? She had told Lady Rathbone about her employer, Mr. Merribone. Would Lady Rathbone tell him, she wondered? Oh, she sighed sadly, there were so many questions, so few answers.

For the next several days, she spent an inordinate amount of time in the front part of the millinery shop, gazing from the plate glass window, her heart lodged in her throat as

she strained for a glimpse of . . . of what? Then, feeling
guilty for shirking her duties, she would throw herself head-
long into her work once again. Apparently word had got
out among the *ton* that she had returned to London, and
was once again designing bonnets for Mr. Merribone, for
the shop had been doing a brisk business. And, while she
did enjoy the few moments she was able to focus fully on
a new design, or enjoy a particularly pleasing result, the
free feeling never lasted beyond a few minutes, then the
breathless longing would settle about her again.

Thoughts of Lord Rathbone were never far from her
mind. Despite the memory of those last awful moments
with him on the balcony, she missed the gentleman fiercely.
She knew he had only behaved as he did that night out of
anger. He had not meant to hurt her. Beneath his wounded
pride, Lord Rathbone was first, last and always, a gentle
man.

As Chelsea walked to and from work those next few
days, she found herself gazing overlong at every gentleman
whose path she crossed, at every carriage that clattered by
on the cobblestone street. Upon reaching the shop door
every morning, her eyes already felt blanched and tired
from having searched so diligently for Lord Rathbone's
handsome face.

When that long week had dragged nearly to a close, she
was about to give up. If the gentleman were in London, he
did not mean to see her. Otherwise, he would have already
come.

Late that afternoon, Chelsea was seated in the workroom
of the shop, just beginning the task of securing a pink satin
rosebud to the crown of an Oatland Village bonnet, when
she heard an unusual sound coming from the front of the
shop.

A gentleman's voice. Other than that of Mr. Merribone,
a masculine tone was not a common occurrence in a millinery establishment.

Recognizing this deep timbre, Chelsea's heart skipped a beat. Unnoticed, the pink satin rosebud slipped from her fingers to the floor.

When she heard Mr. Merribone ask the gentleman if he was looking for something for his wife, Chelsea's hand stole upward to the golden locket clasped around her neck. Straining to hear Lord Rathbone's reply, her fingers curled tightly about the warm, heart-shaped metal.

"I am not a married man, Mr. Merribone," she heard the gentleman say. "I have come to inquire if you know the whereabouts of a Miss Chelsea Grant?"

Chelsea's heart stood still.

"Indeed, I do, sir. Miss Grant is my chief designer," he said proudly. "Would you care to meet the young lady, sir?"

"Is she here now?" Lord Rathbone asked, his tone sounding quite anxious.

Her pulse pounding in her ears, Chelsea did not wait for Mr. Merribone to summon her. Springing to her feet, she flew through the curtained partition into the display area of the shop. Lord Rathbone's tall, elegantly attired form seemed to dwarf the tiny enclosure. A tremulous smile skittered across Chelsea's face.

"Lord Rathbone," she murmured, "I thought I recognized your voice. How lovely to see you again, sir."

"Miss Grant." Liquid brown eyes found hers and held the gaze.

Pinned beneath the look, Chelsea found it difficult to speak. "H-how is Lady Rathbone getting on, sir? Well, I hope."

"Very well, thank you. She misses you frightfully." He paused, then said quietly, "As do I."

Chelsea felt her heart lurch fitfully to her throat. Though there were so many she things she wished to say to him— that she missed him fiercely, that she loved him beyond all reason—she knew she could not speak.

The moment of strained silence between them grew.

At length, Lord Rathbone cast a gaze about, his eyes taking in the feathers and frippery. A few customers were browsing in the shop—a matronly looking woman and a young lady. Strangely enough, they both seemed more engrossed in the small drama unfolding before them than the prettily decorated bonnets scattered about.

Chelsea was also sharply aware of Mr. Merribone still hovering closeby, taking in every word that she and Lord Rathbone had uttered. "Did . . . business bring you to Town, sir?" she finally managed.

"Yes, indeed," Lord Rathbone replied. "I arrived only this morning and went straight to the House."

Chelsea gazed at him expectantly. "Parliament?"

"Yes." He nodded.

"And you presented your petition?"

Rathbone nodded again.

"I expect it was well received."

"Yes, yes it was."

Chelsea smiled broadly. "That's wonderful news, sir."

"Yes . . . it is . . . ah, is there . . . ?" He appeared to be quite uncomfortable, his eyes casting about for, a bit of privacy, perhaps? Suddenly, he said, "Perhaps, I could persuade you to take tea with me this afternoon, Miss Grant. It is close on tea time now." He turned toward her employer. "I shall return her to you promptly in an hour, sir."

Mr. Merribone was already shaking his head. "I am sorry, your lordship. Miss Grant is not allowed to leave her post."

Chelsea turned wide eyes on her employer. "Mr. Merribone—"

"Out of the question!" Mr. Merribone was adamant. "You will return to the work bench at once, Miss Grant."

Staring aghast at the man, Chelsea stood fixed in place.

"Perhaps I could call again later," Lord Rathbone suggested. "When will Miss Grant be free, Mr. Merribone?"

"Six of the clock would suit nicely, my lord."

"Now would suit better, Mr. Merribone," Chelsea retorted, oblivious to the tittering sound her answer elicited from the two women in the shop, who were still vastly interested in the proceedings. "Suddenly, I feel quite parched," Chelsea said, fixing what she hoped was a speaking look on her employer. "A cup of tea would be the very thing to restore me. I shall just go and get my bonnet, Lord Rathbone." With that, she swept past a dazed Mr. Merribone and disappeared into the workroom.

Lord Rathbone's lips were still twitching when she reappeared, hurriedly tying the green grosgrain ribbons of her flat chip bonnet beneath her chin. With a final nod to Mr. Merribone, she took the arm Lord Rathbone offered and together they exited the shop.

"Do you always take such command of a situation, Miss Grant?" he asked, guiding her through the crush of people promenading on the busy flagway and toward the black lacquered coach parked at the curb.

"Not generally." Chelsea smiled up at him. "Though I must say I firmly believe now, that being honest and straightforward is the best policy."

"I see. It appears we are once again of the same mind, Miss Grant." He handed her into the closed carriage, then climbed in and settled himself beside her. "To that end"—he gazed into her upturned face—"may I say straight out that I am deeply sorry for my shocking want of conduct that last evening we were together at the castle. I regret that my . . . ahem, wounded pride and my anger . . . caused me to behave in such a deplorable fashion toward you. Can you ever forgive me, Miss Grant?"

The smile on Chelsea's face was warm. "I have already forgiven you, my lord. But, have you forgiven me for my part in the unconscionable trick Alayna and I played on you?"

"Indeed, I have." His dark eyes locked with hers, then he smiled. "Well, then, what would you like to do now,

Miss Grant? I admit, I know very little about London." He glanced out the window. "Is there a tea-room nearby, or . . . ?"

"I should like to marry you, my lord."

Rathbone's dark head jerked 'round. "So, that is how it is, is it?" His lips began to twitch once again, greatly delighting Chelsea, whose boldness had surprised even herself. "As it happens, Miss Grant," he went on, "I came to London for the express purpose of asking you to marry me."

"I thought you had business in Town," Chelsea countered

"Making you my bride, *is* my business." His tone was sincere and affectionate.

But, suddenly, Chelsea's eyes clouded over.

"What is it, my dear? Do you not wish to marry me?"

"I . . . there is something I must tell you, sir. Something that . . ." she lowered her gaze, "perhaps you will not wish to marry me, afterward," she concluded quietly.

"I can think of nothing that would cause me to change face on that head, Miss Grant."

"Nonetheless, I must tell you, sir. I shall not be guilty of deceiving you a second time."

"Deceiving me?"

Lord Rathbone's brow's pulled together as Chelsea, in measured tones, told him all about the ugly rumor that had circulated in Brighton regarding her famous Grandpapa Andover and Miss Farringdon at the academy.

"Ah, I see. And I take it is that is the same frightful scandal which that silly woman at the ball was alluding to?"

Chelsea nodded.

"And, I expect my cousin Alayna has been doing her part to keep the rumor alive. Is that the case, Miss Grant?" He did not wait for a reply. "I suspect that is also how she persuaded you to assist her in deceiving me, is it not?"

Chelsea did not answer. She merely lowered her lashes. "If you do not wish to marry me, sir, I shall understand."

With a gloved hand, he reached to gently lift her chin upward. "Of course I still wish to marry you, you little minx. Whatever might have happened half a century ago between your grandpapa and his lady love makes not a whit of difference to me. I assure you, no scandal, not so much as a hint of one, will follow us across the sea." His voice became a whisper. "You will always be safe with me, Miss Grant."

Chelsea's brown eyes brimmed with happy tears. "In that case, sir, my answer is yes."

Rathbone feigned surprise. "Fancy that. I was about to give your proposal the exact same answer."

Chelsea laughed aloud. "Indeed, we are of the same mind, sir. I predict we shall get on quite well together as man and wife."

Lord Rathbone leaned toward her. Chelsea knew he meant to kiss her, but instead of giving him leave to do so, she held up a hand to halt the action. "There is something else I should like to ask of you, sir," she said.

"And what might that be?"

Chelsea's gaze turned solemn once again. "I should like to hear you say that you love me. *Me.* Chelsea Grant, and not . . ." she did not finish the sentence.

Ford's eyes became especially warm and understanding. "You are saying you grew weary of hearing me call you by . . . another's name, is that the case?"

Chelsea nodded.

"I love *you,* Chelsea Grant. I love you with all my heart."

Chelsea's breast swelled with joy. "And I love you, Rutherford Campbell." Her chin begin to tremble and her eyes to brim with moisture. "I shall love you always and forever, and I am so very sorry for the—"

"Hush!" He put a finger to her trembling pink lips. "We shall never speak of the deception again. Though, if it had not happened, you and I would never have met. And, my dearest Chelsea, I would sooner die that not have you by my side, forever."

Her lips trembling, Chelsea swallowed her tears.

"Well, then," he said, smiling down at her, "that leaves only one last thing to settle between us. Where shall we go for tea?"

Chelsea tilted her golden head to one side. "I have it on good authority sir, that Honduras is quite nice this time of year."

Ford laughed aloud. "Honduras is it, my dear."

Then, with love shining from his dark eyes, he gathered Chelsea into his arms, and kissed her very, very tenderly.

Chelsea made a mental note to tell Mr. Merribone that she'd been offered another position. One that would last a lifetime.

Author's Note

In 1787, William Wilberforce became the leader of the anti-slavery movement in England, though his Parliamentary Bill for the abolition of slavery was defeated, due in part to the pressure exerted by men who stood to profit from the shipping of Africans to British colonies.

In 1805, the importation of slaves into new colonies was forbidden, and in 1807 Parliament passed a General Abolition Act which extended the measure to all British possessions.

Still, according to Henderson in *An Account of the British Settlement of Honduras,* gangs of Negro slaves were still being used in 1809 for the cutting and shipping of mahogany trees and to work sugar plantations throughout the West Indies. In fact, documented proof exists showing that as late as 1829, slaves were still being offered for sale at public auctions.

It was not until 1833 that all slaves in the British colonies were finally set free.

—Marilyn Clay

Dear Reader,

If you are like me, you also feel an overwhelming longing to experience life as it was in the romantic time-period known as the Regency. Then, a real man was a gentleman, right down to his polished Hessians, and a proper young lady still blushed when caught staring overlong at milord's broad shoulders—not to mention his thigh-hugging inexpressibles!

For me, the pull was so great I simply had to delve deeper, to learn more about the past I found so intriguing. Not even travelling to London, or visiting Brighton and Bath, was enough to satisfy me. I had to know more! From this longing grew *The Regency Plume,* a bi-monthly newsletter dedicated to accurately depicting life as it was in Regency England.

Each issue of *The Regency Plume Newsletter* is full of fascinating articles penned by your favorite Regency romance authors. If you'd like to join me and the hundreds of other Regency romance fans who experience Prinny's England via *The Regency Plume,* send a stamped, self-addressed envelope to me, Marilyn Clay, c/o *The Regency Plume,* Dept. 711-D-NW, Ardmore, Oklahoma 73401. I'll be happy to send you more information and a subscription form. I look forward to hearing from each and every one of you! In the meantime, I hope you enjoyed reading BRIGHTON BEAUTY, and will want to read my next Regency romance, FELICITY'S FOLLY, coming out in March of '97! Thank you!

Sincerely,

Marilyn Clay

ZEBRA REGENCIES
ARE
THE TALK OF THE TON!

A REFORMED RAKE (4499, $3.99)
by Jeanne Savery

After governess Harriet Cole helped her young charge flee to France — and the designs of a despicable suitor, more trouble soon arrived in the person of a London rake. Sir Frederick Carrington insisted on providing safe escort back to England. Harriet deemed Carrington more dangerous than any band of brigands, but secretly relished matching wits with him. But after being taken in his arms for a tender kiss, she found herself wondering — *could* a lady find love with an irresistible rogue?

A SCANDALOUS PROPOSAL (4504, $4.99)
by Teresa DesJardien

After only two weeks into the London season, Lady Pamela Premington has already received her first offer of marriage. If only it hadn't come from the *ton's* most notorious rake, Lord Marchmont. Pamela had already set her sights on the distinguished Lieutenant Penford, who had the heroism and honor that made him the ideal match. Now she had to keep from falling under the spell of the seductive Lord so she could pursue the man more worthy of her love. Or was he?

A LADY'S CHAMPION (4535, $3.99)
by Janice Bennett

Miss Daphne, art mistress of the Selwood Academy for Young Ladies, greeted the notion of ghosts haunting the academy with skepticism. However, to avoid rumors frightening off students, she found herself turning to Mr. Adrian Carstairs, sent by her uncle to be her "protector" against the "ghosts." Although, Daphne would accept no interference in her life, she *would* accept aid in exposing any spectral spirits. What she never expected was for Adrian to expose the secret wishes of her hidden heart . . .

CHARITY'S GAMBIT (4537, $3.99)
by Marcy Stewart

Charity Abercrombie reluctantly embarks on a London season in hopes of making a suitable match. However she cannot forget the mysterious Dominic Castille — and the kiss they shared — when he fell from a tree as she strolled through the woods. Charity does not know that the dark and dashing captain harbors a dangerous secret that will ensnare them both in its web — leaving Charity to risk certain ruin and losing the man she so passionately loves . . .